Also by Gretchen K. Wing:

The Flying Burgowski

"… a compelling novel that weaves together fantasy elements with the dark, absurd, and sweet aspects of a family's ordinary life. Alcoholism, divorce, and sibling relationships are touched on realistically and often hilariously; everything is seen through a young teen's point of view…although adults will be moved too."

—**Miriam Angress**, author of *How Water Speaks to Rock*, and other plays

"Gretchen Wing has a natural talent—a very distinctive voice, great timing and a good punch, creative imagery, and a super sense of humor. I absolutely loved the story…a sensitive and imaginative tale of one girl's struggle to deal with the junk she's been handed by life."

—**Michelle Isenhoff**, author of the *Divided Decade* trilogy, and the *Song of the Mountain* and *Taylor Davis* series

Headwinds: *The Flying Burgowski, Book Two*

"…a thrilling plot that keeps you on the edge of your beanbag chair (which is a hard thing)."

—**Erik Weibel**, Thiskidreviewsbooks.com

THE FLYING BURGOWSKI

BOOK THREE

ALTITUDE

Gretchen K. Wing

MADRONA BRANCH PRESS

ALTITUDE

MADRONA
BRANCH
PRESS

www.GretchenWing.com
info@GretchenWing.com

Book cover and interior design by
Robert Lanphear
www.lanpheardesign.com

Library of Congress Cataloging-in-Publication Data
Wing, Gretchen K.

Altitude/The Flying Burgowski
Gretchen K. Wing

ISBN: 978-0-9914213-3-6

Printed in the USA

To my men, once again,
Ken, Mac, Casey—
and to anyone who's ever
been locked inside a box of any kind

ACKNOWLEDGEMENTS

My Lopez Writers, Suzanne Berry, Brooks, Marty Clark, Iris Graville, Kathleen Holliday, Rita Larom, Ann Norman, Lorna Reese: Jocelyn's midwives! Thank you for all the encouragement over the years, and the wisdom, and the treats.

Bonny Becker and her YA Fiction Workshop at the Northwest Institute for Literary Arts Residencies: thanks for ripping Chapter One to pieces.

Virginia Herrick, editor: thank you for requiring the best from my story.

Bob Lanphear, book designer: thank you for all the expertise I wish I had.

Anah-Kate Drahn: as you fly away into your own horizon, Jocelyn's hands will always be yours.

Heather Harrison: I appreciate your generous spirit as much as I appreciate your photography skills—and that's a lot.

Jesse Bartlett, Nicole O'Bryant, Patrick O'Neil: thank you all for steering me right on issues of boat rescue, the Coast Guard, and winter fishing.

Juliann Bildhauer: your understanding of immigration law and practices was invaluable to me—and continues to be invaluable to thousands of real people in real need.

Bruce Creps: thanks for the details of Hawaii and Chinese Hawaiian culture, which helped me fully understand the character of Vivian Wu.

Sarah Jessup: thank you for your patience and thoroughness in sharing your knowledge of Mandarin.

CONTENTS

CHAPTER ONE

WORLD'S CLUMSIEST GORGEOUS BARISTA

It was Labor Day, and Dad was laboring through one last Dad Talk when some girl had to ruin his moment by crashing onto our sidewalk café table.

Not with a car, or I wouldn't be writing this. But not like she tripped on the curb, rushing into the café, either. I didn't buy that for a second.

One minute, I'm watching Dad's shadow on the tabletop in the bright fall sunlight. Dad's saying, "You know I'm not wild about this boarding school thing, Jocelyn, but since I've just spent the morning carrying all your stuff up three flights—"

"Which no one asked you to," I put in. "I *said* I'm fine. The roomies could've helped."

"No offense to the roomies, but one of 'em didn't look like she could lift more than her purse. And the other wasn't exactly offering. But since you're all moved in now—"

"The roomies are fine! I'm fine. It's all good, Dad."

He sighed his Difficult Daughter sigh and tried again. "I'm trying to say, Joss, that when all's said and done, I guess I'm glad you're here. It's good to see you back on a path toward—"

Next minute: *CRASH.* Out of nowhere she fell. Right smack onto our lattes.

Mugs shattered on the bricks. Pigeons flapped. Something pink whomped my chest and hurled me backward in a tangle of black leggings and black hair. My chair tipped; my skull clonked my purse, barely avoiding fracture like the mugs. Then I was on the sidewalk, squinting straight into the sun.

"Omigod, miss! Are you okay?" Dad scrambled up, a tall shadow between me and the sky. A second later, my breath heaved back in that sickening rush I know from a couple of crashes I've had on windy days. I tasted sour coffee. The world refocused.

Here's what I saw: bright pink high-tops flailing from under Dad's chair like a pair of naked bunnies in a trap. "Oh, my chair flipped," said Mr. Obvious, bustling to free the bunnies. Which were attached to legs. Which were attached to...

...well, a girl. Black hair pulled back above high, wide cheekbones I'd kill for. As Dad ignored me to help her up, I saw dark eyes, Asian-shaped—and red as hell. She'd been crying. Not like she just crashed onto a metal table, though I doubt that helped. Crying like her face had time to go blotchy, or would have if her skin weren't so golden.

I noticed I'd stood up, still staring. She was gorgeous.

Also bleeding; a small stain widened through the elbow of her long-sleeved T-shirt. The shirt said "Bean There, Done That"— the name of the café.

"I'm so *sorry!*" Her voice was as delicate as her bone structure. She tried to pick up some mug-shards, but Dad grabbed her arm, pushing up the sleeve to clamp his napkin over her scrape. "Thank you, thanks, I'm okay. I'm *sorry.*"

"Perfectly all right, miss, just an accident. You'll be fine. Joss, you okay?" Dad finally remembered to ask. He's too used to my crashes. I nodded and stood there like a dork.

"What happened?" I managed. "Did you jump off the fire escape up there, or what?" *Not to be rude, but if that was a suicide attempt, it sucked.* And I barely got to taste my coffee.

"No, I—just *totally* tripped on the curb, I do that all the time," the black-haired girl mumbled, trying to hold Dad's napkin on her elbow while fixing her ponytail. "I am *totally* sorry, you guys, I'm late for work, I'll go tell Jason to re-do your coffees..." and she disappeared into the café.

"Whoa." Dad used our napkins to mop coffee-splatter from his chair, but made no move to sit back down. "That was one hell of a stumble! Poor kid, wonder how she functions." He looked at his watch. "Hey, Joss, much as I'd like to start over with a fresh brew..."

"You have a ferry to catch." I picked up the largest of the mug-shards. Dalby Islanders always have a ferry to catch.

Not me; I'm a Mainlander now.

But my heart was still jittering from the barista-girl's crash. *Tripped on the curb? B.s.—no one gets that airborne from a stumble.* No one gets that airborne, period... except people like me. People who actually fly.

That's crazy. What are the chances? Flyers are, like, one in a million.

Nuh-uh, there's two of us on Dalby Island alone!

Only 'cause I inherited Mom's powers.

Right, all that sweet Flying Burgowski quality time we've been having—NOT. But what if this girl...

This girl's got no powers—unless you count her looks. Forget it. But I felt my flight-engines begin to hum.

Funny—they're starting to whirr again as I write this, just remembering.

Forget it, Joss. Write about your Coffee With Dad before that girl wrecked it, okay?

Okay, fine.

Even though "sixteen year-olds really shouldn't do caffeine," it was Dad who suggested a café when Parent Orientation finished up at school—ahem, I mean The Horizon Academy. All this weird, old-fashioned Boarding School lingo I get to use now: "Dorm." "R.A." "Dean." But hey—my choice, right? Horizon Academy Early Start Program = high school classes + Coastal

Washington University classes = early high school diploma + Jocelyn's escape from Dalby.

I know, I KNOW. What's to "escape" from, when you live on a beautiful island with a great family and, oh yeah—you can fly?

It's just...since That Awful Summer, my happy old Flying Burgowski magic hasn't been working. Not the flying part. The happy part.

So Dad should've been thrilled to get rid of me. But I guess he was feeling mushy, about to say 'bye till Thanksgiving.

Coastal U Buccaneers apparently keep a whole block of cafés in business, but Bean There, Done That had the sunniest outdoor tables, and who knows how much more sun we'll get here in "Wet-ville?" Not like Wattsville's any wetter than Dalby Island. But when's the last time I sat around a café with Dad at home?

Dad muttered about "turning into your mother" when I ordered a latte, but he got one too. Note to self: don't apply to Bean There for a job. The pissy blue-haired barista guy didn't even look at me—too busy snarling how he was "FINE with working twenty-five minutes past my shift! Viv can take her sweet TIME."

As soon as we'd shooed the pigeons and adjusted our chairs on the wobbly bricks, Dad started up again: "Sure you got everything for school? For your room?"

"No, Dad, I'm pretty sure I need a crab pot. And some, uh, halibut hooks. For class."

I swear, he pushed his chair back, like, *I knew she needed me!*

"Joke, Dad."

He shook his head, half-smiling. "Still can't believe you're not heading back to Dalby High tomorrow. What's poor ol' Mr. Evans gonna do without you taking over his English class?"

I reminded him I was hardly Mr. E's favorite student by the end of sophomore year. Kinda hard to write that, even now. Getting back to journaling after a whole year off...I don't know. *Oh boy, I get to write about Louis's new girlfriend? Mom's flying shut-down?*

Ooh, how 'bout Whatshisname, Fourth of July, That Awful Summer? Right.

"Well," Dad said, "Mr. E seems to get you, anyway. Best idea you had, letting him in on all that Flyer stuff. He was in your corner all year—"

"—yeah, if 'in my corner' means 'on my case'—"

"—and I still think, if you'd just suck up last year's grades, make your junior year a fresh start…" *blah blah blah.*

I reminded him, A, it was a little late for this advice; B, sending me to Early Start at The Horizon Academy was Mr. Evans's idea, and C, his own parenting job was about to run a lot smoother without weekly teacher phone calls.

So Dad went with, "But Savannah needs you more than ever now—"

"Savannah's doing fine," I cut him off. "Savannah will always do fine. Besides," I added, before he could start again, "It's not like I'm moving to another planet! Mom went a lot farther than Wattsville when she did college."

Dad raised his big ol' eyebrows. "True, Joss. That turned out well, didn't it?"

Wow, snark from Ron Burgowski. Not a good fit.

"That wasn't her fault! Mom was trying to give up flying and it messed her up." *If anything, it was your fault,* I wanted to add—*she was trying to be your nice, normal girlfriend*—but Dad's face stopped me.

"Dad…" I sighed. "Seriously…high school and college at the same time? I'm saving you tons of money. Jeez. Just 'cause no Burgowski's ever done it…"

"No Burgowski's ever graduated college at all," he mumbled. "And your brother's not exactly on that track now, following in my fishy footsteps."

The pigeons edged back, ruffling. I said, "Yeah, well, Lorraine's got enough degrees for all of us." Dad likes when I include his wife among the Burgowskis, even though she didn't take the name. "Plus," I shrugged, "It's not like I'm the first one smart enough for college. You had to help Grampa on the boat. Michael's helping you. And Mom…she got bored with college, right?"

"True." Dad frowned. "Beth learned more from experiencing life straight up." *You mean addiction to pills and alcohol? Right, Dad. Two years after discovering his wife and daughter's powers, the guy can still barely talk about "Flyer stuff." Not that New Improved A.A. Mom has been sharing any Flyer stuff with me either.*

"Yeah, so, you shouldn't take this personally. I just…need to be here now, okay? Dalby is…" *A prison. Dalbatraz.* "…fine."

The pigeons burbled in their weird *Star Wars*-y language. Across the street some girl was chewing out her boyfriend on her cell phone, and a car alarm sounded in the distance. How do people focus in all this city noise?

"I'll be back, Dad. And I'm not giving up flying, so I won't be like Mom. I'll be fine."

People say I have Dad's eyes, big and chocolatey—almost enough to make up for my dishwater hair. But now those eyes disappeared under his giant eyebrows.

"I *know*," I said before the lecture started, "Rule Number One, I KNOW. Dad. I got this. I won't Get Seen. Jeez, I've learned *some*thing about flying in two years."

I expected Dad's response to be *Please, you're as crazy as your mom, just look at last year.* But he surprised me.

"I know that, hon. If you handle Horizon Academy and Coastal U as well as you handle … flying…you're gonna have 'em for breakfast."

"Wish Michael thought so," I mumbled. "He told me only posers go to boarding school."

The eyebrows went up. "Yeah, well, there are more things in Heaven and Earth, Horatio, than are dreamt of in Michael's philosophy."

"What? That's *my* Hamlet quote. Bet you don't even know what it means!"

"Means Michael doesn't know yet what he doesn't know. That's his weak spot." Dad smiled. "Yours too, Jocelyn."

I snorted. "Well, that's lame—how's anyone know what they don't know?"

"They don't." The smile became a grin. "It's everyone's weak spot."

I breathed in the hazelnut steam of my latte. *Be nice. He's about to say goodbye.*

And that's when Dad started with "I'm not wild about this boarding school thing…" And The Flying Barista came down on our lattes.

I know. She didn't fly. She tripped. Or something. I KNOW, all right?

So, Dad's Parenting Moment was over; he had to leave. But my flight-energy still buzzed through me, skittering my heart. "Uh, I just gotta use the bathroom," I said, and zipped back into the café, leaving Dad to pick up our broken-mug mess.

Blue-hair Guy stomped past me and out the door, muttering under his breath. The World's Clumsiest Gorgeous Barista had taken his place behind the counter.

"Hi, welcome to—oh, I'm *sorry*, I forgot your drinks," she said, and turned to grab some mugs. "That was so *embarrassing*," she added, not looking around. Her punchy words floated over her shoulder. "What were you guys *having*?"

"No, that's okay, we gotta go," I said. "But, hey." I realized I had no idea what to ask.

"I'm so *sorry*," the girl repeated. She turned back to the register, but still she wouldn't look at me. "Let me give you your *money* back anyway."

"No, no, don't worry about it," I muttered, and she was off wiping again. Her ponytail hung nearly to her waist. None of the coffee-drinkers in the corner looked up from their laptops, so I leaned against the counter, breathing through my nose. My engines raced. *Idiot.*

I smelled…coffee. Vanilla. Cinnamon. No lily-smell.

I still don't know if lilies are truly the scent of the sky, or just the scent of a Flyer's power. Even Lorraine, World's Smartest Stepmother, hasn't figured that out, in all her research. All I know is, flying makes Flyers smell like lilies.

No way this girl just tripped onto our table. If she'd step a little closer…

"Do you…are you, like, a student here?"

"Yeah," she said, back still turned. Weird that somebody that pretty would get so embarrassed about a little accident. Except I guess it wasn't all that little.

"Oh, cool," I blabbed, "I'm gonna be one too. I mean, I'm still in high school, I'm going to Horizon, but I'm in this Early Start program so I'll be taking classes at Coastal U too, and I'm, like, stoked. I mean, it's pretty cool here, right? We don't have any outdoor cafés where I live." And I leaned across the counter, inhaling. *Still just coffee…*

She tossed a tiny frown over her shoulder, like who wouldn't if some strange chick came sniffing at them? "Oh," she said, and turned back to her wiping.

So much for asking me, "So where do you live?" and us sharing our life stories.

"Jocelyn." Dad stuck his head into the café. "Ferry."

"Okay, so, I'll see ya," I said lamely, and headed back into the sunshine to say goodbye to Dad.

I could've stayed to get my replacement coffee. I could've sat there until Barista Girl *had* to turn around and talk to me. I could have made a real friend in Wattsville, like I used to have on Dalby.

Or I could get a grip. Another Flyer, falling into my lap? Gimme a break.

"Joss, honey." *Oh jeez*—Dad was taking my hands. "You take care of yourself, okay? Call us tonight after dorm orientation."

"Okay." His hands were so big and warm. I know he wanted a hug. A year ago, he would've gotten one. But a year ago, I wasn't the kind of girl who ditches her family and friends for boarding school. I squeezed his hands and let go.

"I'll be fine, Dad. Don't miss your boat."

CHAPTER TWO

BOUNDED IN A NUTSHELL

To: LouisTheRed@gmail.com

Hey, Louis. You know, this would be a lot easier if your mom believed in freakin PHONES. But I probably won't send this anyway. What's the point when you can't even read it till you get to school tomorrow and sneak onto email? I want to talk to you NOW.

So it's my First Night At Boarding School. I mean Academy. SO weird. Dude, I live in a dorm—Nutschel Dorm. Seriously. Sounds more like "Mitchell" than "nutshell," but still it's kinda like Hamlet, "bounded in a nutshell." ☺ It's all red brick, like everything on this campus, with ivy even. There's Curfew, and Sign-in, and a Resident Advisor—I mean, "RA." We call her the Raging Aardvark 'cause she looks like one, and she went OFF when my roomie asked how old she was.

Yup—I got ROOMMATES. Two of 'em. Dawntae reminds me of your mom—she brought cookies just like Shasta would. Except Shasta would never use sugar, and Shasta's skinny where Dawntae's, like—not. But she's super nice. Also REALLY into Disney, like she's six instead of sixteen. But whatever!

The other one, Rialta? I know, right?—sounds like a hotel.

Her family probably owns some. She's got seriously nice clothes, like this suede jacket she let me wear to dinner. Savannah would just die. Rialta's into Harry Potter too, like: "Hermione's the best female character in all of literature." (Tae only saw the movies.) I think Rialta and I can be buds—Tae doesn't get my jokes at ALL. But Rialta's folks paid extra for the single room in our suite, so Tae and I share the double. Still, I like my top bunk. You know me and heights, right?

About that. Dude. Remember that last time I took you flying? Yeah—me neither. That's how long it's been. That's what I really wanted to say to you, Louis: What is up with... the whole not-flying-Air-Joss-anymore thing?

Don't give me that "I'm too heavy for you" crap. I can still fly Michael, and he weighs like two of you. Well, not anymore, now you're all buff and Incredible Hulky. But I could still fly you, Louis.

Why didn't you want to? Cuz of Erin?

Why didn't you come say goodbye? Erin too?

Is that how it is now?

-- Are you sure you want to delete this message? --

Can't believe I started writing Louis last night. How pathetic is that? Just, after our Welcome to Horizon Program, Rialta and Dawntae went to the Ice Cream Social, and all of a sudden "social" was the last thing I wanted to be, ice cream or not. So I ended up lying on my bunk like a moron, staring at Tae's poster of Disneyland fireworks. Which of course made me think of the Fourth of July. So I rolled over, and there's my fam and all my buds, smiling from that photo-collage Savannah made me, Louis's hair sticking up all Red Rooster-y, as usual.

Jeez. I'm psyched Louis has a girlfriend, seriously—good for him. But couldn't she have let him say goodbye?

Ah, give it a rest, Flying Burgowski. Study for your math placement. No more Savannah to help with math.

I should go flying.

Yeah, right. Wattsville's a city. You'll get Seen in your first two seconds.

The sun'll go down soon. I could get on out there before the roomies get back.

No. Study.

OK, fine—math. Looks like a pretty sunset, though.

I made it halfway through my practice problem set before the sky darkened and I caved.

The good news: Our Raging Aardvark and all the girls on our floor were Socializing ice creamily, so I didn't have to make excuses. More good news: Wattsville's not terrible for flying. The Horizon campus is close to the waterfront, this maze of grungy alleys and warehouses, no stores or restaurants drawing nosy people out to See me. Weird that Horizon Academy lets us tender teenagers live so near an area you could stash bodies in.

The bad news: Flying didn't whoosh those draggy home-thoughts out of my system.

Well, it did at first. I mean—*flying*, right? Step, step, *schooom*—straight up, no tree limbs to dodge like my takeoff spot at home, nothing but flight-energy pouring from my chest to my fingertips. And the sky! Yeah, the wind over the warehouses smells more like cigarettes and garbage than lilies, but mixed with diesel and fish—Dad-smells. And I got a good feel for the borders of my safe flying range, once I turned my back on the bay: whoops, there's the Coastal campus, landscaped all the way up the hill, with little pathways and benches perfectly designed for Coastal Buccaneers to spot Flyers. So I will NOT be flying over Coastal U. I zipped back down to the safe, dark warehouses, feeling pretty damn smug.

Mom couldn't handle this. College is when she met Dad and gave up the sky. But me? I'm in my habitat.

I didn't fly long—down the waterfront to a power plant and back, maybe fifteen minutes. It was still dusk when I coasted into a particularly garbage-y alley to land.

"Dusk"—Louis loved saying that word. And boom—right back where I started.

Under the streetlights, I walked the few blocks to Nutschel Dorm, feeling the flight-power drain back into my chest, thinking about emails I wasn't going to send.

The roomies wanted to know where I'd been. Let's hear it for all that lying practice with Savannah back home.

"Girl, you missed out!" Dawntae greeted me with a hug. "We did this ice-breaker thing with toilet paper, cracked me up." She stepped back, big warm eyes like Dad's, holding my shoulders. "Mmm, you smell fine! Hook me up with some of that."

"I went to scope out the shops in town," I told them.

Rialta hesitated for a second before hugging me too, one-armed. "Pretty pathetic shopping, right? Well, maybe not compared to what you're used to on your island. Ooh, I didn't mean to sound like that," she added.

Didn't you? "It's okay. I like thrift shops better anyway." *Considering that's pretty much all Dalby has.* "How was the ice cream?"

"Forget that, Joss, you shoulda seen the guys," Dawntae grinned, smoothing her already-smooth 'do. "Telling you... Horizon Hotties, that's what's up. My girl Rialta already snagged herself one."

"Oh, stop," said Rialta, blushing. *Oh boy, another friend in a relationship.* "But Jossie, seriously, you *should* have been there. The Raging Aardvark asked about you. We told her you weren't feeling well, but next time..."

"It's Joss, not Jossie," Tae reminded her.

Hate saying it, but Rialta's right, I need to be careful. "Thanks, guys, I'll be a good little girl next time," I told them. "Want some tea?"

So we hung out, all Boarding School-y, drinking my peppermint tea. Dawntae laughs with her whole body, but sarcasm dies with her—she just cocks her head till you feel bad for trying. And Rialta...she'd rather talk about *her* stuff. Her family goes to Hawaii every Christmas! Maybe she'll take me along sometime.

"Journaling is cheap therapy," Mrs. Mac said in middle school. And I chose last year to ditch this notebook and screw myself up even worse. Well, guess what—I finally feel like writing. Must've been that home-smelling tea we were drinking, 'cause when I turned out the light last night, my stupid brain got stuck on this day from Sophomore Disaster—I mean Year. I should be writing about my new classes and stuff, but I gotta get this out of my system. Therapy time.

In a Hamlet nutshell: there was this guy, summer before last. Made like he liked me—I mean, *liked* me. Big joke: all he wanted was to zap my Flyer powers, and Mom's. 'Cause he and his uncle are Standers and that's what Standers DO.

Mom and I disempowered Mr. Stander Uncle before he disempowered us. He went ballistic and attacked Mom; she sued his ass and won some bucks. Helped Dad put a down payment on his new fishing boat, *Flyer*. Happy ending to the summer, right?

Then school started and the year went to hell.

I guess Louis figured out how much I wanted Whatshisname. I guess that's why he disappeared on me. With Savannah's baby coming, I was too distracted to notice how little Louis and I were hanging out, and when I did? Too late.

And Mom...You'd think after grounding herself for fourteen years, she'd want to do nothing but fly with her flying daughter, right? And she sure did at first. But ever since the Standers—I don't know what her deal is. Kinda hard to talk it out when neither of us wants to remember that scouring humiliation. And that's enough about that.

Cheap therapy, huh? Tell that to my stomach. Feels like someone's practicing knot-tying.

Keep writing.

Fine. Saturday, middle of last May. Halibut season had just re-opened, and Lorraine and Dad were having this huge argument about whether it was safe for him and Michael to take the boat out. Well, for Lorraine, "huge argument" means speaking at normal-people volume instead of whisper-trails. I was finishing breakfast and the kitchen was tense, like back when Michael used to be the problem. Now the problem was the weather forecast.

"Ron, they're calling for gusts up to forty miles per hour. Does that sound safe to you? Be honest." I remember the smell of Lorraine's peppermint tea. And toast, which I was munching while clearing my plate. Lingering over breakfast did not appeal.

Standing at the back door, Dad and Michael exchanged looks like they were Lorraine's little boys instead of husband and stepson. "The *Flyer* did fine when we took her out last week, hon, and those winds were even higher," Dad said. Usually "hon" works its magic on Lorraine, but not this time.

"But that was just motoring around in the bay! You didn't go out in the Strait, did you? Where, I'm guessing, the fish are?" Lorraine tossed her long, silvery braid over her shoulder. "Come on, Ron. You know better."

Whoops, overkill. Dad may have a bull's physique more than a bull's temperament, but that last sentence? Red cape.

"What I know *better* is how much I owe the bank, okay?" Dad's eyebrows hunkered low. "What I know *better* is how fast the bank will take her back if I don't get out there and catch some fish. Wouldn't that be a great thank-you to Beth for helping me get back on the water?"

"Plus," Michael put in helpfully, "if we lose the boat, you'd have to work at the store again, right, Dad?" He snagged an orange from the fruit bowl and tossed it into his grungy daypack. "Only this time you wouldn't own it. And Mom might have to work there too."

Gotta hand it to the bro—that was some skillful hyperbole. If her ex-husband's boat got repo'd, Mom wouldn't lose her accounting job just 'cause she helped him buy it. And Dad could always fish on someone else's boat; he's not prisoner to the Quik-Stop Convenience Store since selling it a year ago. But Michael's right about us needing money. Forty-foot fishing boats are spendy, and Mom didn't get *that* much from her Mr. Howe-neck-injury settlement.

I could see various arguments racing across Lorraine's face—that's how upset she was, 'cause I can't usually read her. But that's when the phone rang.

Lorraine snatched it up with a look that told Dad, *Don't you dare leave.* But Michael, big Mr. Almost-Graduated Working Man, tossed his hair out of his eyes and headed for the back door.

"See you at the dock, Dad," he muttered, and slipped out.

Me? I eased out of the kitchen, wishing Dad wasn't blocking the exit Michael took.

"Oh, hi, Norm," Lorraine was saying into the phone. *Norm? He'll always be Mr. Evans to me.* "Yes, we have a minute. Do you want to talk to Ron?"

She's a smartie, my stepmom. She talked to my teachers all the time. But the phone made a fine anchor. She handed it to Dad and stood watching, hands on hips, as I made my getaway through the living room.

Yay for our new house, yay for the money from selling the store. No more dodging customers while escaping from our adjoining kitchen—yay for a real front door. Which I fled through. Though not before hearing Dad say, "You're kidding. She ditched the whole English *exam*? Can she even pass now?"

I needed to fly in the worst way.

Literally. The best way is when the energy fizzes through you like your blood has sparkles, and boy, you better elevate fast if you don't want to explode. The worst way—that's what I was doing. Escape, with eggs and toast turned to cement in my stomach. I launched vertically from the front porch like Ironman—harder than one-two-three takeoff steps, but better than smashing into a tree trunk —and rocketed over the woods. I flew at treetop level in fast circles, happy not to live smack in the middle of Dalby Village anymore. But not happy about anything else.

You thought they wouldn't find out? Cs are one thing. Skipping an entire Julius Caesar *Unit Exam means a big fat F.*

Dad thought those disastrous days were over, the year before, when Michael and I stumbled through two months of high school on the mainland, trying to live with Mom. Back on Dalby, I'd been a total angel through the rest of ninth grade. Then That Horrible Summer happened. Fourth of July. I got through August by re-reading Harry Potter book seven every time I couldn't un-snag the memories of Whatshisname's face, or voice, or breath. I know *The Deathly Hallows* by heart. Then sophomore year started. And I...

What do you want to call it, Flygirl? Fell apart? Took over Michael's role? Started Acting Out?

Anyway, the downhill slide that had started in September was hitting bottom last May, and I needed to get the hell out. So I flew to the edge of the village, landed behind our old store and walked to Louis's.

Dalby Village was livening up like it always does on Saturdays when spring brings the tourists back. I skirted the Farmers' Market, turning my head quickly to avoid Mrs. Mac, who would've said a lot more than "hi" to her former favorite student. *Mr. Evans tells me you insist on reading* Hamlet *to yourself instead of* Julius Caesar *with the rest of the class. Why on earth? You do know you have to pass Sophomore English before you can take my AP class?*

I know I know I KNOW. What a moron—couldn't even skip like a normal tenth grader, had to sit there defiantly reading the play Michael was struggling with in Senior English. *Why on earth?*

I don't freakin' know, all right? Except...Julius Caesar was a pompous ass. Hamlet was depressed, hemmed in, pissed off. *"Denmark's a prison."*

Hamlet I could relate to. And Louis, I remember thinking grimly, could be like Hamlet's bud Horatio. Louis would fly with me and help me sort out what to do about Mr. Evans. Or not. Louis isn't really about advice. But he'd listen like Horatio until I figured it out.

So, what I said in that Louis-email I never sent? It's true, I don't remember the last time we flew together. Sure wasn't that breezy day in May.

"Hey, sweetie!" Louis's mom, Shasta, sang, like she's done since I started barging into their kitchen at, like, age seven. She was washing dishes with her partner Janice. "Is it a party, then, Joss? You guys want to make cookies?"

I hugged Shasta. "Party?" *Ohhh...Louis has company.* My stomach, relaxing from my Shasta-hug, tensed again. "No, that's okay..."

Louis had been hanging around with Erin a lot—duh, they had practically all their classes together, like freshmen do. But since when did they hang out on weekends?

Can I get something straight? I *like* Erin. She's a soccer stud, and she's pretty much caught up to Savannah in geometry since she bumped up to our math class. She laughs at my jokes. She helps Louis with Algebra. And writing. And everything else I used to help him with.

Just, I was REALLY hoping to fly with Louis right then.

"Hey!" they said together as I stepped into Louis's teeny room. They were sitting hip to hip on his bed.

"What rhymes with 'metaphor'? We're writing Mrs. Mac a birthday card," Erin added, patting the bed for me to join them—like it was hers. I sat, squinching her and Louis closer together.

"That's what I 'said it for,'" I responded automatically. *Great, forgot Mrs. Mac's birthday too. Self-centered moron.*

"That works," Louis grunted. His new, manly voice gave me a little jolt back then. Well, it still kinda does—not that I've heard it since I bumped into him at the store a week before leaving. Not that I ever heard it saying, *Have fun at boarding school, Joss, I'll miss ya.*

Knock it off, Flygirl. Tell the story.

"'Sup?" Erin chirped. She was in pigtails, wearing her green softball uniform—yeah, she's a pitching stud too.

Me and my Horatio-buddy are NOT up, with you here, I thought. "When's your game?" I countered, looking at their feet parked side-by-side like cars in a cozy garage.

"Oh, like, an hour." Erin stood and stretched her arms, and Louis, on the bed, did the same, as if they were connected by an axle. I knew he'd grown taller and more muscular because, duh, when a person flies doubles with you for over a year, you get to know their body—damn, that sounds wrong, but I KNOW what I mean. It's just, he stopped feeling like the same ol' shrimpy Louis a few months ago, but that was totally okay because he still WAS his same ol' self. But last May, I was surprised to see how *toned* his arms had gotten. He was still getting over the shock of being good at baseball.

"Oh." I felt like I had to offer some reason for being there. But why??? Louis is my oldest friend. So I said, "You sure? On my way over, I thought I saw the team heading for the field."

"Oh, shoot! Are we playing at *nine*? Louie, sorry, we'll finish later. Come watch me, 'kay?" And Erin jetted out of there.

"See ya, Erin," I called.

Just—I wasn't used to it then, okay? Louis and Erin. Erin and Louis. It's not like I needed to keep on being his only friend, like I had been for years and years. *But jeez, couldn't he have warned me? "Louie?" Gimme a break.*

"Hey, wanna go fly over their game?" *Lying hypocrite.* I knew perfectly well there wouldn't be a game to fly over for another hour, and flying over a crowd is *verboten.* But Old Louis would have suggested something better, like swoop-overs of Whittier's Bluff, or experimenting with flying just under the fiercest layer of wind, daring it to flip us, like we'd done in...wow. February?

New Louis gave me an un-Louisy smirk. "Seriously, Joss?" he said and stood up. "Yo, my game's right after Erin's. I gotta get dressed."

A chill reached down my chest, even as I felt my face turn red. "Right," I said, like *sure, I came all the way over here to tell you the game schedule.* "Hey, come by my house later if you—you know. Wanna go up tonight." *Awkward lying hypocrite.* I'd never had trouble inviting Louis to fly before.

He tossed his uniform onto the bed. "Whyn't you fly with your mom?"

"She's not really into it these days," I said, flattening the curling edge of Louis's Seattle Mariners poster. He never used to have such boy-stuff in his room.

"Beth? Not into flying?" Louis's frown disappeared as he struggled out of that "Visualize Whirled Peas" T-shirt I'd given him for his thirteenth birthday. "I saw her yesterday over the Spit. Maybe she just doesn't want to fly with *you.*" He turned his back, letting the shirt drop to the floor.

"Well," I said, because *Why yes, you're right, that* is *the problem,* would make me start crying, and *Damn, when did you start hiding your bod from me?*—who says that to their buddy? "Mom's, like, totally independent these days. And I guess flying with me—"

21

"—reminds her of when she wasn't? Or Fourth of July, almost gettin' grounded? Yeah, I get that," said Louis. His bright hair reappeared through his green jersey like a woodpecker in a bush, and my heart cracked a little: *You always get it.* But turning around, he was still frowning. "Hey," he nodded toward his baseball pants.

"Right, see ya."

All I got was a grunt. So much for Horatio.

Shasta and Janice offered me tea on my way out. I declined with a smile and head-shake, not trusting my voice. I walked back into the village. My stupid eyes were burning. My flight-urge felt as dead as my oldest friendship.

But no way was I going home after that ominous phone call. I decided to go browse the half-price shelf at the bookstore. Where I bumped into the last person I wanted to see, after Dad and Lorraine.

Bushy eyebrows appeared around the side of the mystery section. "Well, look who's here," said Mr. Evans.

To: Nevans@dalby.k12.wa.us

Dear Mr. Evans,

I was just writing about you in my journal, but I got too bummed, so I decided to address you directly. I wish to extend my thanks.

Thank you for calling my house so much last year and turning my parents into Homework Vultures. Thank you for setting up all those conferences, especially that last one in May. Thank you for your witty use of *Hamlet* quotes to sum up my attitude: "Jocelyn seems to feel herself 'bounded in a nutshell,' and finding her classes, 'stale, flat and unprofitable.'"

(You were wrong about that, you know. It wasn't just

my classes I was "finding" that way—it was the whole freakin' year.)

Thank you for saying, "Jocelyn needs to have her mind blown, or she's going to drop out next year." Thank you for saying, "What if she moved to where no one knows she's a Flyer, where she can be a normal teenager for once?" And suggesting The Horizon Academy and Early Start at Coastal U. And helping to get me in. Hey, my guy Hamlet went away to school too, right? The thought of that escape literally saved my sophomore year—and yes, I know I mean "figuratively." Put your red pen down. I'm actually being sincere now. Yes, I know I don't need to say "actually." I'm here at Horizon now, making new friends—it's going to be great. As long as I can find a place to fly.

Oh, yeah—thanks for not freaking out when I showed you about flying, last fall. And for understanding about the enemies of flying, and how betrayed they can make you feel. Thanks for telling me I could talk to you about That Awful Summer and Standers and Whatshisname, if I needed to. It's just kinda awkward when you stand there handing me tissues while I babble about how flying isn't the problem. And talking to teachers isn't the solution. I'm sixteen. I'm supposed to have someone of my OWN to listen to me.

Right. I'm not freakin' sending this. What kind of a loser ditches her own diary to email a teacher? I'm going flying. I just

-- Are you sure you want to delete this message? --

"Joss? If you're going to the machine, can you get me a Diet Coke?" Dawntae asked from below, removing her earbuds as I slid off my top bunk. I totally forgot she was there. "Something wrong?" she added.

"Oh. No, I'm…just going to the bathroom."

"Jossie," Rialta's voice floated out from her room, "ask the Raging Aardvark if our hall meeting starts at nine or nine-thirty."

Ha. Still bounded in a Nutschel. Nice try, Mr. E.

CHAPTER THREE

PASSION'S SLAVE

W as this a horrible mistake? The whole boarding school thing?

Didn't mean to ditch the journal for two weeks. Horizon classes are great. I just…don't know what to write about the roomies. Like yesterday in PE.

"Nngghuhhh," Dawntae grunted from the floor. We're supposed to do pushups plank-style, but Tae's plank was warping.

"Thirteen! C'mon, Tae, you got this!" I cheered, mid-crunch, next to her on the squishy mat.

"Easy…for…you to say," Tae mumbled. "Grrrahh!" Her pushup collapsed into a panting mound. "I got the…wrong body type…for this mess."

"No way," I told her, crunching away—flying's fantastic for your core. "Two weeks ago you couldn't do two pushups, and now fourteen? You're in *charge* of that body."

Arms above her head, Rialta glanced over from her tricep-reps. "Jossie's right, Tae—bad body type is no excuse."

That stopped my crunches. "I didn't say that!"

Dawntae's huge brown eyes tightened with hurt. "Yeah, well, 'it is not what is outside, but what is inside that counts,'" she muttered, sitting up.

I'm learning to recognize her little Disney quotes when I hear 'em. "Right—totally. That's what I'm trying to tell—"

"But no offense, Jossie," Rialta interrupted, yanking her weights down, "someone naturally slender like you who can eat what she wants…you're not exactly a useful role model."

Who knew "naturally slender" could sound like a slap?

Then at dinner tonight, picking through her carefully organized salad, Rialta announced: "My dad says colleges don't look at transcripts with Early Start credits."

Do you ever start a sentence without "my dad says"? "Well, that's not what my teacher told me," I retorted, munching my own pile of grated carrots and mini corn cobs. Horizon's salad bar is awesome. "Plus, I'm psyched for my college classes 'cause they sound cool, not just 'cause they're gonna graduate me early."

"My grandma was pushing Early Start." Dawntae sipped her soup. "But she backed off when I got my scholarship. So Joss, you're gonna have, like, a whole new crowd to hang with at Coastal, right?"

"Yes," Rialta answered for me. "But Tae, anyone can totally sneak into Coastal parties."

I chomped hard on the inside of my cheek. "I don't need to hang out at Coastal." *Or do I?* "They just have stuff Horizon doesn't offer. Jeez, I'm taking Mandarin! And History of Modern Slavery."

"But two sets of classes…" Dawntae shook her head. "Not this girl. You go, Joss."

Rialta shrugged. "My dad says Mandarin's a fad; most businesses are looking for Japanese speakers these days."

I stood up before saying something Tae couldn't smooth over. *Maybe bag lunches?*

Rialta didn't notice. "Coastal classes start tomorrow, Jossie? Find out what our party choices are. My dad was in a frat there; he says just stay away from the punch."

Or maybe I could switch rooms. As I bussed my tray I heard Rialta's voice piercing the noise of two hundred dining teenagers: "Y'know that salad bar lady couldn't comprehend 'Green Goddess dressing'? You should at least *understand* English if you're going to have a job around real people."

To: Ginnymama@hotmail.com

Hey, Savannah. You're probably having dinner with your fam. What's up? Not much here. My roommate's a diva--the one with the nice clothes. Dawntae, the other one, she's a sweetie. But when I try talking with her about Rialta, she goes all Disney on me: "y'know, the things that make Rialta different are the things that make her HER." Tough to be friends with someone so un-snarky.

I'm babbling, I know. I'm stuck on Pre-Calc—huge surprise. Diva Roomie has a crush now, Chaz—they're co-editors of our prestigious school paper. So when I ask for math help she's like, "Okay but only for ten minutes cuz I'm meeting Chaz for layout." Like a sexy executive.

But this school's all over you. Skip one class, they make you Write a Letter for your File saying you're Aware of the Consequences of Poor Academic Performance... meaning, how crappy can you get before they yank your scholarship. Don't ask how I know this.

-- Are you sure you want to delete this message? --

Moron. Savannah doesn't do email anymore. She's all texting and Facebook. But some of us have dads who won't pay for texting, and no WAY am I letting Facebook lure me in now. "Academic Performance." Scholarship. FOCUS.

Dawntae's *Aladdin* music is leaking out of her earbuds from the bunk below: *"You ain't never had a friend like me!"*

I should stick some more photos on my wall, all messy and curling, just to bug Rialta.

That one Louis took last year, Savannah wearing Ginny in her front pack— I never noticed Louis's shadow's in the picture. Looks like Ginny's grabbing for his shadow. Savannah's smiling her Queen smile, like, "I know, I'm such a Mother-Woman now and you're just a kid, but I'll still always be your bestie."

Just a kid who flies, girlfriend. I should've told Savannah at the beginning. It's too late now; she'd be devastated that I kept my power a secret for two years. Especially since I told Louis first thing. Now I'm stuck on Planet Flyer and she's on Planet Mom, and there's, like, no connecting satellite. Who'm I supposed to talk to? Even if Louis had a phone...he has Planet Erin to explore.

Shouldn't have written that damn word "boyfriend." Why can't I "delete" my own stupid memories? But Dawntae's humming along with the Genie and I keep replaying stuff.

Cheap therapy, Flying B.

OKAY.

Last June, right after the World's Awkwardest Parent Conference. Savannah and I were hanging out in her messy room with Ginny, World's Cutest Baby. I'd just told her I was ditching Dalby for Wattsville. Typical Savannah: in between texts to someone more interesting than me, she tried to talk me into Seattle, because a) the shopping, and b) University of Washington is prettier than Coastal. "Everything's all gothic, like going to college in a castle."

"Yeah—a castle where King Asshole lives."

"Ah, screw King Asshole. If he's still as hot as he was, I wouldn't mind," my bestie laughed. Then she looked up from her phone long enough to see my face. "I know, I know. Zach Howe is not a nice boy. Joss does not want to go to college with Zach Howe. I got that. Hey, though, are you *sure* he's at UW?"

I reached across the bed for Ginny's stuffed otter so she could suck on its nose. "YES, I'm sure," I told Savannah. *You think I'd let myself lose track of the Stander who tried to destroy my power last summer?* "Lorraine said her professor friend had him in a seminar. He's finishing up his freshman year now." Here came the stomach-knots, right on cue. *Zach could come back to Dalby any time and finish the Stander work he started.*

Yeah—about that. Savannah just thinks Zach "led me on" and broke my heart in the normal way, like Tyler did to her— minus the unplanned pregnancy part. She doesn't know Zach's a Stander, or what Standers stand for. How could she, when she doesn't even know her best friend can fly? I was the first person, after Savannah's parents, to hold her baby, but I still can't tell her what I am. Some bestie.

I leaned back against Savannah's bed with Gin-gin in my arms and nuzzled her silky blond hair. *If innocence had a smell...*

"Okay, whatever." Savannah was back to her phone.

Not my fault I can't tell you, girl—you can't keep a secret to save your life. I promised Mom and Dad and Lorraine that summer: my Flying Burgowski Ground Crew = family + Louis + Mr. E. That's it. Not even Mrs. Mac.

A new scent intruded through the Savannah-smells of dirty laundry and lemongrass lotion. Savannah sniffed. "Jeez, Joss, is that you?"

"Bite me. Here, have a dirty-diaper daughter." I passed Ginny over, stuffed otter and all. *Savannah doesn't need to know Zach's my enemy. For her it's enough that he helped humiliate me in front of the whole town.*

She plopped Ginny on a sketchy-looking towel and started undoing her onesie. "I just hope the hotties you meet at Coastal U are nicer than Zach's cousin."

Yup—I'm officially a crappy friend. It's weird how easy I forget that Zach's cousin = Ginny's dad, a.k.a. Tyler Howe, who ditched Savannah when she got pregnant. Son of Mr. Howe, a.k.a. the piggy Stander who attacked my mom. I guess I just love Ginny so much, I don't like thinking about where she came from. Or the pain Tyler caused Savannah. Or that Zach and Mr. Howe caused me, that disaster of a Fourth of July.

Mom's lawsuit settlement helped. And the Howes' moving off Dalby, disappearing into Seattle—that helped more.

"New topic," I said, watching Savannah ball up the stinky diaper like an expert. "Can we do some geometry? Pretty sure I flunked the quiz yesterday."

"F'reals, girl," Her Majesty, Queen of Math began in exasperation, but then her phone buzzed. "Here—" she patted Ginny's tummy—"you take her, 'kay? It's Nate."

When I finally left, three phone calls and a half-sheet of geometry problems later, I felt a little better about math, and a lot worse about boys. Savannah's heart must've healed pretty fast, and why not? She doesn't have a big fat Flying secret keeping her from getting close to anybody.

I could sure use her help now, though. CanNOT concentrate. Maybe I should try headphones like Tae. *A whole new world…*

This is stupid. I'm calling her.

Savannah: "Girlfriend! Where've you been? Get a damn texting plan! I've Facebooked you, like, fifteen times."

Me: (not pointing out that "fifteen times" = twice in Savannah-speak) "Yeah, I'm off Facebook till I get caught up. It sucks you in, y'know?"

Savannah: "You're the one who sucks. You forgot Ginny's eight-month birthday, she's never gonna forgive you. Seriously, girl, I miss you! What is *up*?"

Me: "Not much." (lowering my voice) "People here are awfully different."

Savannah: "Hold up…No, look, it fell under the crib…Sorry. Ginny dropped her pacifier."

Me: "Oh. Hey, Gin-gin."

Savannah: "So Nate says hi. Wanna say hi, Nate? Well, he's waving." Me: "Nate's over?" *Duh.* "That's okay with your parents? It's like, eleven-thirty."

Savannah: "Nate's the best daddy Gin-gin could have. Aren't you?" (Kissy noises.)

Me: "Savannah, he's not…never mind. You're right; Tyler would've been a horrible dad."

Savannah: "I know, right? He'd have been posting pictures of Ginny on a motorcycle wearing a hunting cap. We *so* don't miss Whatshisname, do we?" (More kissies.)

Me: "So yeah, my one roommate…all she talks about is her dad and the stuff her family does, like skiing, and Hawaii."

Savannah: "They have skiing in Hawaii? Nate's family's taking us there after Christmas!"

Me: "No, I said—never mind."

Savannah: "Joss, what are the guys like? You get a fake ID so you can party at Coastal?"

Me: "Uh, not yet."

Savannah: "Well get *on* it! *Damn.* A college boyfriend? That's just what you need to get Dalby out of your system, and, y'know—Zach and all. Remember that *Hamlet* thing you wrote on your notebook last year? About passion, and hearts? You're just lonesome, girlfriend."

Me: "I can't believe you remember that. *'Give me the man who is not passion's slave, and I will wear him in my heart'*—Savannah, you don't get it, that's not about boyfriends, it's…"

Savannah. "Sure it isn't. 'Passion's slave'? And now you're, like, in college? I'd be all over that."

Me: "Really. I'll be sure to mention that to Nate on Facebook."

Savannah: "Whoa, Snarkypants. This isn't about me."

Me: "Seriously? That's a first."

Me: "Hello? You still there?"

She wasn't.

Whoa. A wave of homesick jealous pissed-off yearning guilt slammed through the phone-silence, and my internal motors revved awake, ready to launch me into the ceiling. Like Zach launched me into that cedar branch on the Fourth of July.

I grabbed my mattress, anchoring myself. *Damn it. "…you need to get Dalby out of your system…Zach and all." Talk about "passion's slave"!*

NO. NO. NO. I filled the page with Nos till the revving eased enough for me to write all this down. Now it's midnight, Tae's asleep and I have GOT to finish my math. Coastal starts tomorrow—just classes, no drama. 'Bout time.

Holy crap, this college Chinese stuff is HARD. What was I thinking?! The words for "horse," "ant," "hemp" and "mother" sound exactly the same to me, but all these hip Coastal Buccaneers are like, *Yeah, Mandarin, no big deal.* I'm never, ever opening my mouth in class.

At least my next Coastal class is taught in English. History of Modern Slavery, how hard can that be? Probably another re-hash of Harriet Tubman. But hey, maybe I can use the class time to catch up on my Mandarin homework. If I stay awake.

Ha. Five minutes after Modern Slavery started, my brain had no room for Mandarin. Too full of shocking slavery facts. Like: up to a *third* of captive Africans died, crossing the Atlantic to be sold. Okay, I kinda knew that, but Professor K made it real. "Look to your right," she said in her commanding voice, like Professor McGonagall in the Harry Potter books, minus the Scottish accent. Kinda looks like her too. "Look to your left." No one was sitting next to me, but the guy two seats down cast me an uninterested glance. "One of you would be dead," Prof K intoned. And suddenly I'm not this awkward white teenager in a class with a hundred university students. I'm part of a dark, chained crowd of despair.

Then Prof K hit us with the *modern* stats.

I'll be honest, I've never heard of Ivory Coast before today, but those graphs from the lecture are still burning through me:

109,000 unpaid workers in the Ivory Coast chocolate industry—slaves! And 10,000 of them are kids. Mostly twelve- to sixteen-year-olds, but some younger. Prof K showed pictures of sad-eyed, skinny boys in raggedy T-shirts raking cacao pods and showing their scars from being beaten.

Not back in the 1700s—right NOW. Nothing left of my mind to blow.

"I'm *never* eating another chocolate bar," said a soft voice behind me.

Okay, I lied. *That* blew the last of my mind. The Non-Flying Barista Girl—talking to me.

"I know, right?" Stupid, but I didn't want to scare her off. Class was over, time to hustle back down to Horizon for math, but I turned around, stretching casually. "Did you know any of that stuff?"

"No," she breathed. She's even prettier when she hasn't been crying. Weird to see she'd been sitting alone, like me. "I don't know whether to start researching or join a *protest* group."

"Professor K'll probably assign us both," I said, total hip College Girl.

"Do I know you?" She narrowed her dark eyes. "Aren't you *Brittney's* roommate…?"

"No, I'm—I live down the hill." *Careful.* "I kinda met you at the café where you…where you work. You, like, bumped into my table. A while ago."

Her face flushed instantly, like someone clicked a remote. "Oh…*shoot.* Yeah. That was *you*? I never did refund your *coffees,* I felt so *bad* about that." Her sentences have these funny little volume-blips. "I was just a *mess* that day."

"It's totally okay. I was saying goodbye to my dad and it was just starting to get awkward, you know? So you kinda saved the day." The lecture hall was emptying. *Late for Pre-Calc again.* "I'm Jocelyn," I added. "Burgowski."

"I'm Vivian. Vivian Wu." She held out her hand so we shook, all formal. She had on a giant blue Buccaneers hoodie, and those same black leggings and pink hi-tops. "Nice to meet—*hey*. I know what. I'm going to work now. Why don't you come too and get the *coffee* I owe you? I'll feel a lot *better*."

Yup—behold College Girl, going for coffee. Ditching yet another high school class. But not like last year. Really. I just needed to talk to someone about that lecture.

We headed down the hill past a pretty fountain made of boulders, past batches of bright-jacketed students, everyone talking on phones and going about their business like there was no slavery in the world.

"We sell a *lot* of chocolate at Bean There," Vivian said. "I wanna pull it off the *counter* now, knowing where it probably *comes* from." The wind was grabbing loose strands of black hair from under her hood and whipping them across her face.

I couldn't help myself. Even with all the shock and outrage swirling through my brain about chocolate-slavery, even with the guilty thrill of my first Horizon class-skip, my main impulse was... sniffing. I thought I caught a whiff of something flowery when Vivian opened the auditorium door, but the wind blew it away.

"Uh, yeah," I said. *Get a grip, it's just perfume. Vivian* tripped *when she fell onto our table, like she said.* "And you can totally see that supply-demand thing. Dark chocolate keeps getting more popular, and the darker it is, the more beans, so...yeah. Crazy increased production."

"So you'd think the plantations would pay their *workers* more, right? Why do they have to trick poor families into sending their kids, and then *keep* 'em?"

The wind took a break. *There—another whiff!* I hurried my feet down the uneven sidewalk; Vivian's a fast walker.

"Well, I guess if people don't care enough to ask about conditions, the whole thing just keeps humming along."

"People like *us*." Vivian stopped so abruptly I ran into her. *I know that smell*. "Dang. Slavery. Human trafficking. Right in my very own *life*time."

Standing at the stone gate of this lush, tidy campus, two thoughts floated, in two distinct colors. Dark gray: *All that misery, so unreal.* And pale pink: *What's real is, I might have found another Flyer.*

"Yeah," I managed.

"You know?" Vivian turned left around the wrought-iron fence that protects Coastal U from the rest of Wattsville. "This reminds me of the Chinese who came to work on the *sugar* plantations, where I grew up. They were practically slaves. My great-great-*grandpa* was one. No one ever talks about *that* part of Hawaii," she added.

"Whoa, you're from Hawaii? How cool is that! I've never met anyone from there."

"Oahu."

"Is that like hello? Well, Oahu to you too. Oh wait, no, that's *aloha*." My turn to go bright red.

Here's how I know Vivian's a way nicer person than Rialta: no eye-rolling. She flashed me a kind smile. "Silly—Oahu's my *island*. Hawaii's more than one, you know."

"'Course. Yeah. Duh." But Vivian was so cool about my ignorance that I got over it. "Hey, I'm from an island too. Dalby. And people don't believe me when I tell 'em the Santa Inez Islands are right here in Washington. My roommate goes, 'Santa Inez? You don't look Mexican.'"

"That's *awesome*." She pushed her hair back and glanced at me. "If you don't mind my asking, how *old* are you? You skip a grade or something?"

"I'm sixteen. But I'm not really a student—I mean, not at Coastal. I'm still in high school." Scurrying to keep up as we entered the old, red-brick part of Wattsville, I explained the whole Early Start thing.

"You must be a total *smartie* then. College classes *and* prep school? Did you get a scholarship?"

"Yeah." *Which I'm now putting at risk.* "Pretty amazing, since my grades sucked last year, but my English teacher stood up for me. Guess they believed him. And I wrote a pretty decent essay."

"You must be more than decent to get into *Horizon*," Vivian said, skirting a group of retired-looking ladies outside an antique store. "And way *braver* than me. I still get *home*sick and this is my second year here."

"Well, I do miss…" *Yeah, Flygirl? What about Dalby do you miss, exactly?* "…my dad, even though he drives me crazy sometimes, being all, you know—daddish."

Another glance. "I just have a stepdad. I don't miss him. I miss…the ocean."

"The ocean's right here, silly!" Couldn't believe how fast we fell into that kind of talk, like me and Savannah. And this girl's, like, nineteen!

"Not *my* ocean." That super-sad smile again. "And I can never get *warm*. At least I get paid to make hot *drinks*."

"That's cool. I mean warm," I giggled. We passed the little movie theater, papered with posters. "I worked at a candy store last year. My friends always came in to eat the broken bits. I guess I miss them too."

"But you're so near, you could go home *any*time, right? Or your friends could come visit?"

I could fly home. Could you come with me?

"My best friend's got a baby, she can't really go anywhere." That baby-scent memory hit me, nothing to do with lilies. "*Her* I miss—the baby. Ginny. Major cutie. Hoping she'll start walking around Thanksgiving so I can be there."

"Ginny? Sweet. Short for Vir*ginia*?"

I grinned. "Ginevra. Like in Harry Potter. She's lucky she's not named Hermione. Savannah, her mom—total Potterhead. Like me."

"Whoa, me *too!*" This amazing girl grabbed my arm. "Harry was like my secret *boy*friend growing up. We'll have to go see the next movie when it comes out. My real boyfriend won't go. I think he's *jealous.*"

"So does your boyfriend go to Coastal too? Or is he back in... Oahu?"

We'd arrived at the café; I looked over at the table where Dad and I had been sitting. *That curb is pretty high...probably would send you flying if you hit it wrong.*

"Oh, he goes here." Vivian yanked the door open and pulled off her hoodie to reveal the brown Bean There T-shirt underneath. "So, Jocelyn? I *love* your name." She leaned over to pat my shoulder as I wrestled off my fleece and—*there it is again. Lily-scent.* "You sit here and we can *talk* more if it doesn't get busy. I'll get your latte. You like a flavor?"

I knew it! She really is—

Wait. I lifted my hand back up to my face. Lilies. I put my hand down; the scent faded.

What a moron. I'm the only Flyer in Wattsville. It's the sky on my own Flyer skin I've been sniffing.

"Hazelnut," I told her, and sat down in the corner.

The café filled up with people escaping the wind. I started writing in this notebook, waiting for Vivian to have time to talk, but I'm an idiot—she's totally swamped. And now I'll have to sweet-talk Rialta for Pre-Calc notes. And re-start my career of lying to teachers.

But so what? This exotic college woman seems to like me! Might not be what Mr. E meant by mind-blowing, but it's pretty freakin' awesome.

And there goes my power again—this time, revs of happy-hopeful-daring-pent-up-crazy. Fly in broad daylight? That IS crazy.

But I'm tired of writing NO.

CHAPTER FOUR

WHAT'S MANDARIN FOR "SURPRISE"?

Not super intelligent, flying before dark, but I've learned some tricks in two weeks, okay?

Number One: Launch straight up from the sides of buildings, using the corner as a blind.

Number Two: Never silhouette yourself against the sky. Fly along rooftops, so you're gone before anyone registers a glimpse of you. Even a lurking Stander would doubt his eyesight. Not that I have to worry about Standers anymore. But since "YouTube Sensation" isn't among my life goals, flying over the Coastal campus or downtown Wattsville = Big No-no.

So, Number Three: stick to the waterfront.

Not gonna lie, those alleys are creepy as hell at sunset, every last piece of trash turning into a shadow-puppet monster. At takeoff I nearly stepped on—*OMG, was that a person?* Nope. Just a nasty ol' blanket. Shaking off that hollow-stomach feeling, I zipped from warehouse to warehouse like Spider-Man—*if Spidey had my mad hovering skills.* I am kinda liking that diesely-fishing boat-Ron Burgowski smell, though. Bet Rialta's dad smells like leather car seats.

Don't know how much more crap I can take from that girl. Maybe that's good—every time I want to smack her, I go flying instead. Last Sunday she said teachers only care about summer vacation—pissed me off so bad I flew for an hour. Found this cool park, down past the power plant, with a little cliff almost like Whittier's Bluff at home. I swooped and circled till I could barely hold my arms out. But when I got back, Rialta was telling Dawntae that single parents should just quit complaining and hire a nanny. Tae rolled her eyes and stuck her earbuds in, leaving me to argue till I needed to fly again.

Tonight's flying-urge was my fault: I mentioned Professor K's research assignment to Princess Privilege at dinner. "So I'm gonna find out about Washington State immigrants," I told her and Tae. "Try and find people from, like, Ivory Coast that I could maybe interview."

Tae: "Right on, Joss. Beats writing AP essays."

Rialta: "Ask them how they feel about taking American jobs."

Me: "They're doing jobs Americans won't do. That's why people wanna hire them."

Dawntae: "I totally need to get a job. Think your friend's café is hiring?"

Rialta: "Good luck with that. Unless you're willing to work for nothing like Jossie's immigrants."

NO ONE calls me Jossie. But Rialta's like, "if *I* think it, it must be right." She could be a Stander, minus the homophobia part. A social-class Stander—stomping on anyone less entitled.

So I was flying tight circles above the warehouses, my exciting Friday evening, skipping study group and trying not to think about Rialta, and Standers. You'd think a Student-Centered place like Horizon would be more flexible about switching roommates. Dean Williams didn't even try to *look* sorry when he told me, "Sorry." Probably thinks it's more Student-Centered to make people room with people they want to smack.

Whoa! Something screamed from the darkness in front of me; my left fingertips caught an extra wash of air. *Stupid city seagull— it's all about them.* Just like Rialta.

"Jossie, seriously." The roomies came back from study group just after my flight and we'd all settled into homework positions, but now Rialta was frowning in her doorway. "I can hear your laptop humming from here. Can't you get a quieter one?"

"Oh, sure, I'll get a new computer." From my desk in the living room I beamed my best smile. "Or you could get a nice, cheap one that hums too. They could harmonize."

"Want my earbuds?" Dawntae the Human Bridge offered from her bunk.

"What I really want," Rialta said, hands on hips, "is to know when you're planning to take this place seriously, Jossie. I mean—someone cared enough to give you a scholarship, but you still just skip class or study group whenever. I bet my dad would totally buy you a new laptop if I asked. But you'd probably make some smart comment."

"Your dad sounds like a total sweetie," said Tae. "Jossie" was too busy being speechless.

"And you can quit looking like that, like you're better than me 'cause you have this bleeding heart," Rialta continued. "Know what your problem is? You think just because *you* think something, it must be right." She slammed herself into her room.

I turned to Dawntae. "Can you believe her?"

But Tae shook her head. "Seriously, Joss? You do bring the drama when someone doesn't see things your way. Tetchy! Try being the only person of color in your Honors classes for, like, your whole life."

Uhhh...

"You know, when Rialta gets going, I just count Disney characters in my head till she shuts up," my roommate added. She stuck her earbuds back in and opened her Spanish text. "Gotta find your mental Disneyland, Joss."

Vivian was *thrilled* to see me at Bean There, Done That. "But how come they let you out so late? Don't you guys have *curfew*?"

"On Fridays we can stay out till eleven. I know," I added as she glanced at the clock. "Better drink fast, huh? I just had to get out." *And I'm too tired to fly—wish I could say that out loud.* But I'm over my stupid what-if-she's-a-Flyer obsession. Sometimes people just need someone to talk to.

"So...decaf with hazelnut?" Vivian started my drink without waiting for an answer.

"Can I ask you something?" I leaned on the counter like I did that first day. "Do you have any friends who know Mandarin? 'Cause that class is kicking my butt, but the people in there are kinda intimidating."

"Are you kidding?" Vivian raised her voice over the espresso-hiss. "I speak Mandarin! My mom's Chinese. She taught me a lot. What do you need to know?"

"Oh, y'know, just...everything. *Sheh-sheh*," I said, wrapping my hands around my latte.

"Well, that's a start! *Bié kèqì*—you're welcome. I can't teach you much from here, I gotta start closing soon." Back to her endless wiping. "But I can *totally* help you later."

You're already helping. "That would be great. So..." I sipped my coffee, still standing dorkily. "I was wondering...when you first got here, did you call home a lot?"

Vivian stopped wiping: eyebrows up, shoulders sagging. "Yeah. For like a *year*. My mom made me stop, too expensive." She gave herself a little neck rub. "Feeling homesick?"

I nodded and sipped. Jack Johnson sang softly through the speakers, something about sunset on the beach.

"I still do too," Vivian said. "Real Hawaiian music makes me cry, and even songs like this? Sometimes I skip 'em."

I cleared my throat. "So...you get used to it? Because, y'know, Horizon's okay. And Coastal's awesome. And home's not..." *the same anymore? Something rotten in the state of Dalby?* "I mean, I don't wanna leave. It'd just be nice to..."

"To know you won't always feel like this" Vivian said, real low. "Yeah, I wouldn't count on that. Going off to college is different for us *island* girls."

Whoa. My brain did its two-color processing thing. Dark blue: *She means you're never gonna get over feeling lonely.* Bright yellow: *She thinks I'm like her!*

"Really?"

Vivian wiped. "I dunno. I mean, your island's small and Washington-y; mine's big and *tropical.* But they still have their own ways that no one here gets, right?"

"Right! And you can't explain that to anyone who—"

"—hasn't been *part* of it—"

"—growing up there, talking about the mainland like it's another country—"

"—which it totally *is,* because we're *island* people," Vivian finished. We smiled at each other.

Yeah, but Flyers are their own special island, my brain muttered. "Wish they'd let me live on your campus."

"I *know,* right? You could room with me! I'm totally living alone right now 'cause the roommate they assigned me dropped out, like, the first day."

"What? Why? You didn't choose your own roommate?" *Why don't you have close friends after a year at Coastal?* I did not ask (dark blue). Bright yellow: *She'd room with me!*

"Well, I asked for a single," Vivian said, wiping again. "But Coastal's gotten crowded, so..." Her smile slid back to sad. "My *boy*friend's happy I'm alone again."

"Doesn't your boyfriend keep you company?" Vivian's face did that instant-red thing, so I added, "Oh jeez, I don't mean like that!"

"He comes over a lot," she muttered. "But we're...we don't believe in..."

Wow, almost as awkward as Savannah sharing Tyler details. "It's okay, I get it," I said, looking away. The three other people in the café were packing up.

"Sorry for being so *private*." Vivian fussed with her loose strands of hair. "I have to get over it, I know."

"I can relate," I mumbled. Jack Johnson switched to a minor key, so wistful. "There was...this guy. Summer before last. Totally did a number on me. My best girlfriend keeps wanting to talk about him. But..."

Vivian nodded energetically, setting hair-strands loose again. "It has to be *your* idea to talk, right?" Another glance at the clock. "I know you have to go, but..."

"It was stupid," I heard myself say. "He was older—your age, prob'ly. He made me feel like... he could see who I really was. I thought..." *I thought I was done thinking about Zach.* No flight-revs this time, but my stomach burned sourly. "I thought he was in love with me."

Vivian regarded me steadily. "But?"

"But I'm a moron. I was barely fifteen. He had other things in mind. Not *those* other things," I added quickly as Vivian frowned. "It's hard to explain." *Yeah, Standers vs. Flyers—ya think?*

She crossed her arms over her "Bean There" logo. "Just tell me as much as you *need* to."

What if I need to tell you about my powers? "Thanks—I mean, *sheh-sheh*." A bouncy song by the Shins started, one from Louis's playlist.

"*Hěn hǎo* —good job! I know what," Vivian breathed. "Why don't you meet me in the library tomorrow to work on your Mandarin? And our Modern Slavery outlines too. Whadd'ya *think?*"

I think I might not care if no one here understands the Flying Burgowski, as long as someone understands Joss.

"Cool." I finished my latte, feeling warm all the way through. "Meet you—when?"

"Ummm...two-thirty?" my friend said. "I'll be in the second floor reading room. And if it's okay, my *boy*friend will join us, we usually study together. He's a smartie like you."

Ah, yes, the boyfriend. What'd I expect? Vivian's no more available than Savannah. Or Louis.

"Oh, shoot—curfew." I dropped four dollars on the counter, but Vivian surprised me by reaching across the money for a half-hug.

"Thanks," I said, 'cause *Can you hold still and let me smell you better?* sounds creepy. And I'm over that anyway. With four minutes to spare, I raced for Nutschel, prepping my story for the Raging Aardvark about meeting a long-lost friend. We Island Girls have our ways.

The *boy*friend was late; fine with me. Vivian had taken over the end of one of those giant tables. People were talking in low voices—you don't have to whisper like at Horizon. I waved to a skinny Indian girl from our Slavery class, and she waved back. But Vivian wasn't sitting with her; she was saving a place for me. The whole room was lit up golden from the high windows, matching my mood.

"So I gotta write three paragraphs in English about my home, a friend, and a problem—our three new Mandarin words," I told her, turning on my pathetic laptop, *"but in each paragraph I have to use four other Mandarin words. It's a vocab icebreaker."*

"Sounds more fun than my Anthro," said Vivian. "Go for it."

"'**Number One**,'" I read aloud from my laptop. "'**Home.** *Jia. Jia* **is a small island. I live with my** *fu qin*, **who's a fisherman, and my** *ge ge* **Michael who's trying to be a fisherman too. My** *mu qin* **lives pretty close to us; she and Dad are divorced but nowadays they get along fine,'** *since Mom quit substance-abusing and finally told her ex she's a Flyer.* "'**I have a—**' What's the word for stepmother?"

"Hòu niáng," said Vivian. "You never told me that. Do you... get along with her?"

Oh, right, Vivian has a stepdad she's not wild about. "Lorraine's fine," I said. "She's..." *Wise. Learned. Responsible for my fighting off the Standers.* "...very quiet."

Vivian nodded, frowning. "Lucky. My stepdad is the opposite of quiet."

Her face told me not to pry, so I went back to my paragraph. "**'I have a *hòu niáng* who is a librarian and a terrific cook.'** Okay, one down, two to go." Then I noticed the girl at the next table gazing at me, like it was Library Storytime. "I'll just read to myself," I murmured.

"**Number Two. Friend. *Peng yu*. I have two best *peng yu*.**" *Or do I, anymore?* "**One is Savannah, and she had a—**"

"Hey," I asked Vivian, "is baby a different word if it's a boy or a girl?"

"It's just *bao bao*. Girl is *nu hai zi*, boy is *nan hai zi*." Vivian looked up from her Anthro. "Why're you writing about *babies*? Oh right, your bestie! Baby Ginevra." She shook her head. "It's weird thinking of having a kid at your age. Is your friend very *religious*?"

"Meaning...why'd Savannah choose to have her baby?" I lowered my voice. "She decided she couldn't handle, y'know, an abortion. But her parents totally help take care of Gin-gin. And Nate helps too."

"Nate's the dad?"

"No...it's complicated. The dad's..." *a jerk with a beautiful Stander cousin...* "gone. Nate just stepped up 'cause he's always been in love with Savannah." *Ha—and I once thought Nate wanted me. Fun times.*

"But hey. Back to work." I read to myself: "**...and she had a *bao bao*, a *nu hai zi* named Ginevra. My other friend is Louis, who's a *nan hai zi*,**" *which never used to be a problem till he got himself* *an actual girlfriend,* "but he doesn't own a phone—a *diànhuà*, or a computer, so it's hard to stay in touch." *Even if he wanted to.*

One paragraph to go. Bent over her book, Vivian was fiddling with her ridiculously silky hair. *Funny how Louis's hair looks like red velvet but feels so scruffy, pressed against my temple when we swoop...*

I shook my head, hard. "Number Three. Problem. *Wen ti*. A big *wen ti* for me is getting all my—"

"Hey, Vivian, do you say 'work' when you mean 'homework'?" I asked. "Sorry to keep bugging you."

"*Gōngkè* is 'homework'," and don't worry," she murmured. "I *love* this. Reminds me of Mom. I haven't seen her in over a year."

"What?! Don't you go home over the summer? Or for Christmas?"

"No, I stay here and work," Vivian answered. "It's really *expensive,* going home. And things aren't that great there."

"How can Hawaii not be great?" But I knew the question was stupid.

Vivian's face closed up. "Is it okay if we don't talk about it?"

"'Course," I muttered. "...getting all my *gōngkè* done because I have two sets of—" "Is 'teacher' different from 'teachers'? Sorry."

But Vivian smiled again, her cheeks a little flushed with—who knows? Maybe bad memories speed her heart up like they do mine. And my flight-engines. But she doesn't have those.

"Plurals stay the same."

"Thanks." "...two sets of *lao shi*, at Coastal and at Horizon Academy. But luckily it's not a *wen ti* for me to go *jia* for—"

"Shoot, what's the word for 'holiday'? And hey, if you don't go home, what do you do for Thanksgiving or Christmas?"

"Holiday is *jie ri*," Vivian said quietly, "and sometimes a friend invites me home."

"Well, you are totally invited! Come to Dalby with me for Thanksgiving, okay?"

"*Thank* you, that's so nice. We'll see. I may go to my *boy*friend's in *Seattle.*"

"Oh. Of course. Is that where you went last year?"

"No, I only met him last spring in Seattle, and then he transferred here." Vivian pulled out her phone. *"He's not usually so late.* I'll text him. You get back to work."

"...**to go** *jia* **for the** *jie ri.* **My** *jia* **is close."** *Close enough to fly home, where nobody cares. Or I could stay here where someone seems to care...if she can spare time from the* boyfriend.

Almost done. I finished aloud: "**I'm also lucky because my old** *lao shi...*" *defended me when a beautiful Stander boy set me up to be accused of plagiarism in front of my whole town and broke my heart...*

Damn it. I am so DONE with those memories. "...**helped me get a scholarship to be here."**

"Oh, my goodness, I forgot to *tell* you!" Vivian burst out. "My boyfriend said he's been to your island."

"Seriously?" I saved my Mandarin masterpiece and opened my Modern Slavery syllabus. "What, like, whale watching?"

"No, not like a tourist, he actually *lived* there! He was surprised when I told him you were from Dalby." Her phone blipped. "Oh, perfect! He's on his way up. Maybe you'll *recognize* each other!"

I looked up from my laptop. "Lived there when? I know everyone our age on Dalby. What's his name?"

I'm an idiot, okay? Why didn't I ask her that on the very first day? Could have spared myself two whole weeks of adjusting to this place, and now I'm going to have to leave.

My friend said his name. But she didn't need to. Because right at that moment the reading room door opened, and there he stood.

"Well, hello, kid," said Zach Howe.

Vivian clapped her hands in delight. "Oh, so you *do* know each other!"

I couldn't breathe.

Zach beamed his golden smile at his girlfriend. "Man, Viv, if I'd struck *you* that speechless, you mighta gone out with me the first time I asked, 'stead of the fourth."

"What are you doing here." My voice sounded weird. "You're supposed to be at UW."

He stepped up to our table, put his hands on Vivian's shoulders. He seemed even taller than before. "Something made me want to switch to Coastal. But I'm flattered you've kept track of me. It's been a while."

I can't stand to write this. Zach's HERE. Walking around MY campus. His arm around MY friend.

I have to go home.

I don't want to go home.

"Nice-to-see-you-but-shoot-I-just-remembered-we-have-a-roommate-thing-at-school," I muttered, stuffing my laptop into my pack under the eyes of that beautiful couple. "See ya."

My fingers were shaking so bad I could hardly punch the phone number. "Be home, be home, be home," I chanted down Campus Hill, away from my enemy. Yellow leaves whipped past my ankles. Storm clouds filled the spaces between buildings.

"You're okay, babe," Mom said when I blurted my Zach's-here-and-I'm-coming-home news. "Stay where you are." I could hear her cat Tion purring in the background.

"How can I? He knows I still fly." It wasn't tears I was swallowing, it was panic. "We stopped him from stopping me, but he still has his powers. Mom, I could practically feel them radiating out of him." A chattery group passed and I lowered my voice. "I can't spend every minute here worrying when Zach Howe's going to pray me down for real."

"Every minute? Are you flying that often?" *Jeez, she sounds like Dad.*

"You know what I mean! How can I fly at all if he might be underneath me saying the magic words?"

"Well, there is that," said Mom.

It's what Standers do, what they've always done, even before those ancient books of Lorraine's started recording it. They're on a "holy mission" to vanquish those they call "deviant"—witches, Flyers, gays. Burning and hanging people, that's not too cool these days, but lucky old Standers: all they have to do is stand beneath a flying Flyer and pray their special prayer to break her power.

Like Zach almost broke mine.

The wind rattled the rhododendrons. "I miss you guys," I heard myself say.

"What? Speak up, babe."

"Nothing. Would we have to repay my scholarship? I dunno how that works."

"Jocelyn. Are you telling me you *want* to come home?"

"NO!" A pair of professor-looking women turned to stare, striding past. "I like it here," I added quietly. "But if I can't fly, how can... Mom, you know about this."

"Yes, I do." She sounded grim. "Which is exactly why you need to stay. Stay and graduate early and go to college. But *fly*. Don't you dare let that little Stander punk scare you away from yourself."

"But how—"

"You'll manage." Now it was her voice quivering. Usually it just gets scratchy when she's mad. "We're *done* with letting people push us around, burn us, hang us, denounce us, pray us down. Flyers fly—we don't flee." I heard her take a deep breath. "You'll just have to fly more carefully than ever, babe. No routines. Find someplace inaccessible. You can do it."

I wanted to crawl inside her fierce confidence. *"Flyers fly, we don't flee"*—hell, she sounded like the dude in *Braveheart*. But...

"Mom, you quit flying for a whole fourteen years! And you disappeared on me again last year." *First time saying that aloud.* "So how'm I—"

"I know, babe." Her voice dropped low. "Couldn't find a way to explain. Turns out those Standers did a number on me too, that summer. Didn't want to make it worse for you, sucking you into my stupid flying issues. But now, DON'T let them finish what they started, okay? Fly for both of us."

Whoa. But raindrops started to splat, dousing my questions. "Okay, Mom, whatever. It's raining, gotta run. Love ya."

I dashed the last stretch to Nutschel as the rain hissed on the asphalt. *Mom has total faith in me. Problem is—Mom's the wildest person I know.*

CHAPTER FIVE

FLIGHT FROM AWKWARDVILLE

Awkward **Conversation Number One,** History of Modern Slavery, yesterday (two days after Zach Howe marched back into my life):

Vivian (whispering): "Hey, you. Why'd you disappear like that on Saturday? And how come you haven't answered my *texts*?"

Me: "Sorry, I…I had this roommate thing. And I don't text, remember? But it was nice to meet your boyf—I mean, it was good to see Zach again."

Vivian: "Really?"

Me: "No."

Vivian: "Right? That's what I thought when you took off. He's…Zach's the guy, right? The one you were telling me about?"

Me: (nodding)

Vivian: (turning bright red) "So, yeah. So. What I wanted to ask…Do you still *like* him? 'Cause …"

Me: "No. No! Vivian, that was, like, a century ago. And nothing happened. And…"

Professor K stopped in mid-sentence to stare at us. So did everyone. We shut up. For a while.

Vivian: (barely moving her lips) "It's just… you said he broke your heart. And I see how other girls look at him. I won't judge, I just want to know—were you guys *together*?"

Me: "Jeez, I was barely fifteen! And that's not even the point."

Vivian: "What is the point?"

Me: "Zach is…And I'm…"

Vivian: "What?"

Me: "I just had a stupid crush on him, okay? We barely even knew each other on Dalby. It was just…a shock to see him again."

Vivian: "Well, I'm glad. I mean thanks for telling me. You totally have to keep hanging out with me, okay? Then it won't be *weird* anymore."

So why don't I tell her? Oh, right! The whole magic Flyer thing, and the anti-magic Standers, to my brand-new non-Flyer friend. That conversation wouldn't be awkward. It would be impossible.

Awkward Conversation Number Two, this afternoon at Bean There (three days A. Z.—After Zach):

Zach: "Hey, kid, this your hangout now too?"

Me: "Uhhh…"

Vivian: "Told you he'd show up if I broke the biscotti! I swear he *hears* 'em break. Here, you cookie monster, eat this."

Dawntae (entering with Rialta): "Joss! You're here! We thought we'd check your place out."

Rialta (looking around): "Kind of alternative, but I can see why you like it. How's their cappuccino?"

Vivian: "Are you guys the *room*mates?"

Me: "Uh, yeah. Dawntae, Rialta—this is Vivian."

Zach: "And Zach. Hey."

Dawntae: "Hellooo." (fake whisper) "Wow, Rialta, I get why she likes the atmosphere here, know what I'm sayin'?"

Me (blushing like a dorky idiotic moron): "Zach's Vivian's… they're together."

Vivian: "But Joss and Zach actually met be*fore*, on her island. Kinda cool, right? Can I start some drinks for you guys?"

Dawntae: "I'd love a hot chocolate."

Rialta: "Cappuccino with extra cinnamon, please. So Zach, does your family have a vacation home on Dalby? We go sailing around there, but I heard there wasn't much to do."

Zach: "I was working."

Dawntae: "And you met Joss? And here you both are! Joss, how come you never told us you had friends here?"

Vivian: "Oh, they didn't really—"

Me: "Oh, we weren't really—"

Rialta: "Uh-huh. That's why Jossie isn't blushing her face off, right?"

Zach (leaning across the counter to rub Vivian's shoulders): "I'm just here for the biscotti. And other sweet things that need taking care of."

That last part? That wasn't awkward. It was creepy.

Mom called me again after lunch; I let it go to voice mail. I know she's worried. I'm sure Team Burgowski's had a meeting about the Return of the Stander. But I don't want to hear again why Flyers don't flee…since that's exactly what I'm doing. Soon as I figure out how to tell Mom. And Vivian.

Awkward Conversation Number Three, later that evening (three days A.Z.):

Sucks that I never learned where Vivian's dorm is. Sucks worse that I forgot my phone.

All those yellowish brick buildings looked alike, squatty rectangles casting sharp shadows in the pathway lights. "MacDougall," said one doorway. *I could stop some random student —Hey, does Vivian Wu live here? What a dork.*

"Hey, stranger." If a movie showed Zach striding out of the shadows like that you'd go, *Yeah, right*—but there he was, suddenly spotlit in front of me. "You headin' where I'm headin'?"

I froze like a stupid rabbit. "I guess."

"Well, c'mon," Zach said as I stayed rooted to the sidewalk.

"Viv's about to leave for work. Unless…" He glanced back, his hair ridiculously gold in the light. "Oh, I get it. You still hate me, huh. Really, Joss? After two years? Thought you'd have moved on."

"It's only been a year and three months," I said idiotically. *Get a grip, Flyer.* "What, you think I should suddenly trust you 'cause your fat ol' Stander uncle's not here to back you up? You're still who you are, aren't you?" Right on cue, my flight-energy started revving in my chest. *No no no, don't let him launch me.*

Zach smiled. "Aren't most people who they are? But yeah—I get you. I'm still a Stander, just like you're still a Flyer. Right? Nothing's changed. I can smell it on y—"

"I don't care what you smell! I mean I do…that's the point." *You messed me up so bad, I practically turned into Hamlet.* "I don't trust you. I don't like you. I want you to not be here." *Damn it—no crying. No flying.*

He put his hands up like a wrestling stance. Vivian said Zach's not on the Coastal wrestling team, but he still carries himself like he's coiled to strike. "Joss. I get it. I know that was rough on you, that time."

"'Rough'? You tried to kill my power. You almost did it to my mom, torturing her with secret letters. And you trashed her house! And Louis's house even worse!" The more images from That Awful Summer flashed past, the angrier I felt. *Good.* "You're a horrible person."

Zach dropped his hands and shrugged. "I'm…I'm what I am, Joss. Told you that summer, I didn't ask to be a Stander. I'm just an instrument, and when we see wrong, we have to fix it. Even if it means being, y'know that cheesy thing, cruel to be kind."

"Wrong?! What wrong? There's so many REAL things out there to fix, like…like slaves making chocolate! And no one's forcing you to go after Flyers and gay people, are they? There's not some Stander council decreeing, like, 'Zach Howe, you are responsible for grounding Jocelyn and Bethany Burgowski, and shaming their lesbian friends.' Right?"

"You know it doesn't work like that." Zach sighed. "Standers learn to trust our instincts, like you trust your mom—only our instincts are to save people."

"But you said you hated being a Stander! You said you wanted me to free you from it. You tricked me." *With a kiss.* That memory sent another surge through me—one with rough, sharp edges.

"I liked you," Zach said. "That wasn't a trick." He looked straight at me. "Still do. And I like that Viv likes you."

I shook my head, fighting the urge to grab a rhododendron as a tie-down. "I can't hang out with someone who does the stuff you did." Then I clenched all my muscles and returned his look. *Stay down, stay down.*

"Well," Zach said. The silence stretched. And he dropped his eyes first. "It's like I said, kid," he continued at last. "I'm an instrument. What I did on Dalby… it was part of a bigger picture, okay? My brother Rory, you, your mom—your souls were… they're in danger. Hell is *real*, Jocelyn. I don't want to get visions of you burning there, like I did when Rory got super-gay."

Zach's face looked so open, so sad. I forced myself to look away.

"I'm a loyal guy," he went on, softly. "When someone I care about is threatened with eternal fire, I'm…*compelled* to save 'em, okay?" He looked up again. I forgot how his eyes remind me of a lion's. "But you did make me think, Joss. People make their own choices."

"Duh," I murmured lamely.

The gold in his eyes warmed up somehow, drew me in. "I mean I don't try to force 'em anymore. I'm just…here for 'em." *Of course you are. Who wouldn't want you?* "Here for Viv," he added. "She's the whole reason I transferred."

Lucky Vivian, to feel that lion-gaze, feel nothing but safe…

"And for you, Joss. I'll always be here for you."

A rush of cold wind smacked me back to reality. "Be wherever you want," I snarled, and turned my back. *Stupid girly moron, looking into his eyes…* One deep breath, and I marched away, clenching everything, ignoring Zach's call behind me: "Hey, weren't you goin' to see Viv?"

Oh, HELL no. As soon as I had a building between me and my enemy, I took off running, straight down Campus Hill, along the lumpy, lamplit Wattsville sidewalks, dodging startled people.

I'll tell her 'bye at the café. Vivian understands homesickness. I ran right past the grungy warehouse district, fighting the wind. Kept running down a service road, following the harbor's curve from concrete to giant breakwater rocks to rough beach, till scruffy alders appeared, still holding on to their leaves. Behind that screen, panting, I finally took to the sky.

"This inaccessible enough for you, Mom?" I snorted aloud. *She'll see—how can I stay when Zach's "here for me?"* It was too cloudy for moonlight, so I wheeled freely above the bay. My poor brain wheeled too, between *I did it! I stood up to him!* and *Thanks, Wattsville—it's been real.* The oil-stink from the refineries fought with the lily-scent of the sky.

But that's the weird part. SCENT. Because when I finally dropped down out of the wind, freezing, and jogged about a mile to Bean There to warm up, Vivian saw me shivering, and right away made me put on her Coastal hoodie. Then she fixed my latte, which I huddled over, waiting for the right moment to say goodbye, till I got warm enough to shed the hoodie and go pee.

When I came back, Vivian had picked up the hoodie from the counter and buried her face in it.

I did not say, *What the hell are you doing?* Because I could only think of one reason Vivian might be breathing in my flying scent. After I'd finally given up hoping!

Vivian's face flamed red when she saw me watching. "Totally need to do laundry," she muttered. "Sorry I made you put this stinky thing on." And she turned her back like she did the day we met.

Ah, right back home in Awkwardville. "Well, thanks for warming me up," I said, offering a five. Vivian waved my money off with a smile, but wouldn't meet my eyes.

If I'm right after all, if Vivian's missing the sky, how can I leave? But her freakin' boyfriend's a Stander. So how can I stay?

Yes she is. No she isn't. Yes she freakin' IS—and I gotta warn her.

Could you BE more of a moron? Go home before the Stander brings you down.

But what if he brings her down?

Idiot. What does a stupid hoodie-sniff prove?

Welcome to Jocelyn's Brain, here in Prof K's class four days After Zach. No need to fasten your seat belts—we'll just be going round in circles for like, ever. *Mr. E will be so thrilled to have me back.*

But Flyers don't flee, they FLY.

Yeah, and Standers bring 'em down.

Vivian (whispering): "Hey, earth to Joss, aren't you gonna take *notes?* I'm totally using this stuff on my Human Trafficking outline."

Me (leaning in, sniffing deep enough to pass out): "Oh, totally... me too." *Gotta leave. Can't leave. Trapped.*

Vivian: "Did she say twenty-five percent mortality or thirty-five?...What're you staring at? I got something in my *teeth?*"

Professor K (interrupting her own lecture): "You know, I never thought I'd tell students this, but would you ladies mind texting your fascinating conversation instead of disrupting my class?"

So we were actually listening to Professor K when she introduced the movie.

"As I explained, we're shifting now from statistics into narrative mode, and from Africa to Asia. This is the documentary on human trafficking I've been referring to. The filmmakers had to smuggle it out of the Philippines. If they'd been caught, these images might never have seen the light. I think you'll agree that they convey, powerfully, the reality of Asian slavery today. It's all about girls."

She lowered the lights, and the film started.

Shattered, I guess the word is. Both of us. In the dimness of the movie I saw Vivian's shoulders shaking, and when the lights came back up, her eyes were red. We looked at each other.

"Whoa," she whispered.

"Yeah."

All those girls, lined up in their skimpy, bright dresses, their shoulders shining in the dim light of their tiny room. They were looking off-camera where their "owner" was yelling at them. All of 'em smaller than me. And that girl in purple, looking right into the hidden camera like she was begging someone to notice her...

The lecture hall emptied in silence. Vivian went to work. I ditched Pre-Calc to run straight back to my inaccessible beach and fling myself into a heavy gray sky. I roared into crazy-tight swirls—like I could make a whirlwind, a funnel cloud to suck up all the ugliness of girls being bought and sold on this same Earth at the same time that I'm flying, so safe and free.

Oh, poor Jocelyn. She doesn't dare leave her only possible REAL best friend. And she doesn't dare stay.

"Trapped?" Ha. I'm FLYING. I'm fed. I'm warm—okay, I'm freezing, but so what? No one has locked me into the sky.

Can't stand this. What's flying FOR? How lame a super-hero am I? Ask Vivian about her hoodie.

Idiot! Let it go about Vivian.

But she's the only one who'll understand why I NEED to help—not Mom, not Lorraine, not Louis. Vivian and I, we're GIRLS.

I felt my circles slowing. I banked toward the warehouses, skimming the trees.

If I could get her back to the sky...put our powers together...

I reached the first ratty rooftop and hovered there, quivering.

Flyers fly, we don't flee. Just show her—

What's THAT?

Not a seagull. This sound was coming from the alley below. A quiet wail—kittens crying. *Was that rusty blue shipping container there before?*

I landed on my old takeoff spot behind the gnarliest warehouse and peeked into the alley. Deserted—but walking down that narrow, shadowed pavement in broad daylight felt more vulnerable than flying above it. From street level, the giant rusty container towered above me, resting on a yellow truck-trailer. The kitten-cries were definitely coming from inside.

Maybe someone dumped a pregnant cat in there. The end of the box was hinged—a pair of doors belted with a big ol' chain and padlock. *Why lock a cat in?*

"Kitty-kitty-kitty?" I called. "You in there? Poor thing!"

The cries got louder. Took shape.

Cats don't cry words.

Two syllables floated from the stinking metal monster. Syllables I recognized from my Mandarin Terms a Traveler Should Know: *"Bāng wǒ."* Help.

I screamed and leapt backward, tripping on a wine bottle. My hands, then my butt, struck asphalt.

"Bāng wǒ!" cried the container.

My palms burned. "What *are* you?" I gasped, standing up—along with every hair on every inch of me.

The kittens screamed. Beneath that nightmare sound, a low, metallic thrum. The side of the container vibrated, ever so slightly.

"Omigod. Who's in there?" Blind panic hit, like it was me trapped in a huge iron coffin. I reached uselessly for the end of the chain, hanging above the truck-trailer's hitch. "It's locked, I can't…omigod."

Do something, Flygirl. "I'll have to get help! Wait there, I'll…" *Where's the police station in this town?*

I tottered a few steps up the alley, then: *You're a mainlander now, stupid—your phone works.*

In my breathless fumbling and punching 9-1-1, the screams fell away. I babbled information to the operator—"Dunno what street, down by the waterfront where it's real smelly, right?"— and dropped my phone into my pocket. "You okay?" I called like an idiot to the container.

No answer. From my pocket, the 9-1-1 operator asked me to stay on the line.

"It's gonna be all right!" I yelled. "Help's coming!" I gripped the bottom left hinge of the container in one hand, trying to worm my other hand around the edge of the door. *Like I had a USEFUL superpower—mega-strength to rip this thing open!*

Silence.

"Oh, please," I murmured, and laid my cheek against the cold metal.

From inside, a faint echo: *"Bāng wǒ."* And then: *"Qǐng."* Please.

CHAPTER SIX

STRONG GIRLS

Wattsville police are amazing. I'd only seen cops up close once, that terrible time when Mom got assaulted on the mainland. On Dalby we just have Sheriff Gil. The Wattsville guys—well, two of 'em were gals—had the movie-ish cars and dark uniforms with guns, but they also had real smiles. And Officer Lang, with the gorgeous micro-braids, had the saddest eyes.

"You done great, honey," was all she told me, but her face said, *I know, right? Welcome to my world.*

The other lady-cop, the gray-haired one, started scolding me for being alone on the waterfront. But she stopped mid-sentence when a male cop with a big belly used some giant clippers on that container lock.

My heart stopped too.

A wave of sewer-stench rolled from the metal cavern as the doors creaked open. I clamped my hands over my nose and mouth, catching a glimpse of something pale and flailing—*like Vivian the day we met her,* my brain said stupidly. Then I was sitting on the pavement. An ambulance blared up, then another and another, and people in hospital-blue started pushing past me, carrying white stretcher-y things. Officer Lang and Gray-hair went into the container. One stretcher followed, others lined up.

A seagull cried above us—just a seagull, this time. No more kittens. "Oh, please," I whispered through my fingers. The metal cave yawned, dark and terrible, behind the crush of rescuers.

Then the first stretcher-board appeared, gliding from the container like it weighed nothing. The crowd of rescue-people parted to let it pass.

At eye level I saw a girl like a doll, black bangs framing a tiny face, eyes closed, peach-colored top, white leggings...or once-white. As my brain processed the filthy stains, the crusty dried blood of her hands, the little girl's eyes opened, right into mine.

"*Sheh-sheh,*" she whispered.

A chain of stretchers followed, but my eyes were riveted on the tiny girl's ambulance as it swallowed her up.

Someone threw a blanket over my shoulders. Shouting and slamming blurred into murmuring and radio-crackle. I heard "ten Asian females." "Heading for Memorial." "Dehydration, one severe." "Chinese translator."

That last word woke me out of my shock. "Translator?" I croaked. No idea how much time had passed since my frantic phone call.

Officer Lang was resting her butt on her car, writing on a clipboard. "Be right with you, honey. Can we bring you to the station to take your statement?"

I cleared my throat. "Uh, yeah. And uh, I think I know a translator."

"What, Chinese?" She crinkled her eyes at me. "Huh. Department's got one on a list somewhere, but if you know somebody...call 'em."

So I did.

When Vivian joined us at the police station an hour later, Officer Lang explained the situation in about eight seconds: "Your friend discovered a group of trafficked Chinese girls who'd been locked in a shipping container and then abandoned by their smugglers. She saved their lives." Gonna remember *that* forever, every word.

On the drive to Memorial Hospital, me and Vivian in the back, Officer Lang gave us a mini-lecture about the local increase in girls "trafficked for the trade." Vivian nodded, so I pretended I knew what "the trade" was. *Something from class...sweatshop labor?* And I pretended not to notice Vivian closing her eyes, inhaling my Flyer scent.

The official police translator met us at Memorial, and Officer Lang spent our waiting room time telling him what was up. I didn't catch his name; he was a young-faced guy with a pointy beard and a nice suit, and he was really from China, so he spoke way better Mandarin than Vivian. But turns out, we needed more than Mandarin.

Three hours after their rescue, only one of the girls was recovered enough to interview. It was the same peachy-pink girl I'd seen, only now she wore a Minnie-Mouse hospital gown. In that big bed, she looked even more like a doll—a very sad doll with an IV line in her arm, staring fixedly at a print on the wall of baby ducks in a basket. The nurse gave us fifteen minutes, like they do in movies.

Translator Guy sat down beside the bed on a yellow plastic chair, but the tiny girl made a whimpering sound and shrank away from him. He looked helplessly at Officer Lang.

"Here, let me," said Vivian, tapping Translator Guy on the shoulder. He shrugged and gave up his seat. My friend leaned toward the little girl and murmured something in Mandarin. I recognized "*nu hai zi*,"—girl—but I couldn't understand the rest, which Vivian was saying over and over, like casting a spell. Maybe she was. I was starting to feel hypnotized when the girl finally reached across with her non-IV'd hand to grab Vivian's. She chirped some words, nearly too soft to hear, and Vivian nodded.

"She's ready," she said.

And the doll-girl was. Her story bubbled out, barely audible, but constant as a fountain. As Translator Guy leaned in to hear,

Vivian kept nodding and squeezing that hand like a miniature pump.

"Her name is Chuntao," the guy narrated. "It means Spring Peach." *Wow, that fits*—so in my mind, she's Peach now. Through translation, here's what Peach told us—or told Vivian, clinging to her hand.

"My family lived in the countryside and came to the city to find work. Huainan. My parents and my brother got jobs in a bean curd factory, but I was too little. So they took me to a bakery. I had to wash all the dishes and polish the machines and clean the floor. It smelled good there and I could eat bun scraps, and my parents were happy when I brought my pay home at night. I was helping.

"But one day some lady in a beautiful red coat came and said my parents had sold me to her company, and I had to come along. I cried because my parents wanted me to go away. And I didn't get to bring my shirt with the kitten on it. I had to get in a brown car full of bags of noodles and boxes of cans. I asked where we were going and she yelled at me like the bakery boss did. She said shut up or she would leave me in the next city. So I was very quiet."

Vivian blinked hard against tears. I realized I was doing the same thing.

Chuntao didn't seem to notice. "The lady drove for a long, long time, singing with the radio like my mom does, and I fell asleep with all the boxes. When I woke up it was dark and we were stopping at a gas station, and she took me to the toilet. She gave me rice balls for breakfast, and one of them was sweet. But I was sad because my family wasn't there. Even though they didn't want me. And I never got another sweet rice ball."

I'm never snarking about my parents ever again.

The tinkling syllables flowed on, shadowed by the translator's harsh English. "The red-coat lady took me to another city and left me, even though I was quiet. But there were other girls there. We stayed for a long time in a little upstairs room. There were mats on the floor and the windows were painted over with brown paint. The girls said we were going to the beautiful country to make lots of money for our families. First there were three girls, then five, then eight. Then ten girls. There were only five mats so we had to take turns sleeping, but the toilet was down the hall, so it didn't smell. We told each other stories about our families. Biyu said she had a twin brother who died. Her parents sold her because she brought bad luck.

"An old lady with big glasses unlocked the door two times every day and brought rice and vegetables, sometimes with egg. The food was good, but she told us not to ask questions if we wanted her to keep coming. Then she'd line us up for the toilet—nothing to see, only the dark hallway. The girls were all older, but most of them were nice, especially Fung. Fung said she'd be my family in the beautiful country. Fung called me 'little sister.'"

Chuntao paused; it felt like the whole room was holding its breath. But Vivian handed her cup over—also decorated with Minnie Mouse—and unclasped hands a moment for Chuntao to sip from the straw. Translator Guy drank from a bottle of water. Only when the sad duet continued did I remember to breathe.

"Then a different lady and a man with a beard came. He looked like my uncle but he had a strange accent, and he smiled too much. They made us get into a van. It was white, and I sat on Fung's lap. We drove a long time, to a city that smelled....sharp in my nose. We came to a place of giant metal boxes. Miles and miles of them; they smelled like the grease my grandfather puts on the wheelbarrow, and there were gulls everywhere. Fung said we were by the sea. The man-like-my-uncle and the lady led us inside one of those boxes. It was bigger than the room we had been living in, but made of metal.

"They said how lucky we girls were, we were going to get rich. There were more mats laid out in rows, with blankets, and they said, 'See how soft!' One blanket had Snow White—we saw that movie once in my village. There were boxes of water bottles, it looked like hundreds. They showed us how to use a plastic bucket for…(Chinese Guy said she wouldn't say the word, but she meant 'waste'), and they gave us bowls and spoons, and two flashlights and a metal fan. They showed us how to put new batteries in. Then they closed the doors with a big clang."

My hand suddenly cramped and I realized I was squeezing the hard rim of my seat.

On and on the soft voice played, mercilessly. "I cried because it was so loud, and so dark. Fung turned on a flashlight, but the other girls screamed at her to save the batteries. So it stayed dark, and it was so hot and stuffy, even with the fan. I sweated and cried for a long, long time, until I fell asleep, and when I woke up it was still dark, and I was terribly thirsty, but the girls only let me drink a little bit of water, even though there were hundreds of bottles. So I went back to sleep on the Snow White blanket.

"The day we went into the box was September tenth—Fung said it was her birthday. The next day—I think, because we could see a line of light around the doors—that's when the whole box-room moved. It shook and then it lifted up somehow, swinging like a big, slow yo-yo. Then down, and another scary clang. Lots of clangs. I tried so hard to sleep but I couldn't.

"But I guess I did sleep because after a long time, the floor started to feel like when you cross a shaky bridge, only bigger and…wavier. It didn't stop. Lots of girls vomited, but I never did. Every night the doors opened for a minute; we knew it was night because we could see stars but no sun. Never any sun. A man set down a bucket of soup. I lost my spoon and the girls wouldn't let me use the light to look for it. But Fung let me use her spoon. They took our stinking bucket every night and gave us an empty one, but it was too small for all of us, it was always overflowing. Fung and Meili could not stop vomiting, even when the big girls screamed at them. The fan was so small, all it did was move the horrible air around. And all those water bottles, they got empty so fast and then they just rattled."

Chuntao looked up and blinked as though surprised to see us all there. Then she dropped her eyes to finish her story.

"I counted sixteen nights of soup. Then the terrible rolling that made Fung sick, it stopped. We felt ourselves jolt, then lift, clang down, lift again, clang. The clanging never stopped hurting my ears. We heard a truck sound, and we moved, but pretty soon we stopped again and the motor went off. We heard men shouting. We heard some shorter clangs, then the truck started and drove away. Then it got quiet."

Vivian helped Chuntao take another drink. Translator Guy drank too. Officer Lang and I were statues.

"The soup stopped." Chuntao's voice dropped to just above a whisper; the translator leaned closer in to hear. "So I couldn't count the days. I was so hungry. No one came to empty the waste bucket. No one came at all. Then Fung got very hot and begged for water, but there were only three full bottles left and we were all so thirsty. We heard drums on the roof, and the girls said it was rain. Water, so close to us! We all tried banging on the door. It made our hands bleed. We all screamed. We prayed. I tried to fill my mouth with spit, but I couldn't make enough. No one came.

"When we ran out of water, we stopped praying out loud. But I never stopped praying in my heart. Fung started breathing like an old machine. I thought she was dying, but I didn't know what to do. No one came."

For the first time in her story, Chuntao looked up and directed her delicate syllables at me. Chinese Guy translated, "But then someone came. So Fung must be all right, isn't she? Can I see her?"

That's when the tired-looking nurse bustled back in. We all had to go. This child needed rest. Her friends were fine. *If "fine" means "I really don't know and I wouldn't tell you if I did."*

No one spoke on the drive back to the police station. But when Officer Lang invited us to milk and cookies "for your good deeds today," we accepted. Nothing more weirdly reassuring than Oreos.

"That girl," I said to Vivian, "I didn't think she was gonna talk at all. What did you say to her?"

Vivian unscrewed her Oreo and smiled. "I said, 'You're a strong girl. You're so, so strong. Now you need to *help*.'"

I smiled back. Vivian just gave me the words I need to coax her back into the sky. *Hell with Zach.* When she understands what he is, she'll say that herself. And then, we two strong girls will find a way to *help*.

Mom's voice: "Hi, you've reached the person you were calling. I can't come to the phone right now, or you know what? Maybe I can, I just don't want to. Leave me a message."

Me: "Mom, I know you're there. It's Wednesday night, you just got home from work, you're watching some black-and-white movie and eating, like, a bowl of capers and Parmesan 'cause that's all you've got in your fr—"

Mom: "I'm eating homemade spaghetti, thank you. And the movie's in color."

Me: "Oh, I'm so glad you're home! You won't believe what happened today when I went fl—"

Mom: "I'm fine, thanks, and how are you?"

Me: "Yeah, yeah, sorry, Mom—how are you? It's just, it's so crazy, I just got home from the police station. ..."

Mom: "Police station? Are you all right?"

Me: "I'm fine! Everything's fine! Well, it isn't..."

Mom: [sighing] "Figured something was up since you've been ignoring my messages."

Me: "Sorry. I meant to call, but then...I've been kinda nuts, trying to decide if I'm staying here or not—"

Mom: "Really? Is it Zach?

Me: "Yes, but no—but never mind, Mom. This thing just happened. I'm a hero!"

Mom: "Uh..."

Me: "Seriously! I rescued a bunch of girls who were locked in a shipping container! Chinese girls, real ones—I mean, from China! Vivian translated their story—well, she tried—but really this one guy the police hired did it, and you know what's funny? His name really is Guy! And Peach was scared of him, but she talked to Vivian, but he's really a nice guy. Guy is. Isn't that crazy?"

Mom: [pause] "Uhhh...what's crazy, babe, is how you're telling this. Could you maybe start at the beginning?"

Me: "Okay. Sure." [deep breath] "I was down on the waterfront where I used to fl—"

Mom: "Hold up. Are you in your room now? Can anyone hear you?"

Me: "Oh, I'm sitting at my desk, but it's okay, the roomies are gone. Omigod, Mom, you would not believe what Rialta said when I told her!"

Mom: "About rescuing Chinese stowaways?"

Me: "They're not stowaways! I mean they are, but they didn't stow themselves! That's what I told Rialta, 'cause the first thing out of her mouth was, 'Oh, wonderful. Looks like a border fence isn't enough to keep those people out.' *Those people*—like they're all the same. She's so bitchy, Mom. She's—"

Rialta: [opening the door of her single which I'd thought was empty] "She's right here."

Mom: "Uh-oh."

Me: "I...better go, Mom. Call you later."

Rialta was shaking. Even in my horrified embarrassment I could see that.

"No, go ahead," she snarled. "Tell your mom how your bitchy roommate's been helping you with math since day one. Tell her how that bitch's dad pays full tuition so the school can give you a scholarship you don't even appreciate. Or how you try to turn Dawntae against me. Tell her that—*Jossie*."

"I'm…" My mouth was a desert.

"Sorry? Right! You're only sorry I heard you, sorry Tae's not here to tell you how wonderful you are. That's all you want from your friends, right?" She marched over to my doorway; her face had gone blotchy. "I've heard you on the phone—all you talk about is you! Why ask about them? Only Jossie matters!"

I swallowed. Embarrassment was revving into anger, and my flight-engine revved with it, pushing me to my feet. "That's totally not fair—and who said you could listen to my phone calls?"

"Who *said*? D'you ever hear me talking to my people? No, 'cause I'm careful." Rialta leaned against my bedpost, turning her back.

"Or you just leave a message 'cause Daddy's not home," I snapped. *She's being so unfair!* I braced for her attack, but Rialta dropped onto Dawntae's bed as if her knees had dissolved, and burst into tears.

My engines shut off, like Harry Potter had waved his wand and Stupefied me. I didn't think people like Rialta cried.

"Now who's a bitch," she choked, hands clenched over her face. "You don't even know—you never ask—how I'm—what the hell do you care?" The bunk bed shook with her sobs.

I forced myself to go sit in Rialta's general neighborhood, on the other end of Dawntae's Princess Jasmine quilt. "Rialta…" I said helplessly.

"It's my *birth*day!" she burst out, and sat up so straight she bumped her head on the bottom of my bunk. "I'm seventeen!

And nobody even answered when I called. You shouldn't have to call on your own birthday!"

"Oh…no. That's just not right. Happy birthday," I mumbled.

"They did this last year too. Threw me a Sweet Sixteen at the golf club, but Dad went out of town and forgot to call, and he promised it wouldn't happen again, but it's always gonna happen. They don't care about me…like *you* don't," she finished fiercely, just when I was thinking of scooting closer.

"I care," I muttered. *Yeah right—the lady doth protest too much, methinks,* said my brain. "But hey, your folks'll call later, right? I mean, maybe they're out right now getting you a present."

"They aren't even 'they' anymore," Rialta managed to say around an attack of crying-shudders. "Dad's sleeping at his office. My brother texted me. But Mom and Dad won't tell me 'cause I don't even count. That's why I'm here."

She flopped toward me on the quilt, crying and hugging herself like a little kid. I patted her shoulder, cautiously, and she kept crying, so I kept patting. For a long time.

Long enough for my arm to start aching, and my heart too. *Poor little rich girl*—jeez, what a cliché, but it's true! If I'd tried to see past her politics and her bossiness I might've noticed.

Rialta sat up with a shivery sniff. I went into our living room, grabbed her mug and filled it from my water bottle, giving her time to pull herself together. She gulped it down without looking at me. Hunting for tissue, I found a clean Dalby Dolphins T-shirt and handed it to her. Rialta wiped her face, then surprised me.

"Thank you." Her voice was hoarse but she looked straight into my eyes with her red ones. "But I'm not sorry for what I said."

"I am," I told her. "Sorry for what I said, I mean." I sat back down on the bed. "I didn't know that I didn't care. How you felt. About stuff."

Rialta blew a giant honk of snot into my shirt. That seemed to be her answer.

"I'm not gonna change how I feel," I said finally. "And you're not either, prob'ly. But if you don't agree with me, I'll... I'll at least try to ask why. Okay?" It was getting awkward, babbling my new resolution while she stared at me.

"Okay," Rialta said, smoothing her hair. "My dad says—" Couldn't help it, my mouth twitched—*oh, shoot*. But then she half-smiled. "I know, I say that a lot, right? I'm a total Daddy's Girl."

"Well, me too," I said, remembering my own dad saying, *"You don't know what you don't know."* "So, like, if you think those Chinese girls got themselves smuggled on purpose...why do you think that?" *Damn, this caring-about-what-people-think stuff is hard.*

"Oh, I don't really," Rialta said airily, standing up to stretch. "They're probably victims like you said. I just wanted you to see the bigger picture, the threat to our economy and our way of life, if America just keeps letting everybody in. I feel like...like America's soul is kind of at risk." She gave a very un-Rialta-ish giggle. "And I want to save it."

Whoa. Souls at risk? Sounded like Zach Howe.

"Well, it's how I feel," my roommate added, shrugging. "You wanted to know."

I did. And I do. Because Zach still thinks that way. He told me himself—he sees the "bigger picture." He's "compelled." He practically admitted he transferred here to "save" Vivian.

But here's what's funny: that thought doesn't make my flight-power swell like it used to. The only swelling's in my sore heart. For the first time, Rialta has me kinda-sorta understanding—not just her, but my enemy.

We were still talking, carefully, about immigration, when Dawntae came back and announced we were taking Rialta out for birthday ice cream. So it was nearly curfew when I remembered to call Mom back.

This time I used my own private roommate-proof "phone booth," huddled behind the Nutschel rhododendrons. I told her about the scene with Rialta, and more about Peach and the other Chinese girls. Then I told her about Vivian smelling her hoodie. "So I'm not leaving, Mom. I just gotta find a way to tell her."

"Yes, you do." Typical Flying Burgowski Mother—didn't argue the idea that hoodie-smelling = proof of Flyer status. "Or *show* her. You've found a good, remote spot?"

"Yeah, this gnarly beach. I quit flying near town since I saw Zach. I just happened to finish up by the warehouses today or I never would've..." My whole body goose-bumped. "Whoa..."

"What?" Mom asked into the long silence.

I faltered, "Peach made it sound like the container had been abandoned for a few days." "*No one came to empty the waste bucket. No one came at all.*" "If I hadn't quit flying over the waterfront 'cause of Zach, I could've rescued them so much sooner..."

Mom talked me through the guilt-wave that slammed me cold. Flying, not fleeing... blah blah blah. She's right, Officer Lang's right: I did save ten girls. And the limits Standers put on me ain't exactly a hardship like human trafficking. I just wish I felt as strong as she and Officer Lang made me sound. Strong as I'd be if I had Vivian to be strong with.

CHAPTER SEVEN

THE ARMADILLO METHOD

Hey, I'm famous now—thanks, local TV interview lady. And thanks for not asking what I was doing at the waterfront the day before. Or why I didn't get there days earlier to end the girls' nightmare.

That interview was yesterday. Today, Prof K called me to the front of the class to praise me as "Coastal's own slavery-fighting heroine." Kinda super wonderfully embarrassing. But I took advantage of Heroine Status as Prof K switched into lecture mode.

"Can we hang out tonight?" I whispered to Vivian. "Or will Zach be around?"

Vivian blushed swiftly but didn't argue. "I'll tell him I'll see him later—after your curfew, okay? So you can come over. Wow, Joss, we have so much to *talk* about!"

Yes, we do.

Vivian opened her door that evening looking apologetic. "He just stopped by," she whispered. As my heart bolted, she added, "Eli, you get to meet my friend *Joss*!"

I took a breath of relief. A skinny guy was getting up from his seat on Vivian's bed.

"Hey, the hero girl," he said, shaking shiny black hair out of his eyes. Chinese? Korean? Embarrassing not to know. Dalby Island's awfully white. "Good on ya, kid."

Vivian was wearing a furry red sweater that covered her butt. She's always so bundled up—even Rialta's commented in her clueless-racist way, "Asian girls are so curvy, she oughta show her stuff more."

"Hey, Joss," Vivian said brightly, "Eli was just telling me Brady's band is playing tomorrow night—Skanky Skallers. We could all go!" Her phone blipped and she frowned.

"Skanky what?" A second later, Vivian got another text. *Never seen her ignore her phone before.* "And who's Brady?"

"Skanky Skallers. They play Ska," Eli said and I nodded, like sure, I know what the hell Ska is.

"Brady's lead singer," Vivian said. Another text chirped; she blushed.

"Aren't you gonna—"

"I *told* Zach I was visiting with Eli," she murmured. "He can just wait."

A pulse of flight-power zapped through me: *Go, girl!* "And who'd you say Brady was?"

"My boyfriend," said Eli.

I nodded again. *Oh, man. Does Vivian know about Zach's homophobia?* Another zap: *Zach never apologized for vandalizing Louis's mom's house 'cause she's a lesbian.*

Another text. In the awkward silence, I studied the bright watercolor prints on Vivian's wall: *Flowers of Hawaii.* At the fifth text, Vivian shook her head and turned her phone off. Eli and I shared an ironic glance.

"You guys wanna go out for *ice* cream?" Vivian asked. The punch in her voice sounded fake.

"I should go." Eli looked around. "I leave my hat in here?"

"Oh, you don't have to." Vivian looked distressed. "I don't know why... I've *told* Zach you're not interested in me, but still...I guess he just can't help being jealous."

Eli raised his eyebrows at me again. We were becoming best buds without a word.

"Uh," I muttered. *Gotta tell her what her boyfriend is. What I am, what she is. But not in front of Eli, cool as he seems.* "This your hat?" Something a 1920s gangster should wear was hanging on Vivian's desk lamp; I handed it over. "Nice," I added—it did look good on him.

"*Gracias,*" he nodded at me. *Maybe not Asian after all?* "Vivita, don't worry about it. I'm around. We'll talk." He kissed Vivian's forehead—"Later, *chica*"—and bowed himself out.

"Oh shoot, I'm sorry!" I burst out as the door closed. "Didn't mean to scare all your friends away. I mean, I really wanna talk to you, but…you guys were in the middle of something, right?"

"Oh, no, I'm glad you're here. Want some tea?" Vivian stepped into the tiny bathroom to fill a kettle. "Eli's a really good listener. I'm just getting to know him, but he's turning into my best friend here." *Wow, that hurts a little.* "Or he *would*, except Zach's so weird about him. *Guys*, right?"

"Well…" *Where to start?*

"Is *peppermint* okay? I get enough caffeine at work."

"Sure. Smells like my stepmom. That's all she drinks." I cleared my throat. "Vivian… you think maybe Zach's problem with Eli isn't, y'know, jealousy? He knows Eli's not into girls, right?"

"You mean homophobia?" Vivian fussed with teabags. "Zach did say something after *church* last week about Eli 'putting his own twist on brotherly love.' But I thought he was kidding."

Whoa. Zach and Vivian go to church together? Why do I assume I know this girl at all? I shook my head hard, trying to force my thoughts into some kind of order. "Yeah. I mean no, he probably wasn't kidding." Deep breath. "Vivian, when Zach was on Dalby…"

Her face started reddening again. "Oh, I knew it," she murmured.

You knew your boyfriend's a fanatic, homophobic, conformist, Puritan enforcer? I did not ask. "Knew what?" I said instead.

"You're gonna tell me about you and him on your island. I *know* there's something between you guys, I can *feel* it. But it's okay," she added with her sad smile.

"Yeah, there is something." She'd given me an opening. "But it's not what you think. I mean yeah—I lied when I said it was just a little crush. I was totally in love with him, okay?" *Jeez, could this feel more like a soap opera?* "And I thought he felt the same." *That burning kiss under the cedars...* "But turns out he was just trying to..."

Vivian looked horrified. "To get you in *bed*? But Joss, Zach's against all that! He's *saving* himself. You must have totally misunder*stood* him!" The kettle was steaming its head off. She ignored it.

"Not that. Not sex." *...his hands on my cheekbones...* "Zach was trying to break my powers, Vivian. He was trying to ground me."

Her expression was exactly what you'd expect when your friend starts talking crazy. "'*Ground*' you?"

I tried again. "Vivian. Okay. I'm a Flyer. I can fly, okay? And Zach...he's a...he hates Flyers. And gays too. So that explains Eli, right?" *What a stupid freakin' mess.* Vivian's face was pale now, and twisted with confusion. "You gonna turn that kettle off?" I added desperately.

Vivian shook her head and kept shaking it as she poured boiling water into two Coastal U mugs, splashing her bureau-top. The scent of Lorraine filled the space between us. "I don't know what you're talking about," she whispered.

"Flying. I'm talking about flying. You do too *know* that's what I'm talking about," I added boldly.

"You're not making any sense." She wouldn't look at me. "I think... you should go."

"You smelled it on me. Didn't you!"

She dropped onto her bed, abandoning the tea. "You're crazy."

"Want me to show you? I can hover right here." The power

vibrated through me so suddenly I grabbed the edge of her bookcase. *Stay down, don't scare her…*

"NO! "Vivian leapt up. "You need to get OUT of here. Right NOW!" She shoved me toward the door, but I hit the bureau. Tea scalded my wrist as both mugs crashed to the floor. *Just like that first day at the café—*

"You know what I am!" I yelled. "Zach knows, and you do too! And that means—don't let him in too close, Vivian! He'll—"

"Get OUT," she gasped, and I couldn't see her face 'cause she was pushing me out the door, or maybe I was just retreating in a flail of shame and horror at how *I've messed up our friendship forever and the ONE person I thought I could be close to is slamming the door and stranding me in the cold MacDougall hallway and what am I going to do now?*

Shame. Horror. Yeah. But as I trudged down the stairwell, a sickening irony flickered in my gut. My Flyer instincts were right about Vivian. So very right that now she's done with me.

To: Nevans@dalby.k12.wa.us

Dear Mr. Evans,

You really called it, last year. "Jocelyn seems to be perfecting the armadillo method of dealing with adversity"— direct quote, right? Nice tight ball, make the world disappear. Guess what? World's not cooperating. Dean Williams put me on Academic Probation. One more missed class and I am out: "Even if you're on your deathbed, Ms. Burgowski, you drag yourself to Pre-Calculus." Bet you wish you could have used that on me last year.

You know it's your fault I can't come home, right? You worked so damn hard to get me this scholarship. "I'm putting my professional integrity on the line for you, Jocelyn, so don't let me down"—ha, bet you thought I wasn't listening. But now I'm drowning in Mandarin and math and all I really want to do is sleep and sleep and shut out the memory of my only possible Flyer friend shoving me out the door.

She is one, I know it now. Why else come apart like that? I'm a freakin' Flyer genius.

I quit going to my Modern Slavery class. It's been...ten days. Prof. K's probably thrilled Vivian has no one to whisper with now. I did try calling the hospital to see what happened to those Chinese girls, but they put me on hold. I don't care. I just want to

-- Are you sure you want to delete this message? --

Back in my "phone booth" behind Nutschel's rhodies, I punched my home number while tucking in that soft red scarf I stole from Dad. It smelled like his warm voice, telling me *everything's okay, kiddo, you got this.* This looming iceberg of homework. This stupidly ironic isolation. Two weeks now since I lost my friend.

Something was wrong with Lorraine's "Hello?" Her breathy voice sounded too sharp.

"Hey, it's me," I said, wishing I could just ask for Dad without hurting her feelings.

"Oh, sweetie, hi," my stepmother faltered—*yup, she's upset.* The wind howled past my rhododendron-clump like a ghost. "When the phone rang, I was hoping—I mean, I'm sorry, it is wonderful to hear you. I'm a little distracted right now. Very distracted. Ron's—" Lorraine caught her breath and my stomach hardened.

"What? What about Dad?"

"Don't be upset, Joss. I'm sure it's fine. The *Flyer's* just overdue, that's all, and I'm—" she laughed, a little forced gasp—"I'm just overreacting in typical landlubber fashion. I need one of those widows' walks they put on the tops of houses, you know, although it's dark out, so of course I wouldn't be able to see anything..." *Lorraine never babbles.*

"How overdue? Is Michael with him? Can't you call?"

"They don't answer! Ron said they'd be home by five, he and his buddy Aaron, and Michael too. And it's seven-thirty. They shouldn't have gone far, just crabbing...but the wind came up so fast! I want to call the coast guard, but Ron'll be so mad if I... maybe I should wait another half-hour?"

Wait...I have to comfort you? "I'm sure they're fine," I made myself say. "Probably coming in super slow to deal with the waves." I know nothing about boats, 'cause I'm a self-centered diva who can't even remember her dad's a fisherman now. All this time I haven't been calling home, I've been imagining him on his stool behind his newspaper, safe and warm in our old store. Not out on the scary black ocean. "Maybe they're—"

"Oh, thank God!" Lorraine screamed, and dropped the receiver. I imagined myself looking up from the floor like a little kid, seeing my big strong dad march in, my big strong brother right behind him, peeling off foul weather gear, dousing our kitchen with ocean scent. Above, I heard the sounds of hugging and muffled words: "Heyyyy there, honey! What're you crying about? Aren't you glad to see us?"

"Ron, I was so worried!"

"Damn, it *is* late, Dad—told you she'd be freakin' out..."

"Hello?" I called. "Dad?"

"Dude, why's the phone on the floor? ...H'lo?"

"Michael! What the hell? Were you guys, like, lost at sea or what?" *Omigod, I miss you so much it hurts.* But who says that to her brother?

"Joss! You shoulda been there! It was *sick*. The waves were, like, playing with us, you know how Tion bats at her toys? Like *that*, dude! Only *we* were the stuff getting batted. Aaron barfed his head off, but I didn't! I'm a *sail*or!"

He sounded high. No, he sounded like Vivian, the way she underlines her words. *How pathetic am I, pining away for a friend I barely know?*

"You're an idiot, you know that? You guys should've called Lorraine, she was going nuts."

"Oh, we tried a couple times, you know how cell phones are here," Michael said. *Another thing you forgot, Flying Moron.* "But Joss, f'real—what a trip! It felt like flying, y'know? You don't know what you're missing."

I opened my mouth to say, *Yes, I do,* and shut it again. Seeing as how Michael almost killed himself trying to fly with a homemade hang-glider That Awful Summer, seeing as how his only ticket to the sky—his Flyer sister—is fifty miles away, the least I could do was let him enjoy his moment.

Huh. *Flyer sister?* Leaning against the cold brick of my dorm, I admitted it: I haven't flown for two solid weeks. Since Vivian pushed me out. *Zach doesn't have to bother grounding me. I've done it myself.*

"Joss… Joss… Joss…" Dawntae The Apologetic Alarm Clock repeated with each nudge of my shoulder. I ignored her. "Yo, Jossie!" she tried.

"Don't call me Jossie," I grumbled, rolling toward the wall, but Dawntae tossed something rattly at my head.

"I snuck you a little box of cereal. You can eat it on the way to history. You are *not* missing the unit test."

Rialta heaved a dramatic sigh from the common room. "Tae, I am not getting a tardy for her. My dad says you can't help people who don't want to be helped." I heard our door open.

"I'm up," I growled. My Mandarin book was nestling by the box of Cap'n Crunch; must've fallen asleep studying again last night. Yup—still in jeans and T-shirt. "Go to class. I'm coming."

"Nope, not leaving without you. Get your butt outta that bed,"

Dawntae ordered, and kept it up as I slid down and stumbled to the bathroom. "Put your jacket on, it's cold out. Got your notes? I'm quizzing you on the way over. You got this, Joss." *Jeez, she sounds like me in PE.* Rialta waited too, getting her daily eye-roll workout. *Behold The Pathetic Burgowski.*

"So, Jossie, no offense, but how's college even working for you now?" Rialta interrupted Dawntae's Continental Congress questions as we hustled to history class, past flowerbeds full of gold and purple and burgundy. "Don't they take attendance?"

"No," I muttered. We'd had this same conversation, like, ten times in the past two weeks. Since I started substituting naps for Modern Slavery. I poured the last of the Cap'n Crunch into my hand and inhaled it.

"But you're gonna go visit those Chinese girls, right? And write about 'em? That oughta save your grade," Dawntae said loyally. *I love Tae, or I would if I weren't such a self-absorbed Hamlet-girl. Just like last year.*

"Yeah," I lied, not bothering to mention that I'd given up calling the hospital after three tries. The wind whipped my ponytail into my face; it smelled funky. I may not have washed it for a while.

"Well," Rialta reached for the outer door, "you're lucky everyone's so nice, Jossie." She swiped at her own glossy strands of hair. "Or maybe not. Maybe if the going got tougher, might make you get going, y'know? Oh, hey, Chaz!" And Rialta ditched us to join her new sorta-boyriend who's hot as hell and pretends he doesn't know it.

"Explain the economic causes of the North-South tariff dispute." *Dad and Michael didn't drown. No one's yanked my scholarship. The roomies have my back...and so does Team Burgowski.* "Trace the establishment of the bicameral legislature from its English roots." *Louis even emailed— "'Sup?" counts as email, even if it does sound like Erin.* "In your opinion, did the Three Fifths Compromise represent a departure from, or a modification of the Declaration of Independence? Support with evidence." *And I saved ten girls, right?*

Sweet ol' Rialta's comment burned slow, but it burned. By the end of the test, both my flight-engines and my conscience were in full roar.

Gotta fly. But first—gotta call.

"NO!" I screamed for once, when the hospital receptionist asked if she could put me on hold. "Don't you dare! I need to talk to a nurse who's taking care of the Chinese girls! I'm...I'm the one who saved them."

Silence. Then politeness. Then a hold with an actual end: a nurse-voice. And news.

"You're the girl we saw on TV? That's wonderful, honey. The patients are recovering beautifully; it's amazing what the body can take. I believe they're being discharged to Immigration tomorrow."

It felt like someone was reinflating my heart. "That's great! Wait—where's Immigration?"

The nurse-voice sighed. "I don't know, honey. Seattle, I imagine. Wherever they can hold nine girls till someone comes to claim 'em."

The heart-pump paused. "*Nine* girls?"

Another sigh. "I'm sorry, honey, I thought you knew. The one young lady who was in such bad shape—she didn't make it, dear. She passed away the day after admission."

"Fung started breathing like an old machine. I thought she was dying, but I didn't know what to do." "Fung? You mean Fung?"

"I'm sorry, dear, I can't divulge names over the phone except to the responsible party," the nurse-voice said. "If you talk to the resp—"

"No one's responsible." My voice sounded hollow. "I mean they are, but they're gone. I don't know who to talk to."

"I'm so sorry, dear," she repeated. "But do come visit the other girls before they're discharged, I know they'd love it. We're going to miss them."

"Ohhhhhhhhhhhhhhhh," I sighed as the first blast of salty wind hit my cheek. Louis used to make that sound when we got airborne. And Jocelyn makes that sound after two weeks of grounding, then two hours of trying not to launch through English and PE...then another guilt-wave.

My waterfront avoidance may have cost a girl's life.

Over my Inaccessible Beach, circling low in a bright break of sun, my body gradually unclenched. And finally, finally, my brain rose out of its two-week fog to face the day.

Want to make sense of this? Talk to Vivian.

She doesn't want to see me. Two weeks—she never called.

Never mind flying. Tell her about Fung. Get Modern Slavery notes. And maybe then... flying.

You can't help her if she doesn't want help—Rialta's right. And Zach's probably taken her down by now. Assuming your Flyer-senses are correct.

They are. I know it. Why'd she cry like that? Like Mom must've cried, at that same age, till she started using pills to drown the pain.

It was Mom's choice to give up flying—now it's Vivian's. She's in love with a Stander. If someone's in quicksand, do you wade in there to pull 'em out?

Know what? I'm DONE with those stupid arguments. Going back to Prof K's class tomorrow. I'll tell her I've been sick or something. And I can sit by myself. Vivian doesn't have to know about Fung *or* Flyers.

You know when Harry Potter has to explain to Professor McGonagall how he's been thrown off the quidditch team for doing what she warned him against? Prof K wasn't buying my excuses any more than McGonagall bought Harry's.

"The deadline for midterm make-ups is past, even were I to extend you one," she told me crisply in the minutes before class. We were standing beside her lectern, the same spot where she'd presented Joss the Heroine three weeks ago. "Ordinarily I'd counsel you to accept the failing grade you've earned and concentrate on passing your other classes."

My stomach, already shriveled since walking into the lecture hall, turned into a raisin. "I understand," I muttered. *Great, Vivian's last view of Joss: total humiliation.* "And I'm sorry I..." My throat closed and I hefted my daypack to go.

"I'm sorry too, Ms. Burgowski, but let me finish." Prof K's voice stayed quiet, but it stopped me. "I said 'ordinarily.' Your circumstances are pretty far from that. As are your opportunities."

"Ma'am?" I've never called a teacher that. But I've never had a teacher like Prof K.

"You've made real-life contact with a topic that's only been theoretical for everyone else in this room. Almost everyone. You've not only saved trafficked girls, you've spoken with them."

"Actually, I didn't manage to save all—" I began, but Prof K cruised past.

"You have those girls' trust. You can now make their case study your project. That's worth more than a passing grade."

Dawntae was right! "Omigod, Professor, I'll do whatever—"

"Will you?" Prof K cocked her head, looking super bird-like in those big blue-framed glasses. "If 'whatever' means fighting your way through the swamp of federal bureaucracy we call Immigration? Endless phone calls? Tracking the girls to whatever detention center they're in? Filing the paperwork for visitation rights? Traveling to Seattle or God knows where?"

In seconds, adrenalin was flushing away the dregs of my two-week depression. "I'll do that."

"No, you won't," said Prof K in a cold-water voice. "Not alone, or you'd have done so already." *Two weeks and one dead girl before I made it past Reception...yeah.* "You need a partner." She glanced at the clock. "Time for class. Here's what I want you to do. Go sit with Ms. Wu. Don't talk, for once—" a tiny smile flickered across her stern face, "just take notes. Then after class, the two of you, come back to my office and I will prepare you for your excursion into the swamp."

My face must have shown my blankness. Prof K frowned.

"We've talked, Ms. Wu and I. She's invested in the fate of the trafficked girls too. You need her language skills; she needs your boldness. And yes, Ms. Burgowski," she added as the clock buzzed the hour, "she says she's ready to work with you, as long as you want to work with her—or some such silliness. Go sit."

CHAPTER EIGHT

WHAT A PIECE OF WORK

"Hi," Vivian whispered as I sat down.

I took a deep breath and spoke to my daypack. "Prof K wants to see us after class and I actually can 'cause I don't have math, but don't you have work?"

"I switched shifts." Vivian's smile warmed the space between us like a tiny heater. "I texted my manager when I saw you come in."

It's been a long time since I was hugged and cried on by a girlfriend. Having it happen in a professor's office didn't make it less wonderful.

Turns out Prof K thought Vivian and I were a couple who'd broken up. Who knew she even had an embarrassed-face? Sharing a laugh at her expression felt even better than the cry-hugging. Then I told Vivian about Fung, and we cry-hugged again.

Then we got to work.

In her office clutter of manila folders and photos of people laboring at horrible jobs, Prof K diagrammed the Immigration Swamp—a mess of agencies with scary-sounding names. "The hospital would have discharged them directly here," she said, pointing to the top of the chart. "But next they'll—"

"Is that the place the nurse called Immigration?" I interrupted thoughtlessly. "Where is it? Why wouldn't they tell me anything?

I don't even know their names! Or how old they are, or where they come from! Shouldn't I know that? What if they send them back to China without even telling me?"

Vivian looked horrified. "Oh, they would never…" Then she glanced at Prof K. "Would they?"

Our prof nodded briskly. "That's exactly what they'll do. Ordinary citizens, even good-hearted ones, have no say in this. Lawyers, on the other hand…" She smiled, and wrote a name and phone number at the top of her scribbled chart. "Call this woman. Worked immigration for ten years. No one understands trafficking for the trade like Dee Hightower."

Vivian and I looked at each other. "The police lady used that term," I said. "'Trafficked for the trade.' What does that mean?"

Prof K held us in a hard gaze. "What it sounds like. The sex trade."

*That little doll face in the big, white bed…her baby-bird voice…*I knew the girls were trafficked for slavery. But I thought that meant working in some dark, sweaty factory. Not prostitution. Like those Philippine girls in that documentary.

The sex trade. Right here in Wattsville.

My stomach hurt. I glanced at Vivian. Didn't know her golden skin could turn so pale.

After Prof K dismissed us, we only got as far as the steps of her building, warm in the October sun. We sank down under the weight of WAY too many emotions.

"Whoa." The sun felt so magnificent, I had to clear my throat. "Uh, where d'you wanna start? I can call that lawyer…"

But Vivian put her hand on my knee. "Joss, you need to know something. About me. But it's also about the girls." Her dark eyes stretched wide with appeal. "When I was little, my favorite pretend game was *flying*, okay? I'd tie this bedsheet around my shoulders for a cape, *totally* sure I could fly off the roof if my stepdad would let me up there. But he hated it when I asked. He hated lots of things."

"Uh-huh." Intense eye contact is hard.

"He beat me," Vivian said, dropping her hand and her eyes. "Whenever I even said the *word* 'fly.' So, that time when you—"

"*Beat* you?"

"With his belt. Yeah."

"For talking about flying?"

She laughed shakily. "Oh, other stuff too. But that was a biggie. Yeah. So. When you yelled at me that night, it…you know. Kinda pushed some *buttons.*"

"Is that why you—"

"But that little girl, Spring Peach," Vivian interrupted me, "she looked the way I used to feel, okay? Helpless. And now hearing Prof K…I can't stand it, Joss." Hand on my knee again. "We can't let them send those girls back."

"You'll make this your project too?" The sun got even warmer.

"No, mine's still about slavery in the chocolate industry. But *yes*, Joss, I'm gonna help you track down those girls and interview them."

"Vivian, that's awesome! I thought you'd totally ditched me after what I said that night about—"

"But." My friend made a face as stern as our professor's. "Let's just talk about the girls, okay? None of that, y'know…crazy stuff. Kinda done with that."

Couldn't help myself. "But Zach…"

"Nope, *done*," Vivian snapped. "Leave Zach out of it." I felt my cheeks light up, and her voice melted back down. "I know, a good friend would talk about everything. Sorry. I just…we need to focus on the girls, and all the ugliness out there. It's not about me."

Later, I took myself flying in the nice early darkness, circling over the alley where the girls' prison-box was. Thinking: *So much needs fixing. Is this how Zach feels?* And remembering Vivian's words: *"...all the ugliness out there. It's not about me."*

Probably didn't spend EVERY minute of the past week on the phone, but that's what it felt like. Taking stupidly slow notes as Prof K's lawyer friend gave me advice on who to call and what to say in order to get access to the girls. Stumbling through explanations to immigration officials. Stuck on hold. More explanations. *Immigration Swamp is right.*

"Not about me," I kept reminding myself, on the bus to the government offices in Seattle, then sitting down across the desk of the scary official with red hair like Louis's and eyes like the Wicked Witch of the West. I bussed home in a state of shock from the stack of papers I had to fill out. *What the hell's a notary public?* But FINALLY, one week and a thirty minute bus ride later, Vivian and I were walking out of the swamp and into the Immigration Detention Center.

"What're you muttering about?" Vivian asked. I'd grabbed her arm without realizing it.

"'Not about me.' Been saying it all week," I answered, staring at the building's plain brick front. *How can a prison look so much like a library?* "Lame, I know."

"Not lame at all," my friend said. She patted my arm. "Let's go meet some girls, okay?"

Not gonna admit it to Rialta, but man, it was tough learning all those girls' names. Soon as I got home from that first visit, I made myself this little chart based on Vivian's translations:

Chuntao = Spring Peach, nine year-old sweetie with KILLER smile. (Saw it once on our first visit, twice on our second—can't wait to quit counting.)

Lanying = Blue Glitter. Second youngest—ten. Seems feisty— like who wouldn't, with the awesomest name ever!

Ah Lam = Peace. Tied with Lanying for second youngest. Pigtails + that thing they call "lazy eye." (Maybe why her folks didn't want her?)

Meili = Beautiful. She is—but so are they all. I'm calling her Mini-Rialta 'cause on both visits she bossed the older girls into letting her sit next to Vivian. Hard to believe she's twelve.

Hua = Flower. Thirteen. Only one who managed to stay kinda tubby on their horrible trip here. (Can't wait till they let us bring the girls snacks!)

Biyu = Jasper. (A pretty kind of stone, Vivian says.) Fourteen. Name and age are the only words we've heard from her—opposite of Meili.

Xioali = Intellectual. Wears glasses—perfect! Looks like the tiny evil mastermind lady in *The Incredibles*—but she's fourteen.

Jiao = Dainty + Tender. Oldest. Suuuuper long hair. Not real tender; Peach seems like she's scared of her.

Daiyu = Black Jade. Other oldest, and acts like it. Held Peach in her lap.

Oh, and the girl who died, Fung—her name means Bird, Daiyu said, without us even asking. She was sixteen, like Daiyu and Jiao. And me.

That first visit was so intense, I would've needed a different language to describe it. "Nine Chinese girls staring at two American girls across a table while a double-chinned guard watches"—doesn't quite capture it, okay? The only thing worth remembering from that stupidly stiff half hour is Peach's smile when Vivian told her something in Mandarin. Her little face glowed like a spotlit stage framed by a curtain of black bangs.

"What'd you say to Peach?" I asked Vivian as we boarded the bus.

"I told her peaches are my *favorite*."

Second visit two days later—better. We got a whole hour, and Vivian translated more stuff about each girl…except Biyu, who still puckers her face and looks down whenever Vivian speaks to her. And Peach turned her smile on me when I said, "Nǐ hǎo, Chuntao." Peaches are my favorite now too.

Their conversation totally loses me—two months of Mandarin and all I can say is "hello!" But at least I'm writing about it now. So maybe I've learned some kind of language. Shoot—gotta jet up to Coastal. Vivian and I are gonna plan a special Halloween visit for Friday!

Top Ten Reasons Why This Week Rocks:

1. The Immigration Front Desk Ogre is letting me and Vivian bring the girls Halloween candy! Catching the bus in twenty minutes.

2. We got all the girls bits of costumes. Peach gets a "Hello Kitty" kimono, and she's gonna just *die*. Well, she's gonna smile— which makes me just die.

3. Prof K's lawyer friend Dee Hightower called ME—asked how it was going and said the girls have a shot at a "T-Visa." (I'll explain about those later.)

4. When I told Prof K my Modern Slavery project had shifted from documenting human trafficking to actually getting the girls T-Visas, she looked me right in the eye and said, "Good for you. You're doing something *real*."

5. Louis CALLED last night from Mom's house, 'cause Mom invited him to use her phone. He said he missed me. (Well, really he talked about how hard Mr. Evans is. But later, Mom told me she asked, "So, you miss flying Air Joss?" and he said, "yeah.")

6. Back to Halloween: Vivian's taking me to a Coastal party tonight! She promised Zach won't be there. I'm skipping the Horizon dance, which I one hundred percent need to since Rialta's BF—or ex-BF—Chaz started hitting on me behind her back. (That part doesn't rock—poor Rialta, like she needs

this. But she let me and Tae hug her after Chaz ditched her at breakfast, and she's not mad that I'm partying up at Coastal without her. She's even lending me her whole "interview outfit" for my LAWYER COSTUME: fitted maroon suit, matching pumps, hose. I look amazing.)

Okay, I can only think of six. But that's six more reasons than last year, when I spent Halloween in my room, re-reading *Harry Potter and The Deathly Hallows*. I'm stoked.

Hey, almost forgot, here's Number Seven: when we got home from our second Detention-land visit, Vivian hugged me—and she smelled like one giant lily. Well, like a lily that needs to be tossed from the vase—kinda sweet-sour. So she might not talk about flying, but I'm one hundred percent sure she's DONE it... or tried to. Can't wait till she's less skittery and I can bring up the forbidden topic again.

Time to meet my secret Flyer friend and catch our bus. Happy Almost-Halloweeeeeeeen.

Vivian's costume: Wonder Woman. "So I started my Twitter campaign," she said, hooking her tinfoil-cuffed arm around the pole as the bus rounded the freeway ramp. "About slavery-free chocolate. And I'm writing letters to the Bean There owners to get them to sell the *good* stuff and educate people when they come in the café. How hard is that? But freeing the girls?" She squinted at me doubtfully from under her magic tiara. Pretty funny, 'cause I'm sure Wonder Woman never felt doubtful. "Isn't that...out of your league?"

When I pitched my idea to Prof K yesterday, I expected her to say exactly that. But she was totally encouraging, in her McGonagall way. "If Dee Hightower says the TVPA might apply to the girls" (ahem, that's the Trafficking Victims Protection Act) "then getting them Temporary Visas would effectively 'free' them,'" she said, frowning. "But you'll need real legal help, not just phone consultation."

So I told Vivian, "Prof K said she'd ask her friend to take their case for free, as a personal favor. The Hightower lady sounded kinda uptight on the phone, but when she sees how professional we are…"

"Joss, you know that's just a Halloween costume, right? You're not gonna wear it to meet the lawyer, are you?" Wonder Woman adjusted her tiny cape and pulled her big red sweater farther down her thighs. "She knows you're just a kid, and so do the Detention people. And I told you, I can't keep coming out here, I have to work."

"I know, I know," I said. "But watch: I bet this suit makes 'em treat me like a real lawyer, like Ms. Hightower. Bet she looks just like that." I pointed to an ad across the bus aisle: a white lady with her hair in a bun like mine standing on the words, "NEED A LAWYER?"

"Damn, how do they handle these shoes? My feet kill already."

Vivian bit her lip. "Shoot, I'm messing up your plan. I look the opposite of professional."

"You look powerful," I said. "Remember what you told Peach in the hospital, about being strong? They all need to stand up for themselves, or they're going straight back to China. Ms. Hightower said T-Visas are hard to get."

Wonder Woman stared out at the passing suburbs. The other passengers in the bus stared at her. "That's something else I don't understand," she said finally, still looking out the window. "Wouldn't they *want* to go back to China? They're so young. And they all have families."

"Families who sold them, Vivian! They'd just turn around and sell 'em again. Maybe they're all doing the best they can like Prof K said, but whatever—they can't afford to take care of their daughters. That's why the girls are here."

Vivian shivered. "You're right," she said softly. "I just can't stand thinking that. I mean, I'm not wild about going home myself, but it's not like my mom would ever have *sold* me... although..."

"What?" Houses were giving way to thick, dark forest, but I doubted Vivian was seeing it. "What're you thinking?"

"My stepdad." Her voice dropped even lower. "There was a time when I was, like, Peach's age—I think he would've sold me if he could."

"What?"

Vivian shrugged, rippling her little satin cape. "I was...causing trouble for him."

"You? You never cause trouble for anybody."

"I know, right? I always want to be nice. But when my stepdad messed with me, I couldn't be nice anymore, and he thought my mom might notice."

"'Messed with' you?" A knot was forming in my stomach. I wanted to grab Vivian's shoulders and make her look at me. "Like...?"

Her lips barely moved. "Like it sounds." *Prof K's words.* What you say when you don't want to say.

"Omigod. Did you tell someone?"

"I just did."

I made myself breathe. "Jeez. Vivian. No! I mean, you didn't tell your mom? She didn't see what was happening?"

"She must have. But she never did anything," Vivian whispered. "That's how come I couldn't tell her. She would've pretended everything was fine."

"Not believe her own daughter? That's messed up!"

"Shh." Vivian finally looked around; the other riders quickly glanced away. "Mom's afraid of him, Joss. She always has been."

"They're still together? After all that?" I could not keep the screech out of my voice.

"It was a long *time* ago." The bus slowed for our exit, out in the middle of nowhere where they keep Peach, and Meili, and a hundred other sad people. "When I got, you know, *mature*, he wasn't interested in me *that way* anymore. So I was okay as long as I didn't make him mad."

How much more ugly stuff do I have to know about? *Yeah, Flygirl, it's not about you, remember? Act the way you're dressed.*

Deep breath, low voice. "Vivian. Did he actually rape you?"

Wonder Woman's lip trembled. I looked away to give her some space, and the bus drove through the entrance gate before she answered. "I don't know. I've tried so hard to forget, it's almost like it didn't happen."

And now I'm forcing you to remember. What kind of Temporary Visa keeps you from being deported back to a nightmare?

The bus stopped at the low, brown-ochre brick building. Vivian added softly, "But I'm afraid that..."

"What? You can tell me." *"You're a strong girl. You're so, so strong..."*

"Nothing." Vivian shook her head so firmly her ponytail swished my shoulder. "C'mon, let's go teach the girls about Trick or *Treat.*"

Peach lit up like a jack-o-lantern—*I thought only Louis could grin like that.* Then she flung herself at me. Her arms attached behind my neck like a human front-pack.

"Whoa!" Peach weighs nothing, but I wasn't ready for the flinging part. By the time I peeled Peach off me, the rest of the girls were clustered around us, squealing with excitement at our gifts, even quiet little Biyu. In about three seconds, Meili was stylin' in this gold velvet cape from Goodwill, Hua was wearing angel wings, and Lanying had jacked Vivian's tiara to go with her sequined vest. Then they discovered the candy at the bottom of my daypack and the squeals turned into shrieks. Just like Louis and me, pigging out on Valentines-Day-sale Reese's Cups, back when we hung out.

But the real hit? Crayons. Rialta helped me pay for 'em, and paper too, but it was Vivian's idea: "When I'm with the little kids at Sunday school, all they want to do is *draw!*"

Turns out Chinese girls are pretty much like Washingtonian ones. The squealing stopped as abruptly as it started. Oh, they kept the costumes on, and the candy turned into wrappers, but five minutes after the art supplies came out, Vivian and I were looking at nine black-haired heads bent in total concentration.

Peach, in the metal chair next to me, guarded her drawing with the sleeves of her "Hey-lo Kittee" kimono. Her feet dangled a few inches from the floor. "Ask her what she's drawing," I told Vivian from around the Tootsie-Pop Peach stuck in my mouth.

They exchanged a few musical words, Peach never looking up from her paper. "She says it's a surprise," Vivian translated, smiling. *How* am *I going to do this without her?* Across the gray plastic table, Ah Lam held up her own drawing and asked a question.

"It's beautiful, kiddo." My Dad-language must've translated, 'cause Ah Lam smiled and chattered something and went back to work on what looked like her pig-tailed self in a golden castle. Glancing around our little circle of art and sugar, I saw another castle; a feast; a lime-green mountain with stick people on the tippy-top. "Huh," I told Vivian, "They're all drawing, like, fantasy pictures."

"That's what Ah Lam said: 'It's my *dream* house.' Poor little things," Vivian murmured, popping a SweeTart. "I used to do that too."

"What, draw your dreams? Cool idea. Man, I should've done that when I first started having my flying dreams—" but Vivian did her insta-blush thing.

Idiot. She wasn't even allowed to pretend *to fly.* "Sorry, never mind." I looked around at the girls. "Uh, what's Meili saying?"

"Something about candy," Vivian said, her face fading back to normal. She chirped to Meili, who chirped back, making Vivian smile. "Oh, wow! Meili asked if we had any *li hing mui*—I *love* that stuff! My mom used to get it for me."

"You eat Chinese candy in Hawaii? What's it like?" Meili watched me hopefully, so I passed her a Baby Ruth.

"Dried licorice-plum. It's *awesome*," said Vivian, and her face went all faraway again. "When we lived with my grandfather, after my dad left, we ate Chinese food all the time. It was, y'know … just *food*."

"Never thought of it like that." *Wow, I've learned more about Vivian today than I have in the last two months.* "But your dad wasn't Chinese?"

At my side, Peach glanced up. Her wistful expression beneath her bangs was a miniature of Vivian's.

"No, some white guy. I never knew him, Mom never talked about him." Vivian picked up a purple crayon, started drawing wavy lines. "But Grandfather was so *angry* when she married another white guy, he never let us even visit." More purple waves. "Not that my stepdad would've."

"Whoa." *I know it's not about me, all right? Just not sure how much more I can handle.* Peach looked up again and softly repeated, "Woh."

I cleared my throat. "Your stepdad sounds like…"

"Yeah. He's a piece of work. I read that line in Senior English, and I thought—*yes!* Now I know what to call someone who—"

"Hey, that's from *Hamlet*! He's my fave! 'What a piece of work is a man'—kinda says it all, right? Except," I added, "seriously? Your stepdad sounds more like an evil sonuvabitch."

"Sunn-avah-bit?" Peach echoed, and Vivian and I lost it. Peach laughed too, a tinkling sound, and when the rest of the girls started, no one would think we were anything but a group of Disneyland-happy gals on a sugar high.

The guard stuck his head in then to remind us visiting hour was almost over.

"Chuntao," I said to Peach, "show me your drawing, kiddo. We have to go, but I'll be back real soon, okay?"

Peach pushed her drawing forward and Vivian gasped. There was crayon-Peach, in her Hello Kitty outfit, flying across green hills, arms extended like Superman. Like the Flying Burgowski.

"Oh, how *pretty*! Good job—*hěn hǎo*," Vivian gushed. But she couldn't cover the shock in her voice.

"Whoa," I said for the zillionth time. "That's her fantasy? How crazy is that?"

"Not crazy at all." Vivian started picking up crayons. "I told you, I used to like to pretend too. And you *still* like—"

"Vivian." I grabbed her arm. "I can fly for real. It's not a fantasy."

She looked at me with her eyes Hello-Kitty-big. "Could we *please* talk about this later? We're having such a good time."

All the girls were watching. I let go, and smiled. "Okay, fine. Just tell me," I added, "how do you say 'flying' in Mandarin?"

"*Fēi*," she muttered, and dived under the table for a crayon.

"*Fēi* Joss," I whispered to Peach, pointing to myself. Then I stretched my arms out like Superman. Peach mimicked me, smiling. Vivian reappeared, and I quickly folded Peach's arms back down.

"Okay! Time to roll. C'mon, girls, let's sing the Clean-up Song. '*Clean up, clean up, everybody everywhere…*'" They joined in, sort of, and busily collected crayons and candy-wrappers.

Vivian's right: we are having a good time, even though man is a piece of work and horrible things happen to sweet, wonderful girls.

And she's right about something else: we *will* talk about this later.

CHAPTER NINE

THAT SAVING THING

Guess what else about Vivian: she's allergic to shrimp. Her dorm-room ramen collection is all chicken and beef. "My grandfather thought I was just being picky," she said, pouring hot water into our ramen-filled mugs. "He kept making me try shrimp. Mom made him quit after I had to go to the *hospital.*"

"Huh." I stirred my noodles. I'd been trying not to blurt questions the whole bus ride back from the Detention Facility, blabbing about Rialta and Chaz. And even that topic died when I said something stupid about boyfriend choices. So we'd switched to food chat. "Why didn't you just say 'no thank you'?"

"I didn't want to hurt his feelings. I loved my *gong-gong.*" Vivian sighed, joining me on her fuzzy blue couch.

Oh, jeez. Coupla chicks hanging out, pre-Halloween party—we're supposed to be having fun. I cast around for a topic to unlock her face from Sad Mode.

"Hey, your flower-posters? Is Hawaii really like that, flowers in people's hair and all?"

Finally, a smile!

"Well, yeah," Vivian said. "It's no big deal, they just grow. And they smell *amazing.* When I first got here and smelled a rhododendron, I was so disap*pointed*! I used to wear a plumeria behind my ear." Her hand reached up, finding the Wonder Woman tiara instead of a flower. She removed it, setting it on top of the high heels and hose I ditched as soon as we got here. "Flowers make me happy."

Happy's good. "Maybe you can tour me around Oahu someday," I said. "Not sure I totally believe regular people live in a place like that."

"Well, look who's *talking*! Isn't Dalby Island a big tourist place too?" Vivian blew on her noodles and sipped. "I bet those tourists feel the same way about *you* guys."

"Dalby?" I laughed, trying and failing to hitch Rialta's tailored skirt up high enough to sit cross-legged. "Dalby's got, like, two teensy hotels. But you'll see if you come for Thanksgiving, right? Think you can?"

Vivian sipped again. "Well, it's not like I have to ask anyone's permission. Mom and—the Piece of *Work* won't be expecting me." *Wow, snark? 'Bout time!* "Zach's invited me, I just have to make up my *mind* if I want to go to his place."

I forced myself not to yell *NO!* Leaning back in the squishy cushions, I focused on the Hawaiian flowers. "So," super casual, "you think you're gonna?"

"Well. Here's the *thing*." I heard her mug being set down, then Vivian was quiet for so long I had to look at her. "Joss. Can I tell you something…super private?"

My ridiculous Flyer engines stirred—*is this how a Stander feels, sensing the power?* I rearranged my legs, clamping myself to the couch. "Of course."

"Remember I told you Zach and I are, you know…waiting?"

"Not having sex, you mean?" *So much for not blurting.*

Vivian blushed but looked relieved. "Zach believes sex is for marriage, and I was like, 'that's *fine*,' because I've never really been into all that. I mean all through high school I just *kissed* guys, and if they wanted more, I broke up with 'em. *You* know, right?"

I nodded like, *sure, girlfriend!* without adding, *Actually, I've only ever been really kissed by your BF who happened to be trying to destroy my power, and oh, guess what, that's exactly what he's gonna do to you.*

"But last week, when we were together?" Vivian continued softly, looking at her knees. "Zach kinda...pushed us a little farther, if you know what I mean."

"Oh, totally," I said. "So, can't you just tell him you don't wanna, like, lose your virginity yet?"

"But I *do!*" Vivian burst out. She covered her face. "I want him so *bad,* Joss! You have no *idea* how hard it was to stop!"

Nope, no idea—unless the sex urge is anything like the flying one. I crossed my legs and leaned down hard with my elbows, fighting the revs.

"But...I mean, if you want to, and he wants to ...who cares? Just use a condom, right?" Bright yellow thoughts: *Wouldn't Savannah be amazed, I never talked like this with her!* But flashing red: *No, no, Zach just wants you to lose control and fly.*

I cleared my throat. "What are you afraid of?"

There are so many things Vivian *should* be afraid of that her answer stunned me. "I'm afraid I'm not actually a virgin," she mumbled between her fingers. "And Zach will be able to tell."

My flight-fuel thinned away. "Because..."

"Because." Tears welled up in Vivian's eyes. "What if I really *was* raped, Joss? When I was little? That still counts, right?"

"Ohhh." I scooted across the couch and threw my arm around her caped shoulder. *Self-centered diva, stressing over losing your Flying friend—how 'bout what she's dealing with?* "No, no, Vivian, that's different! That was child abuse, something you survived, something you should get help with. Who cares what Zach—"

"Zach's so old-fashioned. I've heard him talk about other girls. He'll say I'm a *slut.*" She choked on the word, head down. "And he'll break up with me, and I'll..."

"You'll WHAT?" I bounced to my feet. *It's not about you, Vivian needs comfort*—but my Flyer fears took over. "You don't need Zach! What kinda jerk calls you a slut if you're not a virgin? Vivian, listen to me—Zach doesn't love you, he just wants you, but not, like, sexually…well, yeah, probably that too, but he really wants to ground you. Forever. It's what he does. He tried it on me—no, cut that out!"

Vivian clamped her hands over her ears, but I grabbed her tinfoil-cuffed wrist and pulled, forcing her to hear. "The Piece of Work's three thousand miles away, he can't hurt you anymore. You can be your real self here. Your real FLYER self. But—" Vivian stood up, pulling me, and we did a weird little struggling dance—"not—if Zach—gets his—hands—on your power!"

"Let go," she wailed.

"Not till you admit it—you're a Flyer! Not till you promise you'll protect yourself from the guy who wants to keep you down!"

Vivian folded then, literally: knees to the floor, head to her knees, dragging me with her. I put my arms around her satin shoulders while she cried. *Damn, first Rialta, now Vivian—I'm getting good at this*, said Joss's Old Brain, still all about her. New Brain muttered, *You f---in' idiot. Now she's gonna drop you for good.* But even as she sobbed, Vivian only shook her head—no kicking me out this time. She let me pat her and stroke her hair. And when she finally sat up and wiped her weirdly un-blotched face with her cape, all World's Saddest Wonder Woman said was, "Whoa. I can't believe I told you that."

I sat back down on the floor. "Uh…I'm not, like, a therapist. You should probably…"

Vivian sniffled. "I know. I'm a mess. I kinda hoped it would all go away if I just met the right guy. And Zach seemed perfect, 'cause he's so…*different*."

"Yes, he IS." *Now—can I be a good Flyer friend AND a good friend?* "That's what I'm telling you, Vivian. Did you hear what I said about your powers?" And I held my breath.

But Vivian only frowned, and sighed. "I heard. You're crazy, Joss, and you're totally wrong. But I get it." She sighed again, shakily. "You're trying to tell me it's okay to be like you." I opened my mouth and shut it again. "Strong, I mean—not afraid to talk about…flying, if that's what you're into." Another sniffle, still not looking at me.

"But…I mean thanks, but…this stuff is REAL." She shook her head, leaning back against the couch, and I pressed harder. "Vivian. You don't have to admit you're a Flyer. But you never *will* be if you don't trust me about Zach."

Head-shaking. "No. I just need to talk to him."

"Vivian, no!" I jumped to my feet, revving again. "Talk about what?" *Wow, didn't know Vivian could glare.* "Okay, none of my business, but just…be careful, right? Denying the Flyer stuff doesn't make it go away! Just ask my mom!"

"Of course I'll be careful," Vivian said with dignity, ignoring the 'Flyer stuff,' mom and all. "I just need to let Zach know I want to keep things *slow* between us. And so I probably won't go with him for Thanksgiving."

"Don't say 'probably.'"

"Definitely, okay? But I owe him that. Zach's a *sweet* guy, he'd never hurt me. I just don't want to hurt *him.*"

"Vivian…" *Too much to say. Nothing to say.*

She grabbed her phone off the couch. "I gotta do this now before I chicken out." Texting. "So, Joss, you can *totally* hang out here while I go over to Zach's, okay? I'll meet you at the party in, like, forty-five minutes? Hull House? It's two buildings over, the cinderblock one." She looked up apologetically. "I'm such a bad friend. And you're so good for making me *do* this."

If I could make you do anything, you'd delete Zach's number. "You're not a bad friend. I'll hang out…unless, wait—Zach's not coming to the party, right?"

"No, Zach doesn't believe in Halloween. He's funny that way."

I threw up my hands. "Vivian, that's what I'm telling you! That's his brand of religion—hating witches and weirdness and Flyers and queers, trying to 'save' us—"

"*Please* don't start, Joss," she interrupted, more pleading than angry. Her phone buzzed. "Oh, wait, Zach says he's coming *here*. Maybe you should…"

"Oh, hell yeah, I'm outta here. See ya at the party." I snatched up my borrowed shoes and hose, and only my constricting lawyer suit kept me from flying out the door and down the stairwell. *I can't see Zach now; he'll know I've warned Vivian about him.*

Don't be a moron—he's not a mind-reader!

Like it matters. Sooner or later he's gonna launch her and pray her down. I need to make her see.

I need Flyer advice. I need my mom.

But as I pulled my phone out, exiting MacDougall Dorm, this thought finally caught up to me: *Vivian's grounded herself just as thoroughly as Zach the Stander wants to. So what's left to warn her about?*

"Mom," I heard myself say. *She'll end up like Mom, killing her flight-urges with alcohol and pills.* Self-grounding is way more awful than losing your powers to a Stander. And Vivian has even more pain in her background than Mom did. How could she medicate herself out of that? She NEEDS the sky.

"'Scuuuse me—did you just call me 'Mom'?" a voice drawled. Some guy was walking up to me. "Sweet. You can be Dad. Family's important." It was Vivian's friend Eli, with the fedora. No Halloween costume, just black jeans and hipster plaid shirt. "I'm goin' up to see Sister Viv, wanna come? Or were you just there?"

"Hey, Eli," I faltered, coming out of my little Flyer trance. "Uh, yeah, and Zach's heading over, so I decided…"

"Good on ya, lassie, remembrin' me nayme an' all," Eli replied in some kind of Aussie-Scots mix. "Ye'll have to remoind me o' yers, eh? Metcha up there, what—a month ago? Wondered why I never saw ye agaiyn, till Viv told me ye don't actually goooo heeerrre."

"Yeah, kinda." *No point explaining; gotta call home.* "I'm Jocelyn. Well, good to see—"

But Eli took my arm. "Why, Jocelyn, lass, what's yer hurry?" *Is he drunk?* "I'm feelin' the need o' some company just noo, and *not* the Fair Zachary. Come an' bide a wee at my place, eh? Don't worry, yer safe wi' this harmless queer lad." *Or maybe high? Doesn't smell drunk.*

I needed advice. I needed to fly. *But I also need to talk about my friend with someone who knows her.* "Uh, okay, I'll hang out some. I'm s'posed to meet Vivian in..."

"You're dressed different," Eli interrupted without a trace of accent, walking us round the corner. *Weird—I feel safer already.* "And why're you barefoot?" He stopped and peered at me, his black forelock shining in the lamplight. "You okay, Miss Jocelyn? No?" he added before I could answer. "Good. 'Cause I'm not either."

Two zombies on ladders were trying to hang a bedsheet banner across the Hull House entrance without killing themselves—not something zombies should worry about. "Welcome to Hell House!" it screamed in blood-drippy letters.

Eli let loose a colorful curse involving baboons and ducks. "So much for going to my room. Didn't think those troglodytes would've started the party already."

"You live in Hull? I'm supposed to meet Vivian here in forty-five minutes anyway."

"That's special." He cussed again, in French. "Never mind. All we need's some peace and quiet. I'm taking you to my happy place. C'mon."

I glanced at Eli. *What could be the happy place of this human chameleon?* "Uh, maybe I should..." *go flying after all? Yes.*

"Nonsense, lassie." Scottish again, Eli re-took my arm and marched me away from the party, skirting a vampire girl writing "Happy Hulloween" on the sidewalk while her vampire boyfriend fondled her butt. "Ah need yer cooompany. Ah'm a single gay boy tonight and Ah doooon't like it one wee bit."

"Oh. Where's, um..." I searched my brain for Eli's boyfriend's name as we wound up Campus Hill into thickening trees.

"Brady? Ah, *scheisse*," Eli said, and stopped so abruptly I lurched into him in the darkness. He dropped my arm to mash his fists into his eyes. "I am so DONE with this f---in' emotion. Every time I say his name! And it's been a f---in' week already."

"Oh," I said. At least I knew what was jangling him. "I'm sorry. Were you, like, together a long time?"

"Two f---in' years," Eli said bitterly. "He texts me on our second anniversary: 'I need a break.' Like being my guy was a f---in' *job*. F--- him."

"Uh-huh." Only once before have I talked relationships with a guy: my crush Nate, when he was crushing on Savannah. *Didn't think it got more awkward.* "Hey, hold up, I need to put my hose and shoes on, my feet are freezing."

Eli gave a whole-body shiver and slapped his arms. "Righto. You never said why you're barefoot. You have a tiff with the lovely Viv and run outta there?"

"No." I sat my tailored butt on the cold walkway and began working Rialta's hose back up my legs. "But Zach was coming over and I didn't want to be there."

"Then you're not like most ladies," Eli remarked. He dug in the pockets of his skinny jeans. "'S'amatter, you don't enjoy watching The Fair Zachary suck Vivvo's face off?"

"Right." I scrambled up to rearrange my skirt. Eli ignored me and lit a joint, eyebrows arched like an elf's in the flare of the lighter. He took a long toke, eyes closed, and offered it to me.

"Oh—no thanks." I've never been tempted since Savannah made me try pot when we were thirteen, but Eli looked so morose—an Asian Hamlet in plaid—I felt bad for refusing. I took his flannel arm and tucked it under mine. "Hey, what about your happy place? You are one sucky tour guide."

Good thing Flyers aren't scared of heights. 'Cause Eli got me high all right: high on a plywood platform barely big enough for us to sit back-to-back, feet dangling, halfway up a fir tree. Turns out Eli's happy place is the campus ropes course at the top of the hill, this crazy high-altitude park for trapeze artists or monkeys, totally off limits without a licensed—and un-stoned—instructor. Not that Eli gave a *scheisse*.

I can fly, I can fly, I kept telling myself all the way up the splintery ladder. It wasn't cold for the end of October, but up at squirrel height I turned into goose bumps. Hard to hug yourself warm when you're hanging on for dear life.

Sitting back-to-back up in a big, swaying fir tree reminded me of flying with Louis. Or maybe Eli's artificial relaxation got to work on my awkwardness. "So…does Zach, like, even speak to you? 'Cause I know he's totally homophobic. Or maybe tons of people are here?"

"No, people are cool." Eli's voice floated coolly. "Zach's the weird-ass. Cannot for the crazy life of me get what Viv sees in him. Besides his radiating hotness."

"I know, right? But that can't be all of it—Vivian's deep." *And so's Zach…admit it, Flygirl.* "So she won't talk about him with you either?"

Our tree crackled and popped over Eli's response, and I clutched the edge of the platform—*I can fly, I can fly.* "…not into sharing the gory details of her love life. Unlike yours truly," I heard him finish.

"So how's a gay love life different?" I blurted. "Is it, like, more about the sex?" *Can I blame that on his fumes?*

Behind me I felt Eli inhale, hold, exhale. "How am I s'posed to answer that, Jossalass? How's *your* love life different?"

You mean, besides not existing? I didn't say, settling for "Good point." But something danced at the edge of my memory. "You just fall in love, right? So why do some gay people have to be all in-your-face about being gay? 'Cause that's what makes people like Zach get all uptight about 'em."

That's it—Zach felt he was struggling to save his gay brother's soul. That's why he came to Dalby! And Zach's homophobia was my first hint of his Stander-ism. A hint I ignored.

Another wind gust made our tree groan. My hair whipped my face, escaping its tight lawyer-do. Eli snaked his hand back to pat my thigh. "Why're some hetero couples all in-your-face about being hetero? Did you see those vampires back at Hull?"

"Good point," I murmured again. "Zach's not uptight about hetero PDA. It's the whole thou-shalt-not thing, right? The way the Stan—I mean, the way people like Zach read the Bible, they feel like they have to be against whatever-it-is. Gayness. Other religions." *Flying.*

The wind sent a puff of pot smoke across my face. "Why do you care how Zach feels?" Eli wanted to know.

Good freakin' question. "I dunno. I was arguing with my roommate and she said something about saving America's soul, and that made me wonder, how would it feel to be, like, the guardian—of your fellow human beings."

"Ya lost me there," Eli said sleepily. The tree creaked. *Rock-a-bye baby...*

"Well, like, what if I thought that joint was really bad for you—I mean not just your lungs, but bad for your soul?" I was thinking out loud, trying to get a grip on what's hurt too much to dwell on since That Awful Summer. "What if I really believed in Hell—not that stupid Halloween stuff, but real, everlasting torment after you die—and I cared about you and didn't want you to end up there? I'd knock that joint right out of your hand."

"And start a forest fire? Yeah, that'd teach me."

"I'm serious! Zach doesn't hate gays because he's hateful—at least that's not how he sees it. He hates you because he loves you."

Eli snorted behind me. "That is such bull-*merde*. Zach doesn't know me at all. What's he care about my soul?"

"Well, not *yours*." My excitement was starting to warm me. "But his brother Rory's gay, and Zach loves Rory and doesn't want him in Hell, so gayness in general is, like, this big threat to Zach. And the same with fl—" I stopped myself.

"Zach tell you all this? Or have you been chatting with his shrink?" Eli's back pulled away from mine, a half inch of scorn.

I didn't care. *I finally get what Zach was telling me outside Vivian's dorm.* "Zach sees Rory as a victim." I let go the platform to reach back and pat Eli's leg. "And Vivian too—which she is, only not in the way Zach thinks—and—and he wants to save them. Which I can kinda relate to, because I have some people I'm trying to save."

"Okay, this is the worst case of secondhand high I've ever seen." Eli yawned. "Girl, you are making no sense. You might as well partake." The joint, much shorter now, appeared at the edge of my vision. "Whose soul are *you* busy saving?"

"No, I'm good." I pushed the joint away. "Not souls—I'm saving people! From deportation. You know those Chinese girls I rescued—"

"Oh, right right right," Eli interrupted, "Vivvo told me you're trying to get 'em visas to stay here. Good on ya, *chica*. Awesome. But what the hell's that got to do with Zach and his gay brother and gay ol' me?"

"That saving thing! I get it now!" I felt warm and fearless, despite the wind. "I mean, I hate Zach's attitude about gays, but I can actually see how, if he thinks he's saving Rory...it's like, this little girl Chuntao? I found out Immigration granted only two hundred T-visas last year, out of thousands of cases, and all the rest of the people were either sent back to whatever horrible country they're from, or they're stuck in detention, for *years*. And I'm not letting that happen to Peach—I mean Chuntao."

The sky behind the trees was brightening—the Halloween moon fighting free of the clouds. "I *will* save her. And I hate that Zach's such a jerk about it, but he thinks he *will* save Rory." *And Vivian. And me? Does he still care enough about me to ground me?*

Whatever cutting retort Eli would've made I'll never know. From down the hill floated a low-pitched wailing: "Aiiiiii!"

The goose bumps swarmed. We both reached back to clutch hands and Eli swore again, without his usual creativity. "Aiiiiiii!" the ghost-voice wailed again.

"Eli? What the hell's that?" I grabbed the platform with my free hand as my flight-engines tried to propel me off. Eli kept swearing.

"Eeee-laiiiii," moaned the ghost. Coming closer. The clouds chose that moment to ease aside, and bright moonlight filtered through the treetops. And into the wavery moon shadows stepped...a girl?

"Whoa!" The girl's hair seemed to glow, and something glittered before the moon receded. "Eli—you see that? I think Marilyn Monroe's down there. Or her ghost."

CHAPTER TEN

ALTITUDE

M arilyn…" gasped Eli.

The ghost-girl raised her face and called distinctly, "Eeee-liii? You up there?"

In the half light I saw red lips, pearls, and boobs pointed like missiles. But Eli saw—

"Brady." His voice wavered. "You found me."

"There you are! They said you went up the hill—I knew where you'd be," called Marilyn-Brady. "Eli, I *know* you. Your phone's been off. Can we talk, please?" Off came the platinum wig to show a plump, sweet-faced guy who would probably hate to be called that.

Behind me, a shivery sigh. "Okay," my tree-buddy said faintly.

"He says okay," I relayed down to Brady before Eli could change his mind.

Brady squinted up as the moon lit our perch. Being Eli's boyfriend probably means getting used to stuff like finding him halfway up a tree with a lawyer chick.

"Who're you? Do I know you?" The question sounded more curious than bitchy.

I'm a single girl who needs to escape a couple's heart-to-heart—again. "I'm just Jocelyn," I called, reaching for the first rung with my toes. The climb down was less scary, since I was busy wondering what it'll cost to have tree sap dry-cleaned off Rialta's suit.

"Thanks, Just Jocelyn," Brady told me when we were eye to eye. He had his wig back on; probably the only thing keeping him warm in that gold lamé gown.

"For what?"

"For taking care of my guy. He can*not* be alone when he's like this. I'll take it from here," and Brady hitched up his gown and started up the ladder. "Oops, better ditch the heels like you did, right? Heads up!"

As I pulled my own heels back over the shredded hose and headed across the moonlit clearing, I heard murmurs behind me—Brady and Eli making up, or maybe just the trees talking.

Great. Still ten minutes before I meet Vivian at Hull House. Maybe that vampire couple wants to share their relationship issues with me too. But in spite of cold hands and pinched feet, I felt... fortified.

Eli treated me like a regular friend—assumed I had a love life and everything. Vivian let me say the word "fly" without melting down; she's busy right now creating more distance from Zach. And Zach—he's still a threat, but somehow, I get him now, and that makes him...

What, Flygirl?

Vulnerable, that's what.

Oh, yeah? Got a plan to neutralize the Stander before he neutralizes your buddy, or you?

Yes. Yes, as a matter of fact, I do. I stopped short where the pavement emerged from the trees with lamps to guide me down to main campus. A big gust ripped the last effective hairpin off my head, flinging my hair across my face like a curtain, but I hardly noticed. For the first time, I saw a path to disempower Zach.

He whispered it into my ear that Fourth of July: *"I want to love the magic like you do. Get me out of this stupid Stander thing, it's not who I am anymore."* He was lying then, tricking me. And it worked. Vulnerability, a plea for help—I had found it irresistible. And, I knew with sudden certainty, so would Zach. I could be the bait to lure his weakness into the open.

A tingle of excitement pulsed through me. *Crazy idea, maybe impossible—* I needed Lorraine's advice. But if it worked, Vivian would be safe around Zach, and so would I.

And if it didn't…? The thrilling fizz of my idea turned suddenly chilly and I hugged myself.

Nah. It has to. And I clacked down the pavement toward Hull, scheming.

It would probably hurt Vivian some. Maybe a lot. But, like Hamlet said, I must be cruel only to be kind. Zach said it too.

"Hulloween" was starting to rock: music pounding, another banner up, and the vampires and zombies had disappeared inside, probably mixing toxic punch. But my brand-new determination wasn't enough to fake my way in there without Vivian. *And my hair! Need a mirror and a brush. Vivian must have sent Zach away by now.*

Like a confused solo salmon, I weaved through the Hull-bound stream of costumed Coasties, down toward MacDougall. "Hey," I said to three cyberpunk girls I recognized from Mandarin, but they didn't know me behind my Halloween-mask hair. *Mirror, brush—and maybe I can lose these damn shoes at the party.*

From behind, MacDougall looked deserted except for Vivian's light. *Is Zach still with her?* Peering up at the second-floor window, all I saw was the edge of one of Vivian's flower-posters.

…and Vivian's arm. Brushing her hair? Good—if she's redoing her Wonder Woman ponytail, that means Zach's gone, so—wait.

No hairbrush. Her arm was just flailing the air. *What's going on? Where's Zach?*

The next second told me. My friend was grabbing at nothing, trying not to levitate. I've done that. It doesn't work. The rest of Vivian's body flailed into view: Wonder Woman three feet off the ground, desperately trying to keep from bashing her tiara into the ceiling.

And Zach? *There*—the top of his head, just visible above the windowsill. Kneeling. There's only one reason a Stander kneels when a Flyer goes airborne. He was praying her down.

"No!" I yelled, grabbing at a bare little tree to stop my own rush of flight. "Vivian, come down NOW!" *Like she could! She's out of control.* Like I was when Zach launched me That Awful Summer, his power all the more terrible because I had allowed it close enough to kiss.

Zach's head disappeared again, bowed in prayer. Vivian grabbed the top of the window frame, trying to force herself down. *Does she feel that arrow-prick of Stander incantations? Her power leaking away?*

I let go the little tree to scrabble in the cold, damp leaves at my feet. "Get down," I pleaded. *No good—I can't help my friend save the power she's never fully owned.*

But then my fingers closed on a rock: egg-sized, perfect. I hurled it at Vivian's window. The glass spider-webbed. A split-second pause—enough for Wonder Woman to aim herself feet-first, to shatter the window, to escape into the Halloween sky.

"OmiGOD!" A girl's scream pierced the party noise from Hull. "Look UP, you guys—WONDER WOMANS!"

"Whoa!"

"Jesus!"

"What the f---!" I heard below me—suddenly very far below. I was rocketing at the moon.

No time for breath. *I'm a missile on a mission: catch my friend before she flies into orbit.*

For a panicked second I lost her. *Is she landing?* Letting all her fellow Coasties into our secret? Letting Zach purify her soul?

There! Silhouetted against the moon like that old *E.T.* movie, cape and ponytail streaming behind her. *She is Wonder Woman. And a Flyer like me!* And on that rev of joy, I caught her.

Literally: I grabbed her boot and held on. Vivian slowed and leveled her trajectory. She was crying.

"It's okay, Vivian," I gasped, letting go to fly alongside. I reached to pat her shoulder and felt a tear splash onto my hand.

Her whole body was spasming with sobs. Crying while flying? *What fuel is she on? What if it runs out?*

I glanced down—*ohjeezohjeezohjeez*. Wattsville was a little blob of light among farther, larger blobs—Seattle! Tacoma! I was freezing in my lawyer outfit. My lungs ached. *Never ever flown so high.*

Suddenly, lights, red and white, off to our left. More on our right, closing.

"Uh, Vivian? We're in the freakin' AIRPORT LANDING PATH! We need to—" *SCHOOM*—our bodies rocked in the wake of something huge. "Vivian! Gotta get DOWN!"

I slammed my left arm over her back and kept it there, leaning hard. Immediately we pointed steeply down—*too steep!* Our grand view contracted; Wattsville rushed toward us.

"Level out," I yelled.

Steering another Flyer is exhausting, turns out. But effective. Back at normal flight-height, my arms were lead, but I could breathe again. Vivian breathed too, flying out of her personal storm. As we circled slowly, fifty feet above the bay, I removed my hand from her back and she used one of hers to wipe her eyes. She mumbled something.

"What?" I stayed close. Flying with my Flyer friend.

"It's so good." Vivian turned her face to me in the moonlight, red-eyed but beautiful like the first time I met her. She gave a little hiccup. "I keep trying to forget how good it is."

Slow circles above moonlit water. No sound but the gentle slap of the ocean on the docks, the occasional lonely gull, and our own breathing. *It's so good.* Every few minutes I patted Vivian's shoulder, keeping her close, until I heard her lungs begin to relax.

Then I talked: the Flying Burgowski explaining to the Flying Wu about Flyers. What happens to them when they try to deny their power or mash it down. What happened to my Flyer mom: the alcohol, the pills. Divorce. Attempted suicide.

The Flying Wu made sympathetic sounds.

Then I told her about Standers: their mission, their methods. That Horrible Summer. The Flying Wu shook her head and said nothing.

We completed another half-loop around the bay, trading warehouse-stench for salty freshness as the questions built up inside me.

"Okay, your turn," I finally said. "Vivian…why do you fight flying so hard? Now, when you're all grown up and your stepdad can't possibly know?"

She murmured something.

"What?" I flew close and laid my hand on her shoulder.

"Didn't want to be a freak."

"Who told you…?" But I stopped myself. I knew who.

"Didn't want to give in. The feeling's so strong. So delicious." She kept talking to her outstretched arms, chanting almost. "It makes me wild. I can't stop it. I'm so weak."

"Weak? Are you kidding? Fighting the power off all those years without going nuts—"

And that's when Vivian ran out of flight-fuel.

"Oh, *no*," she whimpered, and down she dropped.

No flailing—poor thing hasn't flown enough to learn how to maintain altitude. No screaming either. She just fell, resigned to her fate.

Good thing we were low. 'Cause I'd never have been Superman enough to fly underneath Vivian and catch her. So when she crashed onto the end of a pier, all I could do was land at her side and call her name and pray that a thirty-foot drop onto wooden planks hadn't broken all her Flyer bones.

"Uhhhn," my friend grunted as her breath came back. She held up scraped palms; must've skidded on her hands. But she's tougher than I thought. Here's how she answered my "Are you okay?!": "I'm fine. I just *hate* splinters."

"Are you kidding? You fell out of the sky!" I fussed over her, patting her arms and legs. "How're you not all fractured?"

"Gotten pretty good at falling…" Vivian mumbled, pushing herself to her knees. True: except for her hands, she looked fine. "Least I didn't spill any *coffee* this time."

"What? Is that what happened, back when—"

"I crashed on you at the café? Uh-huh." She spat on her hands and winced. "I just lose power and I have to *ditch*. Isn't that *normal?*"

I didn't know whether to scream with laughter or burst out crying. "Vivian…"

"Oh, *dear*," she said again, and I thought, *What could possibly, possibly be wrong with the world now?* "I broke my dorm room window. You think they'll make me *pay* for that?"

"Uhhh…no way. Vivian, that was…" *me rescuing you, you rescuing yourself, from the Stander!* "… not your fault." A hundred more questions crowded my brain—about Zach, about launching, about fighting back. About, what next??? My Disempowering Plan burned in my chest.

But Vivian couldn't deal with that now. She could barely deal with herself. Who knows if she even heard what I said about Standers? As we shuffled down the length of the creaky old pier, I wondered who was more exhausted.

"No way I can stay in my room now," she said, hugging herself. Her Wonder Woman cape was gone, probably somewhere in the bay. "Campus police must be all *over* it. Shoot, I'm *freezing*, aren't you?"

"Yeah. Oh, I wish I could take you back to my dorm! But our couch is teeny…"

"It's okay, Joss, you've been wonderful." Vivian tucked her hands in her armpits. "Don't worry, I know who I can stay with."

"Who?" I said sharply. "I know you don't mean—"

"Course not," Vivian said, and then gave me my birthday and

Christmas present all wrapped up together: "You were right about Zach. But," she added, before I could start with *How will you keep yourself safe from him? Are you ready to be a Flyer now?* "Joss, I don't want to *talk* about it anymore, okay? I'll stay at Eli's."

Let's hear it for Brady, making up with Eli just in time to clear some space for our pooped-out Flyer friend. Eli must have turned his phone back on; he replied to Vivian's text immediately. "He says I can have his *bed*, he's staying with MM." Vivian frowned. "Oh, I hope he isn't just hooking *up* with somebody."

"No, Vivian—MM is Marilyn Monroe! That's Brady." She looked confused, but took my triumphant smile in stride. "They got back together, just now, while you and Zach…you know." *And Brady thanked me.* Happiness is a great warmer-upper.

I couldn't help myself. As we crossed the street bordering campus, I asked her, "Why…Vivian, I know you don't wanna talk now, but—you *have* been flying. I've smelled you! Is it *all* bad? Doesn't it make you feel a teensy bit free?"

She stopped under a large maple tree, shoulders drooping. "Joss. I'm not like you. You have a Flyer mom." *Oh, so she was listening!* "'Free' isn't a green light in my family, it's a…it's a red flag."

I shook my head helplessly. "How can free feel bad?"

"Oh, Joss." Vivian closed her eyes. She looked exhausted. "You're not gonna ask the girls how they *felt* being locked in a metal box, are you? Some things…you don't want to…"

"Okay. Okay. I get it." *Liar—I don't get it at all.* But I let it go.

We trudged back up to Coastal on fumes, skirting MacDougall in order to avoid cops. Eli came out to meet us behind Hull, where "Hulloween" was still thudding. He kissed Vivian's scraped hands, kissed my forehead, and asked not a single question. "Sorry 'bout the dirty laundry," he said, giving Vivian his room key. "Jossalady, you staying too?"

I wished I could. I wished we could stay up the rest of this wild night, curled on Eli's funky couch, coaxing out Flyer stories. But—curfew. And exhaustion. With the party music seeping through the floor, we picked out Vivian's splinters, conversation limited to "ouch," "dang," and "I know, right?" Even after she snuggled into Eli's bed, me hovering like a mom, all we said was "wow," and "yeah." When Vivian fell asleep two minutes later, I patted her head and whispered, "Welcome back."

Then I staggered back down the hill to Horizon. But wiped as my body felt, my heart was flying.

CHAPTER ELEVEN

GROUND CREW

Who knew a Flyer could refuel on a thought? Tanks drained, beating curfew by a millisecond, I stripped off my lawyer suit and crawled into bed.

"Good party?" Dawntae murmured from the couch, adding, "Rialta's with Chaz, I'm staying up to sneak her in when she texts."

"You're awesome, Tae...sorry, gotta crash," I mumbled, expecting immediate lights-out. But someone forgot to tell my brain.

Vivian's back in the sky! And *boom*—I was charged with the highest-octane energy I've felt since that Fourth of July. Joy, hope, fear—I grabbed my bedpost to keep from flailing like Vivian when Zach knelt beneath her. If Dawntae weren't so sleepy she'd have thought I was having an attack.

Attack. A Zach attack. A brilliant Flyer plan.

Brilliant? Or crazy? I need my Ground Crew.

So I tossed and turned for an hour, hearing Dawntae let Rialta in, then slide into the bunk below. Another ten minutes, and her breathing eased into sleep. Then, as night morphed into morning, I climbed down from my bunk and dressed, super quiet, in jeans, hoodie, fleece and windbreaker. I wrote a note to the roomies in the glow of my phone, tiptoed past the Raging Aardvark's door, and flew home to Dalby.

Navigation's not hard in the moonlight; I know the shape of all the islands. That powerful surge of plans and questions kept me aloft over the shimmering water, the black velvet woods, the bobbing lights of boats in the coves. At that hour, at that height, I was the only moving thing except the wind. But as I dropped onto the wet grass outside Mom's house, my fuel evaporated.

Her clock glowed 1:20 a.m. as I stumbled into her bedroom, but Mom only mumbled, "That's my girl," and made room for me in her bed. I slept like a dead body.

Yay for timing. The party was Friday, so now it was Saturday and Mom didn't have to work. When I shambled into her tiny kitchen it was noon, and she was making grilled cheese sandwiches like, *yeah, I always do this for my kids.*

"All the way from Wattsville?" she demanded. "How long did it take?"

I hugged her hard. Gotta love a Flyer mom. No *what's wrong, why didn't you call?* Oh, she got there. But only after logging all my flight data.

"Time yourself when you fly back," she suggested after I explained I had no idea. "I'm impressed, babe—that's farther than I've ever flown." She dropped another sandwich onto my plate at the kitchen counter. "No wonder you're starving."

I was. "So good," I managed through my mouthful of melted cheese heaven. Tion hopped onto the counter to purr against my arm. *"So good," Vivian said about flying—does she still think that?* "Mom, my friend Vivian—it's true. She's one of us. She flew with me last night."

"You were right! Fantastic!" Mom hopped onto the stool next to mine, knees peeking through her ancient jeans. "Tell me."

"WAY high, we went. Scary high. I think she must've bottled up her power so long, she couldn't handle it." *I should call Vivian. She'll talk about flying now, right?*

"Yup, been there," Mom nodded. "How long d'you think she'd kept herself grounded?"

"Well, I smelled it on her the week before, but kinda sour, y'know?" *Like you used to smell in your not-flying days,* I didn't add. "So she prob'ly hadn't flown since…oh, right, that first day in Wattsville, with Dad! When she 'tripped' and fell onto our table? Broad daylight, out of control—she was fighting it. She told me."

I did some calculations as Tion head-butted me in kitty bliss. "That was Labor Day, so…two months ago?" *Two months. Zach and Peach and now The Flying Wu? Mr. Evans has no idea how junior year at Wattsville has blown my mind.*

"So…where's Zach in all this?" Mom poured me more milk.

"Zach launched her! I saw through her window. All of a sudden she's in the air and he's praying, and I thought that was it! That horrible puncture feeling, the power leaking out…"

Why's she grinning at me? Then I remembered, and grinned back. "But this time there was no Flying Burgowski Mother to knock the Stander down and save the Flyer!"

Mom pumped one skinny arm, laughing a triumphant "HahahaHA! Best move I ever made, babe. And worst move his stupid uncle ever made, going after me. Ron's so happy on that boat—so, thanks, Uncle Doug, for attacking me."

Yup, Mom's best revenge: buying the Flyer *with the Stander uncle's settlement money.* My whole tired body smiled. Mom nodded enthusiastically as I related the epic of Vivian's escape through the broken window.

"So, yeah," I finished, "everyone's power is out in the open. So…"

"…what now?"

"Yeah."

"You're up to something, aren't you?" Mom eyed me over the rim of her mug. "Glad you're here, babe, but I doubt you flew home in the middle of the night 'cause you felt homesick."

"True." Nice thing about New Improved Mom is, I don't have

to worry about hurting her feelings. "But first, Mom, you have to tell *me* something." Deep breath. New Improved Mom is still pretty intense. "You said you had 'stupid flying issues.' You told me on the phone. So, what are they? Why'd you quit flying with me last year?"

She set her mug down and pursed her lips. "You want the quick answer? Watching your kid almost get disempowered by a Stander…kinda messes you up."

"But you fought him off! We both did!"

"Yup. And had a couple of great flights that summer, to celebrate." She smiled a sad little Vivian kind of smile. "Then something must've kicked in for both of us, I guess. PTSD. Couldn't stop thinking about what I'd almost let you in for…those Standers coming after *my* daughter, all because she'd inherited *my* powers. What if they *had* grounded you? They came so close. Then school started. And I could see you turning into me."

I felt a window opening on that dark blur of sophomore year. "But why didn't you tell me? None of that was your fault!"

"'Course not. You think guilt's rational, babe?" Mom shook her head. "I'm a Flyer, I pass it on to you, I felt…responsible. Flying with you just pounded that into me, and talking about it, well…you were having a tough enough time. Didn't want to drag you lower. Stupid."

She took a sip of coffee as I sat there, blinking in the light of her honesty. Then her sorry face gave way to a grin. "But can we get back to your scheme now? If I promise to let you psychoanalyze me later, like maybe in a year?"

Wow. NEW New Improved Mom. I slid off my stool to hug her again. "Okay," I said, chin on her shoulder, "I'm thinking about how to disempower Zach like we did with his uncle. Before he takes Vivian down for real."

She pulled back to look at me. "Go on."

"So if Vivian's a Flyer and she knows Zach's a Stander, she

could work that trick on Zach, what we did to Uncle Doug: drink out of his cup without him knowing, right? Cancel out Stander spit with Flyer spit." I hopped back onto my stool.

"*'Beware ye power of ye witch to defeat ye Goode,'*" Mom intoned—wow, she memorized that bit from the ginormous old book Lorraine had us researching in, hunting down the secret Flyers can use to defeat our enemies.

"Yeah, I told her about Standers, about Zach." *Call her!* "But Vivian was pretty freaked out, Mom. Not ready to hear about defeating anybody." *No, don't call. Back off a little.*

"What? Zach just tried to ground her!"

"Well, she said she'd break up with him…at least I think she did."

"What is *wrong* with people?" Mom's voice scratched up like it does when she's mad. "If she can accept her own crazy power, why can't she accept that someone wants to stomp on it?"

I laughed. "Look who's talking! How long did *you* take to admit your power and fly with me? And Vivian has even worse issues than you did." Not so long ago, saying Bethany Burgowski had "issues" would get your head bitten off. *Let's hear it for therapy.*

"Point taken." New New Improved Mom patted my arm; Tion leaned on both of us. "So. Vivian won't listen to you about Standers? Why haven't *you* tried to get at Zach's cup? The book said if the Stander 'do drinke again thereof' from his 'cuppe' and tastes that Flyer spit—*zap* goes his power. Suck it, Uncle Doug."

Jeez, no wonder Vivian doesn't want to hear this—sounds loony. But it sure worked with ex-Stander Doug.

"Mom, Zach's not an idiot like his uncle. Even at Vivian's café, he didn't get a coffee—paranoid I'd drink from it when he wasn't looking."

"Right. So Zach won't let you do the 'cuppe' thing, and Vivian's not ready to try. Then she's gotta stay away from him till you can convince her." Mom glared like it was my fault.

"Yeah, but even if she's broken up with him—"

"—'if'?!"

"—*now that* they're broken up, she's still vulnerable while Zach's on campus, right?"

"Damn right. And so are you. Even if you don't think you are."

"Maybe," I admitted. Seeing Zach in action last night shook me up, no lie. All that blazing, righteous power aimed at us Flyers. "But he doesn't care about me anymore; it's Vivian he wants to save. He said so! And Mom," I hurried on as she continued to frown at me, "I have an idea I need to figure out with you guys. That's why I came home." I washed my plate, my heart speeding as I prepared to voice my plan. "Could someone—could Vivian defeat Zach by kissing, now that she knows what he is? Wouldn't a big ol' wet kiss work as well as the 'cuppe' thing?"

"But they're broken up, you said! No more kissing." Mom dried my dish automatically.

"If she tricked him, though? Pretended she wanted him back?"

She shook her head, twisting the dishcloth. "WAY too dangerous. Remember what he did to you? And sounds like Vivian's nowhere near as strong as you are."

"But IF," I insisted. "IF she stays away from Zach long enough for me to convince her to defeat him...d'you think a kiss would work? Now that Vivian could do it intentionally?"

"Huh." Mom leaned on the counter; Tion leaned on Mom. My mind flicked back to Vivian. *Did she wake up happy? Freaked out? I shouldn't have left.*

"Maybe," Mom said slowly. "But wait. You kissed him that time and his power got stronger than ever!"

"He kissed *me*," I mumbled. *Hate hate HATE remembering that.* "And it wasn't that kind of kiss."

"Gotta be a sloppy one, huh? Sharing saliva with a Stander," said the Flying Burgowski Mother, hands on hips. "Sounds disgusting."

"Yeah." I shook the memories out of my head and mirrored her stance. "Think it'd work?"

"Don't know," Mom admitted. "But I know who will. Get your jacket—we're going to the library."

Our walk across the Village peeled my heart open. Our old store, where I used to play in the dusty aisles. The Green, lusher than ever after the fall rains, where Savannah and I picnicked last summer when Ginny first started to crawl. The drugstore, where I first met Zach in the candy aisle. And Louis's house, attached to the Co-op. *I'll go over later; he's got soccer now.*

Took us forever to get to the library, since every Dalbian we met, on foot or bike or in a car, stopped to exclaim, "Jocelyn! You're back!"

"Maybe we should wait till Lorraine's off work," I muttered after the fifth explanation of just being home for a visit. "I forgot how nosy people are here."

"Oh, you love it," Mom breezed as we climbed the steps.

Okay, true. Entering the library felt like walking into the happy part of my childhood, before Mom left us. There was the laundry basket full of toys, there was the giant map-of-the-world rug we used to sprawl on during Story Hour, and there, kneeling to reshelve storybooks, was Lorraine the Librarian, World's Least Evil Stepmother.

Since she's also the World's Calmest, I got a kick out of making her jump when I hugged her from behind. But unlike all our village friends, Lorraine didn't pepper me with questions. She breathed me in.

"You flew here," she murmured. The original red of her hair has worked its way down below her shoulders; the rest is a cascade of silver now. "But you're okay."

Mom laughed, plopping herself criss-cross-applesauce on the rug. "You give aromatherapy a whole new meaning," she told the woman who married her ex.

A throb of gratitude hit. *Vivian doesn't have this; neither does Rialta. How did I ever think of this place as Dalbatraz?*

"Speaking of, um, flying," I said, dropping my voice, "I have a question for you. But maybe this isn't the best place to talk?" I saw no one else in the children's section, but Dalby Library's tiny, and sound carries. *Is Vivian in the Coastal library now, studying her Anthro at her favorite table? What if the ex-boyfriend finds her?*

Lorraine nodded, swooping her hair back. "No, you're right— not here." Her whispery voice used to drive me nuts—damn, what a little jerk I was. "How about tonight? Joss, you can drive back to Wattsville tomorrow, right? So why don't you just take the day—go see your friends, relax. Your Ground Crew can huddle up at dinnertime."

"Everyone but Mr. Evans, right?" *He better not find out I'm on Academic Probation.* "You guys and Dad and Michael—I'm cool with that. Want me to start dinner for you?"

Mom and Lorraine shared a look. "Wow, first dishes, now dinner? I like this new girl," Mom said. "What did you say your name was?"

Guess I deserved that.

"Taking the day," as Lorraine put it, should've meant hanging with Louis or Savannah. But I guess I am a "new girl." 'Cause by the time my Burgowski Ground Crew was sitting down to dinner, here's how I'd spent my first Dalby afternoon in two months:

1. Doing a 180 at Louis's house after seeing Erin get out of a VW bug which LOUIS WAS DRIVING—*when did he get his license? And a freakin' car?*
2. Reaching Savannah's voicemail—"Yo, Savannah's wayyy too busy to talk now, leave a message, yo"—followed by the beep, and deciding that cuddling Gin-gin was not worth all the drama I'd face if I went over.

3. Calling Vivian. A bunch. But after the fifth time hearing her soft, generic leave-a-message recording, giving up and moving on to...

4. Lying on my old bed, reading through a year and a half of spiral-notebook journals. My first flight, launching from the rock I named the Toad—that haze of birthday magic. Exile to the mainland with Mom. I even made myself read about that terrible Thanksgiving when she tried to kill herself. Those happy weeks when Mom got back into the sky with me, before the Standers nearly grounded her again for good.

But when I got to the end of That Terrible Summer, the journals stopped. I never realized how bad Zach messed me up, turning into my enemy just when I thought he was about to declare his love. Sounds SO lame. Mom got it right— I spent my whole sophomore year suffering from Post-Zach Stress Disorder.

I wanted to fly straight over to Louis's and apologize for being such a black hole all year. But nope. Not with Erin around. So I used up the time writing this instead.

Far as I know, I'm the only Flyer who ever had a Ground Crew. Most of the "witches" in Lorraine's books bore their secret by themselves, like Mom and Vivian, but even if they had fellow-witches, they sure didn't share with non-Flyers. Ground Crews are tricky, though. I knew they'd shred my plan if I pitched it to them straight. So I didn't.

Over Lorraine's spaghetti, I took my time, telling about Vivian and Zach—and Peach, including her flying-picture. *Gotta get back to my girls! But first...*

"Bottom line," I asked, "if Lorraine says kissing a *known* Stander would work like drinking from his cup, don't you guys think I should talk Vivian into pretending to make up with Zach and, like, smooching with him? Before he figures out what she's up to?"

"Hold up," Dad broke in as Lorraine opened her mouth. "Before we answer, Joss, do you promise you won't slam out the door if someone gives you advice you don't want to hear?" He was smiling, kind of.

Wow, they must've suffered PZSD right along with me. "Yeah, it's all good now," I mumbled to my empty plate. The brass lamp cast a warm glow over the dining table. *How many dinners did I mutter through, last year?* I gave Dad a reassuring nod.

"Damn, another Flyer." Michael's face flushed; he hadn't spoken since I started describing Vivian's flight. "Thought you guys said they were rare," he grumbled. "I'm practically surrounded by 'em. And this new one sounds hot."

"We *are* rare," Mom said firmly. "But that doesn't mean we can't gather by accident. Who knows what brought Vivian all the way from Hawaii? Maybe there's something about coastal Washington that calls to a Flyer—I mean, all these eagles and ravens and seagulls flying around…Gosh, sounds like even your little Peachy girl's got a thing about flying."

"And Standers have an inborn awareness of Flyer-power, right?" Dad continued, looking proud of his new ability to discuss our family weirdness. "So it's no accident Zach's at Coastal now."

"Right, Vivian visited UW, for a concert. That's where Zach met her—guess he smelled her power, like I did." I licked the last marinara molecules off my spoon. "Must be why he transferred."

"How d'you know Zach wasn't coming after *you*?" Michael was still frowning.

"'Cause, duh, he's not *that* magic! He couldn't sense me all the way from UW. It's Vivian he wants to ground."

"How d'you know?" my brother repeated. "You get a good look at his secret Stander orders or something?" He set his fork down. "How's that even work? Who's telling Zach what to do?"

"Good questions." Dad nodded. "Since we're finally allowed to talk about this crazy stuff, maybe one of you experts can clarify:

are these Standers a cult, or what? Are they Christian? I mean, the praying and all…"

All three of us experts answered together.

Lorraine: "Real Christians wouldn't claim them. They're fanatics."

Mom: "They pray all right, but it's nothing you'd hear in a normal church."

Me: "They're, like, the negative reciprocal of Flyers—born into a tiny little tribe."

By the time our answers got untangled, I was clearing plates. Michael grabbed a final carrot from the salad bowl, still frowning.

"Okay, but you never answered my question. Why're you acting like you're safe from Zach? He's a Stander, not an idiot." *Whoa—didn't I say the same thing to Mom?*

"Michael, I'm hip to Zach now. I'll be fine. Hey, what's for dessert?" Two helpings of spaghetti—still hungry. Last night really took it out of me.

"Ice cream," Lorraine replied, and I headed for the freezer. "Joss, the kissing idea has merit."

"There's something about kissing in one of your big moldy books?" Mom asked eagerly. *Knew she'd be on my side.*

"No, but that's not surprising," Lorraine said. "Those ancient Standers considered Flyers witches; they would never have risked their mortal souls by kissing an agent of the Devil. But the literature's very clear: Flyer saliva trumps Stander saliva." Lorraine patted Dad's arm as she reported this.

"So why's Zach not taken down yet?" Michael demanded. "Joss makes it sound like this Hawaiian Flyer chick's been sucking his face off." *Sounds like what Eli said about Zach, up in that tree last night.*

"The Flyer has to do it *knowingly*," Mom, Lorraine, and I all chorused. Everyone laughed except Michael.

"On purpose," Lorraine explained. "That's what the ancient

rules say. Vivian didn't know about Standers before, but she does now. That's why kissing might work, if Zach's too smart to drink around you Flyers. But Joss, it doesn't sound to me as though Vivian is up to the job of disempowering Zach. If he launches her again, how would she stop him?"

Careful, Flying B. They'll squash your plan in a second if you tell 'em.

"She'd have to, like, train her way up to it," I said, plunking a carton of chocolate ice cream on the table. "I'll keep working on her, bring her home for Thanksgiving—if that's okay," I added.

"Good idea," Mom agreed, and Lorraine and Dad added their nods. Michael still looked pissed.

"So," I continued more confidently, "if Vivian stays away from Zach and spends a month in, like, Flyer Boot Camp with me, maybe she could take him down after Thanksgiving." I passed out bowls, same old gold-patterned CorningWare I've eaten sixteen years of cereal from. "Dontcha think?"

"Will she accept your invite?" Mom asked. "I know! I'll drive you back to school tomorrow, babe. You can introduce me to Vivian, Flyer to Flyer, and I'll personally—"

"No, I will," Michael interrupted. We all stared at him; his cheeks had those color-spots he and Mom get when they're mad. "I'm driving you back, Joss."

"Oh, Michael, that's sweet." Mom smiled. "You meet Vivian— reassure her that Flyers aren't all *that* wacko."

"Meet Vivian? I wanna meet Zach. I wanna kick his ass. Ever since that Fourth of July, Joss." Michael stood up. "Can't frickin *believe* you let him waltz away after he nearly got you. If I hadn't had a frickin' broken leg…Frickin' fanatic like out of a movie, and you're talking about taking him down with a *kiss*?"

All the adults spoke at once; Michael ignored them.

"You Flyers—listen to you! If I had your powers, I wouldn't sit there worrying about whether someone was coming after me. I'd go after them."

"I am!" I yelled. Heads swiveled. *Whoops.* "I mean, through Vivian. You can't just bust in there punching Standers, Michael, you have to follow the ancient rules. You have to—"

"Yeah, and speaking of following rules," my brother sneered, sounding like the Bad Old Days, "why the hell are you here if you're on Academic Probation? Aren't you in even more trouble now? Why's everybody so okay with this? Never mind," he answered himself, pushing his chair in. "She's a Flyer. That's all that matters." Michael jammed his Dalby Dolphins cap on his head. "I got band practice. I'm outta here. But I'm still driving you, Joss. First boat tomorrow." He stalked out.

"Does he have to? Can't I just fly back?" *Two and a half hours with Old Pissed-Off Michael?* I sat down weakly. "Why's he even care?"

"Michael needs to feel like a part of this, babe," Mom started. But Dad's eyebrows hunkered down.

"Michael's right—I should have asked you first thing, Jocelyn. You just took off? Without permission? I'm surprised the dean hasn't called." He rubbed his forehead. "Oh, boy, here we go again."

"It's all right!" My turn to pat his arm. "I left a note for my roommates, saying I was crashing on Vivian's couch." I cut Dad off. "I'll call 'em tonight, okay? I'll say I got homesick and took the bus home for a day. Dean Williams won't know, you guys— they don't take attendance in the dorms and I'm not missing class."

"Good," said Mom, but Dad still looked skeptical, and when Lorraine opened her mouth with that librarian look on her face, I thought, *Oh, jeez, if she piles on I'm outta here like Michael.*

But all Lorraine said was, "You planning to serve us that ice cream, sweetie? Or shall we just continue to watch it melt?"

CHAPTER TWELVE

FLYER BOOT CAMP

Michael was too sleepy to chew me out on the early ferry, but he didn't need to. As the boat rumbled away from the dock in the darkness, he slouched into the opposite seat and glared at me. "Academic Probation, Joss—*you*? That's like what I'd be on if I was in college. Get your ass off that."

That was it. That, and his Non-Flying Burgowski stare, full of the longing that nearly killed him That Horrible Summer, when he jumped off Whittier's Bluff with a homemade hang glider.

I'd die for your gift, his face said. *You better guard it.*

We listened to hip-hop in Mom's old Honda as the day dawned gray. Michael's useless for Dalby gossip, 'cause all he does is fish with Dad and practice with his wanna-be band. So I dodged my guilt for avoiding Savannah, and my whatever-it-was from catching sight of Louis, and focused on my plan: *save the Flying Wu*. Entering Wattsville, I clamped my jaw to keep from blabbing.

Outside Nutschel in the chilly damp, Michael refused to come in. "Call your hot friend again," he ordered. "I didn't come all this way not to meet her."

"She's turned her phone off." I let him hear for himself.

Michael cussed. Then—"Wait, she must be at that café, right? Let's go. I'm hungry anyway."

"Michael, why…? Never mind. Sure, we'll go to Bean There."

Five minutes later we were reading Bean There, Done That's "Closed" sign. A gentle rain started tinkling the awning over the door. Michael cussed again.

141

"Shoot, it's Sunday." *So where IS Vivian?* A bright yellow thought—*flying?*— was followed by dark gray: *with Zach?* "Wait— Sunday! She must be at church. Sorry, Michael, I guess we—"

"Sorry, hell," he interrupted, glaring at the thickening drops. "Take me to church."

"Seriously?! Anyway, j/k—she won't be at church, 'cause Zach goes," I told him. *Why won't she turn on her phone?* "And I'm hungry too. Let's get breakfast before my dining hall closes." The morning was darkening with the rain. "You can meet Dawntae and Rialta at least."

But Michael dug in. "I got up early and drove here to invite your Flyer friend for Thanksgiving—end of story," he announced, like a politician at a press conference. "Mom said to," he added, turning back into a grumpy nineteen-year-old.

That melted me. "Michael…" Then my phone jangled.

Michael looked hopeful. "That your friend?"

It was—but wrong friend. "Joss, you are such a HUGE skank!" shrieked Savannah's voice. "Why didn't you come see me? Ginny's SO done with you."

I held up one finger to Michael. He folded his arms, disgusted, and leaned against the café door while my bestie unloaded in my ear.

"Louis said he saw you going to the library with your mom. Damn, Joss, how d'you think that made him feel? How do—"

"I'm SORRY," I blurted, cursing myself for not checking the number before answering. "Savannah, something happened, okay? And I really needed my mommy and I promise I'll tell you all about it, but this weekend was NOT the time, okay?" *Mostly true.*

Savannah's voice slid instantly into the old teammate mode that's made her my best friend all these years. "Aw, girl, I totally get it. You sound super stressed. Just remember, 'stressed' is 'desserts' spelled backward, right? Eat some ice cream. Call me later. Love ya, mean it." And she hung up.

So what do you plan to tell her, Flygirl? She's not Ground Crew like Louis—oh, jeez, Louis…

"So—church?" Michael snapped me back to "Wetsville." Right on cue, bells began to clang melodically, somewhere nearby. An elderly couple in matching tan raincoats hurried past.

"Michael, I have no clue which church Vivian goes to. Plus, I told you, she won't be there. Just drop it! I'll buy you breakfast."

My brother's face hardened. "Oh, boy, breakfast with a bunch of over-privileged high schoolers. Forget it, Joss. I'll get a muffin on the ferry. Thanks for a great morning." He ducked his head and slouched off into the rain.

"I never wanted you to come in the first place! I could've flown!" I scurried after him, drops hitting my face. *Who does he think he is?* "Go on home, I don't need a manager!"

Whatever nasty response Michael would have made was suddenly hijacked. "Whoa! Down the street—is that Zach? Quick, get down!"

He grabbed me and hunkered us both behind a free-standing sign for computer repair—lamest hide-and-seek spot ever. His hair dripped onto my shoulder and I closed my eyes, wishing I could disappear down the gutter like the rain.

"Church is right, he's wearing a tie," Michael whispered. "Well, if I can't meet the Flyer, I'll sure as hell take the Stander."

I yanked him back behind the sign and dug my fingers into his arm. "Michael, don't you DARE," I hissed. "Leave Zach alone."

"Why?" he hissed back, but stayed put. I risked a peek around the sign to see Zach kitty-corner from us, slowing to zip up his bright blue jacket. "Don't tell me," Michael added in a whisper-sneer, "you still want the guy. I can't even tell him to back off? When he brings you Flyers down, you're gonna deserve it."

I bit my lip till I saw Zach stride around the corner. Then I straightened to face my brother.

"First of all: shut up," I told him. "Second, I'm bringing *him* down—but you can't tell the rest of the Ground Crew."

By the time I explained my plan out on the wet sidewalk, the rain was done, the dining hall was closed, and Michael probably had to break speed limits to make his boat. But he hesitated before hopping back into Mom's car.

"Okay, Joss." I got an awkward one-armed hug. "Better get to work."

I hate the expression "lol," but that's what I did when Vivian called me back. I'd spent the day researching temporary visas for Peach and the girls, and studying Pre-Calc and History to get my ass off Ac Pro. Over Sunday roast pork in the dining hall, I was coloring in my lies to the roomies about bussing home, when—*FINALLY!*

Vivian: "You're *there!* I was worried you wouldn't answer."

Me: [after lol-ing] "*You* were worried? I'm not the one who turned off her phone! Are you okay?"

Vivian: "Yeah. It's been a weird weekend."

Me: *You're telling me!* "Uh-huh."

Vivian: "Sorry I didn't call sooner. Yesterday I pretty much stayed in Eli's room. Today I finally talked to campus *police.* They had some weird reports about…well, flying superheroes. I had to lie, said I had no *idea* about that or how my window got broken. That felt yucky. So I've been walking."

Me: "Walking?" *What'd you expect, moron—flying?*

Vivian: "Yeah, while they fixed my window. And Eli and Brady took me out for phô. They said you, like, helped them get back *together* Friday night."

Me: [covering my ear to block the dinner-din] "I didn't do anything. They talked, is all."

Vivian: [choking up] "That's the thing, Joss. You didn't *push* them. You didn't push me, either, about…*you* know…when I asked you not to. You were just *there* for me…when it happened."

Me: "Uh-huh." Dawntae and Rialta had dropped their discussion to stare at me, so I rolled my eyes in a friendly way and stood up to turn my back.

Vivian: "So I wanted to say *thank you*. And I—" Her voice lost out to this annoying girl at the next table who started screaming at this annoying guy.

Me: [jamming the phone to my head] "What? What?"

Vivian: "…wondering, you wanna come over? I got some chocolate. The *non-slavery* kind."

Me: *History essay, Graphic Design project outline, endless Trafficking Victims Protection Act research…* "Sure. Be right there."

Don't know if Vivian's really a crazier Flyer than Mom, or if all those years of trying-not-to-fly have warped her judgement. After thirty minutes of tea and chocolate and Brady-Eli updates in her room, me trying to think of ways to suggest going for a flight some nice day, Vivian suddenly looked me in the eye and said, "So. Can we go up?"

"Uhhhh—now? Sure! It's raining…but hey, it's nice and dark. Yeah, let's go!" *Quick, before she chickens out.*

Chickens? Ha! More like cormorants in a gale. Within two minutes I was soaked and freezing, using all my barely-recovered Flyer strength to stay above the black chop of the bay. And ridiculously happy.

"I went wave-skimming like this back home!" Vivian yelled as we zoomed together a foot above the whitecaps in the roaring darkness. Who knew she could yell? "Feels a lot better with *warm* water!"

How could anyone give this up? "Isn't it hard—" a wave smacked me in the face and I got some altitude, spitting saltwater, "—holding your arms out like that?" Hers were angled out in a Y, not straight ahead like, you know, a normal Flyer. Joke.

"They just go this way," Vivian yelled, and I lost the rest of her explanation in the wind.

"Hey, aren't you cold?" Didn't want this flight to end, but my arms were noodles.

"Freezing!" Vivian laughed. Her hair's even blacker when it's wet. "I just—" She got the whitecap face-smack this time and I yanked at her shoulder as her body dipped dangerously. Leveling out, she let me guide her back to the waterfront, her arms still weirdly splayed. Her landing was really more of a crash, under the rusty awning of an ancient loading dock, but she hopped up laughing again, and finished her sentence. "I just have this *feeling*, when I...do what we just did." Vivian rubbed her wet face with her wetter sweatshirt sleeve. "Like it might be the last *time*. So I don't quit till it quits on me."

"It's called flying, Vivian." I could barely lift my arm to use my own sleeve, but I felt happier than...I can't remember. "What we just did? Flying! Say the word."

"Flying," she whispered, her face drooping.

"We're Flyers. Look at me." She obeyed, looking bleak. "Say it: 'I'm a Flyer.'"

"I'm a Flyer," Vivian sighed. Then she smiled. "And thanks for helping me land without *killing* myself."

"I didn't do a thing!" I hugged myself, shivering.

"Just...flying *with* someone makes me feel safer." She sighed again. "But I *have* learned to stay kinda low."

"But people could See you! Plus, hey—what about Halloween? You almost got us killed! And before you answer," I added, "jeez, girl, can we go warm up? I can't feel my feet."

A starting gate full of racehorses all jostling for release—that's what my brain felt like as we jogged our soggy selves back to Vivian's room with its brand-new window. My dorm's closer, but we needed privacy. She loaned me a dry T-shirt and skinny jeans and her big, fuzzy sweater, so I was warm and happy. Nope, that's a lie: I was warm and crazy from controlling all my unasked questions.

Racehorse Question Number One: *What about Zach?* Vivian had not said his name.

She did talk about her Halloween flight, after trading her soaked hoodie for a dry one, plain gray, and warming the atmosphere with Jack Johnson's Hawaii-mellow voice.

"That night? That was *nuts*. I was out of *control.*"

"Duh!" The Zach-question pulled harder. "So, like…why? What happened?" *How did it feel to be launched by a Stander you love?*

Vivian tucked her wet hair behind her ears and frowned. "It wasn't a fight anymore. The power took over and I was just along for the ride, like a kid in the back seat."

"Yes." *July Fourth—opening my eyes to Zach's, blazing inches away.* "Our magic fights to protect itself," I took a deep breath, "when it recognizes an enemy. Do you know what I mean?"

Vivian winced and dropped her eyes. "No," she murmured.

I stared at her. *Really? Back to the whole stupid denial thing?* In the background Jack sang, *"So don't tell me you might just let it go."*

But a loud knock stopped me from saying anything harsh. The door opened and a shower of white things sailed through the air. One hit me on the head: a miniature human skull wrapped in cellophane.

"Happy Day of the Dead," announced Eli, grabbing Vivian in a hug while Brady advanced on me. Without makeup, he's more Jack Black than Marilyn Monroe.

"Hey, Just Jocelyn." Brady kissed me on both cheeks, then I got Eli—just a hug, too bad. "Whew! Naaaasty out there." Brady plopped himself on Vivian's bed. "Have a sugar skull," he added, tossing one over. "Got 'em in Mexico—they melt your teeth off. We have tequila too."

"Oh, you *guys.*" Vivian smiled warmly, like who wouldn't if they just got to dodge a dreaded conversation. "Joss and I need to study, we can't drink. But sugar?" She unwrapped a tiny skull. "You're supposed to *eat* these? Wow, and you thought Chinese candy was weird, Joss."

"'Sweets to the sweet,' quoth Shakespeah," said Eli, helping himself to the tequila bottle. Today he was preppy: khakis and button-down shirt with pale stripes, no hat. His shiny black hair was neatly parted and pony-tailed. *Maybe being a chameleon's refreshing.* "Saw your boy at church today, Vivvo," he added.

"*You* go to church?" burst out before I could stop it, but that was better than *Zach! Say the name, we need to talk about Zach!*

Eli arched one elf-eyebrow at me. "Mama din' raise no sinnahs," he drawled, taking another pull of tequila. "Seriously, though, our pastor should be, like, the Protestant Pope. Man's brilliant. Keeps me on the straight and narrow—more or less."

Brady rolled his eyes at me. "I know, right?" he said. "Our Eli's a walking contradiction. Who knew this lovely young man could share a pew with...well, folks who disapprove of him. But I tell ya, my guy's a lot easier to hang with after he's been sermonized."

"You sat with Zach?" Vivian asked. Struggling with that image—*Zach and Eli?*—I managed to notice that Vivian looked anxious, even with a candy skull stuffed in her cheek. "Was he, like... wondering where I *was?*"

"Figure of speech, about the pew." Eli sat next to Brady. "We nodded politely at each other, which in my case means 'Hi,' and in Zachary's case means 'Ah, poor Jesus, having to deal with the likes of *you.*'"

Vivian took the candy out of her mouth. "Oh, he's not *that* bad, Eli. Well, okay, he is. But he loves that you come to church at *all.* I just wish..." she gazed at the skull, which couldn't gaze back 'cause she'd sucked its eye sockets off.

"What?" I demanded. "Don't tell me you're speaking to him after"—*whoops, mixed company*—"the other night?" *Damn, finally talking about Zach, and Standers and Flyers are off limits now.*

"He's been leaving messages," she muttered. "That's why I turned my phone off."

Breakthrough. "Well, good," I said. "Vivian…" *Careful, Flying Girl.* "You're not gonna see him, right?"

"You two on the outs? Sweetie, you never said!" Brady gave Vivian another hug. "And you just let me prattle on about *us*. I'm—well, I'm only sorry if you want me to be, okay?"

"I'm breaking up with him," Vivian said from inside Brady's hug, but she was talking to me. "I just haven't figured out how to tell him."

Yesss. "Don't tell him anything. He must know by now." *Zach's left messages but hasn't come barging back?* "We are gonna study, and we are gonna get all caught up on our projects and help our girls and save the world." *And FLY.* "And we are NOT gonna let some guy"—*Stander, boyfriend, piece of work*—"get in the way."

"Cool," said Eli. He stood up, draping his arm around Brady's shoulder. "C'mon, Brade, we're impeding industry here." Pausing at the door while Brady collected goodbye hugs, Mr. Contradiction added, "You're gonna need extra energy, Meess Jossaleeeen. Eat your skull."

As soon as the door shut I turned to Vivian. "So you *are* breaking up with Zach," I insisted.

Her smile vanished. "Yes," she said heavily. "I know he pushes me too far. I know that's not good. And Joss"—up went her hand as she saw my mouth open—"I know you want to pound it into my head about how *bad* he is and how *careful* I need to be, but you know what? I'm getting kinda *tired* of people telling me how to be. So let's just *fly*, okay? Isn't that enough?"

I closed my mouth. Nodded. Ate my candy skull.

Yay for November's early darkness. In between Pre-Calc and Vivian's work shift, we just now squeezed in another over-the-bay flight, and she says she'll go again tomorrow! Vivian's put me in charge of setting our flight schedule. Well, "show me how you stay in *control*" was what she said, but to me that meant Flyer Boot Camp.

Today's drill: maintaining altitude. Wave-skimming in the dark is fun, but not a good strategy unless you like explaining sopping clothes to your roommates. The Flying Burgowski flew all the way to the power plant before figuring out how to express it to the Flying Wu—I mean, it's not like I ever read a manual!

"Tap into the joy," I told her. "That tingle in your blood? Focus on it. Joy levels you out when that other crap wants to crash you or rocket you."

Huh. Guess I've learned something in two and a half years.

Oh, and "that other crap"? Meaning Zach? Vivian turned her phone back on, but Zach's quit calling and texting. Maybe church yesterday did him some good for a change, instead of lighting his Stander fire like it did on Dalby. Maybe I can bring up Standers with Vivian tomorrow. Or Wednesday. Gotta keep that girl level.

Now I'm taking a teensy break from my Human Trafficking report, chilling with Dawntae. She's such a sweetie—she just invited *me* home for Thanksgiving. I'd go if I didn't have Vivian…and Savannah, and Louis, and my Ground Crew… Maybe Tae will invite Rialta when she returns from Future Leaders Club.

Back to work, Flying Girl—your girls need a Leader to get 'em visas to a Future.

But hey, I'm almost done! Got Prof K's permission to skip on Wednesday, so I can go back out to Detention-land and explain the whole lawyer/visa thing to the girls. Vivian taught me how to say "lawyer"—*lushi*. But she doesn't know the Mandarin for, "Even if the lawyer gets you guys T-visas before you turn eighteen, you'll have to split up to go into foster care."

Wonder if Chinese Guy from the police department would help me for free. But the girls still don't trust men.

Speaking of men not to trust…wonder if Zach really is backing off. Or is he up to something? Damn, just thinking about him going after Vivian makes my motors rev.

Now who needs leveling? FOCUS.

Guess what? I don't need Chinese Guy or Vivian. My mad art skills work just fine as translators.

I was drawing with the girls—or rather, circling the table, picking up crayons as fast as they rolled off. They attacked the art supplies like they were starved for 'em. The scent of canned chili wafted over us; it was almost dinnertime. The front desk ogre's getting less strict about visiting hours.

I'd brought stickers too, and Peach had snazzed up her forehead with a shooting star. "Sweetie, not there," I said as she tried to decorate the table leg. "Why don't you finish your drawing? Flying—I mean, Fēi Chuntao!" Yup, she drew herself flying again. This time it wasn't shocking—it was awesome.

"May I have this?" I asked, reaching for her blue crayon. I started drawing Fēi Burgowski into her picture, but Peach sat back, concentrating.

"May I have wa-tah?" she chirped.

Eight other faces lifted from their art. "May I have bassroom?" Meili asked, and the others chimed in.

"May I have candy?"

"May I have ceer-ril?"

"May I have Zhoss?"

"Zhoss" was too busy being blown away to speak. "You're learning English!" I finally managed. "You're amazing! Good job—hěn hǎo! What else have you learned?"

That's pretty much it, turned out, just a request and a handful of concrete nouns. "Security," "self-worth," "hope"—they're not quite there yet. And sad-faced little Biyu has barely spoken a word. But jeez, it's only been two weeks. And "may I have" gave me something to work with.

Before I lost their attention I grabbed a fresh piece of paper (donated by Rialta—thanks, roomie). With the blue crayon (Rialta again), I sketched a table with nine stick figures sitting around it. "You girls," I said, pointing. "*Nu hai zi*. Girls."

Meili repeated, "gulls," then they were all giggling and saying it. Even Biyu! I drew a standing-up person, patted my own chest. "Joss. Me."

"Zhoss," they chorused. *Sounds like the best name ever.*

"Joss and girls have a...umm... *wen ti*. Problem. *Wen ti*." Above the table-drawing I made thought-bubbles coming from all the heads, Zhoss and gulls alike. Inside the thought-balloon I drew an American-style box house: window-squares, door-rectangle, triangle roof. "You girls need—I mean, may you girls have a home—*jia*—in *Měiguó?*" Vivian told me the Chinese name for America means "beautiful country."

Nine faces focused on the drawing of their problem. Jiao pushed her amazing hair back and rubbed her eyes. "May gulls have *jia* in *Měiguó?*" Daiyu, the oldest, repeated softly.

"Great job, Daiyu—*hěn hǎo*! And yes," I nodded huge nods, "Joss says Yes, you may have *jia*, have a home, in America. If you may have..." Bits of my Temporary Visa report spun across my mind: *Church sponsorship? A foster home big enough for nine? A sympathetic judge?* "Money. Qian. Lots of *qian*."

The girls all mirrored my nodding. Even the little ones understand *qian*.

"So Joss will get you that." The blue crayon was a blur as I flipped the paper and roughed out a new box-house, full-sized, across the back, with just enough room to show one tall stick figure—Zhoss—opening the front door to usher nine smaller stick figures inside their *jia*.

Jiao threw her hair back, frowning, but the other eight girls squealed and clapped and Biyu, usually so shy, hugged me around the waist. The responsible half of my brain said, *Are you nuts? Where do you get off promising them anything?* But the Flyer half said—well, nothing. Too busy soaking up these girls' excited hope. And love. And total faith in me.

They all went back to drawing, after that. They used every sheet of Rialta's paper. But as I circled the table, repeating "*Hěn hǎo,*" I noticed something. Peach was still drawing herself flying (with Zhoss, now), and I saw one other fairy-castle like last week, but the other drawings changed. More stick figures, less scenery, and the colors? *Whoa.* Every black crayon in use. Hua hunched over a scene of dark stick figures lying side-by-side on the floor; it reminded me of that slave-ship graphic Prof K showed us in her first lecture. Daiyu had colored her whole page black, leaving only a small corner crammed with figures too tiny to count. And Jiao, the second-oldest, she was drawing...*whoa.*

They have to let it out, I told myself, looking away so Jiao wouldn't see me furiously blinking back tears. *It's called art therapy, right?* Of course Jiao has to draw the dying girl, Fung, with nine figures gathered around her.

They may be learning English and eating healthy now, but these girls are going to need SO much help. Getting visas and decent foster care are just the first tiny steps. When I finished my trafficking victims report last night, I knew this—but now I *felt* it.

When the fat guard called, "time's up," the girls helped me pack the crayons and their heart-rending art into my daypack. One more group hug, then off they went to dinner. Waiting on the bus stop bench in the drizzling dark, I swear I felt the misery of those drawings seeping through my jacket. When it hit my bloodstream—*boom.*

I barely made it around the back of the bus stop before launching into the rainy night. If the skinny lady sharing my bench had looked up from her smartphone, she'd have glimpsed my sneakers clearing the roof .

Following the lights of the freeway from a hundred feet up, squinting against the rain, fingers and ears freezing, I flew back to Horizon with my thoughts in a lame loop. *Haven't even met the immigration lawyer yet, and I've just launched the girls' hopes into space, promising them a house?*

Talk about controlling your altitude! The Flying Burgowski could use a Boot Camp for her brain.

CHAPTER THIRTEEN

WORDS, WORDS, WORDS

I'm such an idiot. That's what I was ready to blurt into the phone, punching Vivian's number with stiff fingers in the darkness behind Nutschel. But when voicemail answered, I remembered: she was at work. Dilemma: change-clothes-dodging-roomie-questions to score the last five minutes of dinner, or give-up-prepaid-meal-to-find-Flyer-friend-and-coffee? Easy choice: the roomies couldn't help with my crazy promise to the Chinese girls.

Get them a house? I'm sixteen! All I know how to get is crayons and stickers! In my damp fleece I bustled down the dark, wet sidewalk to the café, the original, sunny scene of my first intro to The Flying Wu. *Right over th*—

"Hey!" I yelled as a golden head disappeared around the corner.

"Hey, yourself," Zach replied, returning to the lamplight, like he hadn't just tried to dodge out of my sight. He strolled over, easy-peasy, and my engines did their zero-to-sixty thing. *No tables out here for me to grab onto.*

"Good night to be in there," he said, flicking his head toward the café. His damp hair still managed to shine. "Wish I was."

Cockiness, defiance, anger—those I was prepared for. Not vulnerability.

"How's she doing?" Zach seemed to be asking the sidewalk.

"Fine. Busy. But you already know that, huh?" I added, suddenly certain. "You're stalking her! How creepy is that?" I clenched my core muscles harder. *Be cool, Flygirl.* "You think she's gonna launch out that door at closing so you can finish what you started?"

"I don't—"

"We made a deal!" *So much for cool.* I lowered my voice, stepping into Zach's pool of light as the rain thickened. "Last month, in front of Vivian's dorm. You promised you'd leave us alone."

"I said *you*, Joss," Zach said. "What I try to do for Viv—that's between us. If she wants there to be an 'us.'"

There it was again, that wistful tone. Golden eyes, lamplit rain—cue the violin music for the damn movie scene.

Bad guys get defeated in movies, my brain whispered. *What are you waiting for?*

"Hmm." I crossed my arms, all thoughtful, feeling the rain trickle down my scalp. "I think I get that. I mean, if I felt, deep down, like I could only be with a person if they'd quit something—like smoking, right?—I'd try to make 'em quit." A teensy smile. "If I really wanted them. Him."

Super clumsy, but enough. Zach turned his beams on me. "That's the first time I've ever heard you try to understand me. But you don't think flying's like smoking, and neither do I."

"No," I admitted, forcing my voice into a movie-star murmur. "I didn't say I agreed with you." I looked him in the eyes, trying to bat my lashes. *This is it.* My chest quivered, but the Plan I'd hatched at Halloween was protecting me like a Harry Potter shield charm. *Vivian can't do this, but I can.* "I still don't trust you."

"You shouldn't." *Did he move a step closer, or did I?*

"I still don't like you."

"You should."

"I don't want my friend to be with you," I practically whispered.

"Uh-huh," Zach whispered back. I forgot how throaty his voice sounds, close in. "Is that why you're coming on to me?"

The movie scene disintegrated into pixels; my face went fiery. *Damn it—Zach's not an idiot like his uncle, remember?* "I'm not—"

"'S okay, I can stand it," Zach grinned—not quite a smirk. He helped himself to my hand and I forced myself not to pull free. "Maybe while we're having our little standoff, you can help me understand: why's it so hard to accept that a guy has to stand up for his beliefs sometimes?"

His hand's so warm. He just said the word "stand" a bunch of times. What if I kissed him right now? My Plan hung in shreds. *Deep breath, Flygirl.* Then—ringtone. My phone.

I yanked my hand back, snatched the phone from my pocket and opened it. "H'lo?"

"'Sup, Joss."

Have I ever been so glad to hear someone's voice?

"You there?" asked Louis.

"Yes! How are you?" I glanced at the number; didn't recognize it. "Where are you? What's goin' on?" *Other than you saving me from trying who-knows-what with my Stander enemy?* I turned my back on him.

"I'm at Erin's," Louis said. "And I just called to say how much you suck. But you already know that, or you would've come by last weekend."

Zach picked that moment to stroke my wet hair, once, and disappear into the evening. Louis asked again if I was there.

Not completely, no.

"YES. And you suck too. You haven't called me in, like, ever." *Best defense is a good offense, right?* "I was only home for a day, I didn't even see Savannah. And she and Michael gave me enough crap, don't you start. And..." Luckily Louis interrupted me before I told him I miss him like hell.

"Okay, okay." He sounded lighter somehow, but then I'm not real familiar with Louis's phone voice. "Erin heard you'd been here and she made me call."

"Hi, Joss!" I heard in the background.

"So how's college?" Louis asked.

The streetlight above me flickered. My coffee-warmth was long gone and I was standing in the rain talking to one used-to-be friend after being weirded out by—what? *What the hell did Zach mean, touching me like that?* I gripped the phone tighter.

"It's kinda crazy right now, actually. I came home 'cause…" *I'm worried about my new Flyer friend, but that's too complicated for the phone.* "…I'm not doing so great in my high school classes. And there's this project for my college class that's kinda…well, I need a house."

Louis made the only appropriate response: "Huh?"

Get out of the rain, moron—there's a reason they're called mobile phones. I headed for Horizon with Louis in my ear.

"Okay, so I rescued these girls who were being trafficked from China. Like slaves, y'know? I'm doing my college project on how to get them visas. And I kinda promised I'd help them if they're allowed to stay. But there can't possibly be a foster home big enough for all of 'em. So, yeah. I need connections. And money."

One thing about Louis hasn't changed: he still takes time to think about stuff. I walked half a block before he said, "Okayyyy. Chinese girls. Connections and money. Huh. Your mom doesn't have any settlement money left?"

"No, she bought Dad's boat with it." *And thank you for understanding.*

Another half block of silence. I stepped in a puddle and felt the cold seeping into my left sock. Then Louis asked: "What'll happen if you can't find a foster home for all the girls? Are there a lot of 'em?"

"Nine. They'll get split up, which would be horrible, after all they've been through together. Or they'll have to stay at the Detention Facility. People can stay for years." Shoving my free hand into my pocket for warmth, I rounded the stone gates, glistening with rain. "Or their visas run out and they get sent back to China where nobody wants them."

"What about a fundraiser?" Louis suggested. "Like those bake sales we did for Summer Soccer?"

So sweet, my oldest friendship coming back to life…but I forgot how naïve Louis is. Skirting the Horizon dining hall, I was saying, "Uh, cool idea, but a house costs a little more than—" when I nearly bumped into…

"Jossie!"

"Nunh-uh, Rialta, don't call her—"

"Oh, right. Joss! Earth to Joss!"

…the roommates.

"Don't you have any, like, rich friends at that school?" Louis asked in my ear—and the light clicked on.

"Rialta!" *She's hella rich…and she helped buy the art supplies, remember?* "Louis—you're the best."

"What'd I say?" But he sounded pleased. Even better, he sounded like his old self.

"Tell you later, okay? I gotta go. Say hi to your moms for me. And Erin," I remembered to add, closing my phone on his "Okay." I fell into step with the roomies.

"Hey, guys. Rialta, can I talk to you about something?"

"I don't know. Does it involve borrowing more clothes?" Arched eyebrows—bad sign.

"I know, I'm sorry, I promise I'll have that stuff dry-cleaned." *Not how I wanted to start.* We'd reached Nutschel and I held the door for her and Tae.

"You said that two days ago," Rialta commented, avoiding eye contact. *Damn, she's really pissed about that suit of hers.*

"Sorry," I repeated lamely. "I've been ridiculously busy, but I'll get it done tomorrow."

"How are your girls?" Dawntae wasn't having any trouble looking at me as we climbed the stairs. "You do more art with them today?"

"Her girls are fine, Tae, didn't you hear Chaz? That's all he talked about at dinner, Joss, how *amazing* you are for working with them." Rialta braided her hair over her shoulder, still not looking at me as I unlocked our door.

"Not 'amazing,' he said your project was 'admirable,'" Dawntae clarified. *Typical Chaz; what sixteen year-old says "admirable"?* But at least I knew what was eating Rialta.

"Know what? They asked about you, Rialta," I lied. "Both of you," I lied again, generously. "Those girls love the idea that I have cool roommates, like they have each other." *Well, they would, if we'd had this conversation.*

But flattery's a great distractor. Rialta stopped in the doorway of her room. "You told them about me?" She patted her braid. That gave me another idea.

"Yup. Told 'em you bought the crayons and stuff. They want to meet you. Hey, could you do my hair like that? Our hair's so similar, can't believe I never thought of braids." Another lie; I'm just lousy at braiding. But two minutes later, Rialta's Hair Salon was open for business on the edge of her bed, while Dawntae put on Alicia Keys and started making cocoa.

And half an hour later, I had a beautiful, damp French braid, and the girls had their Money and Connections—maybe!!! *And I'd thought the roomies couldn't help.*

"Girl, your dad would just write a check? If Joss found the right foster home, he'd just, like, pay for them to add rooms or whatever?" Perched on Rialta's desk chair, Tae shook her head in amazement, dimples ridiculously deep. "Crazy. But he'd get a tax deduction, right?"

"Of course he would. And of course he'd talk to his lawyers first, and the girls' lawyer," Rialta said, like we were transacting real estate instead of saving nine girls' lives. "They have a lawyer, right? Dad's gotta be convinced the girls aren't, y'know, regular old illegals."

I bit my tongue and stroked my braid. "Sure." Alicia sang, *"I don't worry 'cause everything's going to be all right ..."*

"So you're gonna call him? That's bangin'," Dawntae breathed. "Your dad got a brother I can introduce to my grandma?"

I laughed. "The girls were right, Rialta—you *are* cool." Rialta finally smiled. *She should; this time I'm not lying.*

But my stomach felt skeptical. Rialta's dad, Mr. Daniel Wainwright, might not go for his daughter's proposal to spend his *qian*. He might not even return her call, if Rialta's past experience means anything.

"So you already got the girls a lawyer?" Tae asked. "Dang, Joss, you are *on* this."

"Well...I'm working on that." I got up, the unfamiliar braid sliding off my shoulder. *Yeah...and a foster home who wants nine girls, and a sponsor to impress the immigration judge. Right.* My stomach clenched. "Gotta get back to it. Thanks, you guys."

But when I checked my email, guess what? Prof. K got my back.

From: <u>Krzynowek@ucw.edu</u>

Good evening, Jocelyn. My lawyer friend, Dee Hightower, can meet for coffee next Saturday, the 14th, at Bean There, Done That Café, from 2:30-4. That should be sufficient to lay out all the TVPA requirements for the girls, and determine the resources you'll need for this project—or whether you'll want to hand off to some organization more formidable than an eleventh grader. (Though if I may say so, you appear sufficiently formidable to me.) See you in class.

Hear that, stomach? Connections and money! First (maybe!) Mr. Wainwright—now, a date with a lawyer who sounds like a castle.

"Call me Dee," Ms. Hightower said when we met at Bean There, ten days (and a ton of Rialta-Daddy phone calls) later.

And I did call her that—once I got my voice working. Dee Hightower made my Halloween lawyer costume seem like sweats. Her suit was a svelte glove of royal blue, her nails were glossy daggers, her heels a good six inches. Add the Afro, and "Hightower" is right.

"Call me Joss," I replied, like *sure, I meet for coffee with movie stars all the time.* We sat at Bean There's quietest table; Vivian had the day off, so I saved up details to tell her later. We started with scones and a discussion of hairstyles, since Dee complimented me on my latest Rialta-braid.

"So, Dee." Prof K straightened her glasses. "We've had some advances since my last email. Jocelyn's roommate's father, Daniel Wainwright, has agreed to serve as financial backer, if the right foster parents can be found. From my understanding, that would ease a good fifty percent of the judge's concerns." I made myself stop nodding—*too juvenile.* "That leaves the remaining fifty: sponsorship. Mr. Wainwright's a real estate developer, nothing more. He'll support the girls' housing needs, he might even pay for *you*, Dee, but he's not available as a sponsor. The sponsor has to take responsibility for their transition to…well, Americans."

I nodded again. "Mr. Wainwright's kinda cautious." *But Rialta's request got him talking to her…and to Mrs. Wainwright too, she says.* "So, does the sponsor have to be one person?"

"Good question, Joss, and the answer's no," Dee said. Her voice was warm and buttery. "Church sponsorship is very common. Some churches are so passionate about helping refugees, they've turned into safe havens."

"Refugees? But these girls didn't, like, flee from anything."

"Didn't they?" Dee cocked her queenly head. "Their parents sold them into slavery. If that doesn't qualify—well, wait till I'm done with the judge. We'll make it happen. But as to sponsorship…"

"Do we have any churches like that in Wattsville?" I interrupted. "Sorry. I'm just excited."

Dee smiled, her face glowing, and serious ol' Prof K smiled too. "I'm glad you're excited, Joss. And yes, we have churches like that. One church, anyway. And..." Her smile expanded, dimples appeared, and I realized she and my professor were sharing some happy secret. "...I just happen to have an 'in' with that church's pastor."

"Stop torturing my student, Dee—spit it out," Prof K commanded, looking less McGonagall-y by the minute.

Dee beamed—I understand that word now. "Joss, your girls are lucky enough to have been abandoned in the backyard of the Wattsville Community Church, with the highest-functioning Refugee Settlement Committee you'll ever see in a church our size. One hundred and nine families helped, and counting! Presided over by the Reverend Melchior Gates...my husband."

"Whoa," I said. "How cool is that?" *Lame.*

"So what this means," Prof K pronounced, all business again, "is meetings. First, between Dee and Melchior to work out proposals for the Refugee Settlement Committee, and for Mr. Wainwright. If the Committee chooses to sponsor the girls, and finds the foster parents—"

"Oh, we'll make it happen." Dee nodded.

"—then the next meeting is between them and Mr. Wainwright, discussing remodeling needs for the foster house, if it's found, and working out all the legal details..."

"What about me?" I put in. *So mature.* "Like, what can I do? Not just for my project, I mean."

Both women focused on me—pretty intense. "You've already done a ton, Joss," Dee said quietly. "But going forward: I want you at that Refugee Committee meeting, advocating as unofficial proxy for the victims." *Don't know what "proxy" means; don't care.* "Then I want you meeting with Mr. Wainwright, helping to determine housing needs. And then—oh, hey, Eli! Long time no see!"

In a flash, Dee was hightowering over Eli, who gave her a very sincere, un-Eli-ish hug. His ancient corduroy jacket looked ridiculous next to Dee's suit.

"Look who's talking, Miss Dee. I was among the faithful last Sunday, where were you?"

"Work," Dee said simply, cupping Eli's thin face with her scary fingernails. "Look at this boy, y'all. He is the sweetest, kindest-hearted—I know, honey, I'm embarrassing you. Too bad." Yup, Eli was blushing. "Louanne, you have this guy in your class?"

"Haven't had the pleasure yet," said Professor "Louanne." "Care to join us, Mr....?"

"Eli," I said. His face skipped from embarrassed to pleased, and my heart gave a matching skip. *Idiot—he's not only gay, he's taken.* "Wow, you go to Dee's husband's church? That's wild." A memory flickered: Eli tossing candy skulls, *"Seriously, our pastor should be, like, the Protestant Pope."* "What d'you do there that's so sweet and kind-hearted?"

"Nothing," said Eli, all cute and embarrassed as Dee got him a chair.

"Nothing but run that group of gang kids coming out of juvenile detention." Dee shook her head. "Louanne, it is impressive. They sit down once a week to talk about their issues..."

"Twice a week," Eli mumbled. "There's a lot to talk about."

"Gang members? Whoa," I blurted. "I mean, not, like, gay youth...?" *Shut up, stupid.*

But Eli only grinned at me. "I'm not just a gay dude, Jossalass. I happen to have a brother in prison. So, yeah."

Eli's been meeting with juvie gangbangers. Twice a week. Never said anything about it; wonder if Vivian knows. Or Zach. Who goes to the same church. With Dee's husband. My brain bounced between *Wait, a Stander attends a progressive church which sponsors ex-gangsters and refugees?* and… *Wait—why am I sitting here talking while Eli's out helping people without a word to anyone?*

"Good for you, Eli, and it's nice to meet you," Prof K said firmly. "But Dee, it's time to make some calls, put some dates on paper. We've had enough, at this point, of 'words, words, words,' as Mr. Shakespeare says. Let's make something happen."

I'm in love with all three people at my table. Need to FLY.

Thanks to the end of Daylight Savings Time, I only had six hours to sit on myself before Flyer Boot Camp. I filled those hours by finally catching up on my Pre-Calc in my room *(thanks, Rialta!)* and Mandarin in Vivian's *(sheh-sheh!)* and then…

…ah, glory hallelujah. No rain, no wind, just a gentle ocean that wanted the best for us Flyers. We practiced hovering, and for the first time Vivian got past her engine failure. "I'm doing like you said, I'm thinking about *happy* stuff," she called to me. I was doing the same.

Everything's coming together! Back in the café, Dee Hightower had gotten her husband on the phone, then five other people. "Watch the master work," Prof K had said. By the time Eli left us, giving my head a pat—somehow not insulting—Dee had arranged a meeting of the church's Refugee Resettlement Committee for tomorrow after the service. Then she'd called Mr. Wainwright—well, his secretary—and *boom.* We're all meeting for lunch at the end of next week.

"Secretary said, 'Mr. Wainwright always dines at Gregoire's when he comes to town, so I'll make reservations,'" Dee reported. "You own a tuxedo, Joss? Just kidding."

That happy memory made me zip ahead of Vivian. "C'mon, slowpoke!" I called over my shoulder, and *zhoom*—here came her Y-extended arms in the moonless dark. Vivian has jets.

"Let's go back *up!*" She ascended past me.

"Whoa, whoa, wait!" I climbed to catch her. "Nuh-uh, Vivian, remember last time? It's bad up there, we could hardly breathe. You are NOT ready."

"Don't you always want to see how *high* you can go? I do." She was panting, proving my point, but she leveled out. *Still too high if her thoughts turn dark.*

"No, as a matter of fact I don't," I told her, angling back down so she'd follow. "I always thought my magic was such a gift, I didn't want to push it. Bird-level's fine. I don't wanna be an airplane."

"I guess I always wanted to fly *away* from stuff," Vivian started, but her body dipped suddenly, like someone removed a layer of air beneath her. Her arms sagged. "Oh, not *now*," she wailed.

"Happy thoughts to level out! You're helping me save the girls!" I yelled. "You're coming with me for Thanksgiving!" She thrashed, fighting her fall. *Happy thoughts for* her, *dummy.* "Vivian, you can FLY!"

And she did! Stopped her fall just above the water, leveled out, kept flying, all the way to the pier, where she managed a perfect two-footed landing...and then dropped to her knees, gasping. But as I landed beside her, she looked up and grinned. "I *did* it."

"You did! You kept yourself up." I kind of hugged her back to her feet. "That's how our power works. So if Zach tries to pray you down again—"

Ah, words, words, stupid words. If Vivian were flying I'd have just crashed her by saying that.

"Zach and I are done," she said faintly, pulling away from me.

Deep breath. "You may be done with him, but he's not done with you. Vivian, look at me." She closed her eyes but I pressed on. "You have to prepare yourself, you have to learn about the Standers like I did. You..." *Go ahead and tell her, Flygirl: all about Stander spit and Flyer spit and drinking out of cups and kissing.*

Yeah, right. What good are words when they sound insane? Vivian's eyes were still closed like a little kid shutting out a scary movie.

I gave up. Lorraine's right; Vivian is not up for mounting any attacks. All I can do is keep her away from Zach until I can neutralize his power myself—*if I can get close without tipping him off.* Maybe Vivian could bring me to another Coastal party? *Idiot, that's not keeping her away from Zach.*

"Never mind." I squeezed her shoulder, slightly clammy from the sea air. My heart's a big ol' mushy mess these days—Peach and the girls, Rialta, Louis, Eli, Dee, everyone has me in group-hug mode.

Except for one guy: Zach Howe. It's not a hug he needs. It's a big, wet kiss. But even if I worked up the nerve to hit a Coastal party without Vivian, he'd never let me near enough to try.

Chaz, of all people, showed me how to get close to Zach—by nearly wrecking everything else. Flyer Boot Camp with Vivian ran past dinner hour, and I had to talk my way into the dining hall before they closed. So after setting a speed record for lasagna-snarfing, I was bussing my tray when someone put his hands on my neck from behind. Then his lips.

I dropped the tray and whirled. "What the hell—"

"Oops—sorry! Sorry!" Chaz was backing away, hands up. "Wrong girl. Since when do you wear a braid?" I noticed he was not blushing.

"Since whenever I feel like it," I snapped, feeling myself blush enough for both of us. Plenty of kids were hanging out in the dining hall, looking our way. Including Rialta. Who approached, wearing her own braid and narrowed eyes like a movie Mean Girl.

"Oh, boy, I'm in trouble now." Chaz had the nerve to wink at me before turning to his girlfriend. "Hey, baby. Can you believe what I just did? I thought she was you!"

Rialta ignored him. "Now I see why you wanted a braid," she hissed. "Nice, *Jossie.* You guys plan that? Lots of witnesses so it looks like an accident?"

My turn to go hands-up. "Rialta, no way! He is all yours. Seriously! I would never do that to you." My heart raced. *What if she doesn't believe me? Will she call off Daddy and his offer to help my sweet girls?*

"Seriously, baby, I thought I saw you heading over here. I wanted to sneak up on you," Chaz whined.

"I went to the bathroom," said Rialta. "You didn't happen to notice?" But it was me she was glaring at.

I refuse to be a character in this stupid script. "You know what, guys? You work this out. Rialta, if you really think I'd do you that way, then I…well, you're wrong. You're a good person and I do not. Want. Your. Boyfriend." I wished I still had my tray to slam down. "See you back at the room," I announced with dignity, and swept out of the dining hall.

But as the cold November hit my face, a light bulb switched on in my brain. Thanks to idiot Chaz, I know how to bring Zach down now. And this Plan has nothing to do with words.

CHAPTER FOURTEEN

HAPPY THANKSGIVING

Too bad high school teachers don't assign those old What I'm Thankful For lists. Me and Vivian are heading for Dalby tomorrow—the normal ferryboat way—and I'm assigning one to myself.

I AM THANKFUL BECAUSE:

1. Duh, it's vacation! (In the last two weeks all I've done is go to meetings, go to class, go to the library, go to Boot Camp, go go GO.)

2. Reverend Gates hand picked these AWESOME foster parents, the Carsons. (I got to attend all three Committee meetings with them and Dee. They're both retired teachers, kids all grown up. Mr. Carson introduced himself as World's Best Waffle Chef, and Mrs. Carson has already started reading about China so she'll be ready.)

3. Mr. W is paying for the Carsons' house to be renovated to fit nine girls!!! (Plus he likes my "git-'er-done style.")

4. Dee's got a date with the Immigration judge on December 20. (She says it's AMAZINGLY fast, and aren't I smart for getting her and Rev. Gates and Mr. Wainwright involved?)

5. I AM smart—I'm off Ac Pro! Got a C+ in Pre-Calc. Passing Mandarin. Almost done with my Modern Slavery report. ("Done" will be when the girls get their T-visas—maybe next spring!)

6. Vivian's flying with me every day! (She didn't even waver when I said Zach's name during Boot Camp yesterday. And she deleted him from her phone.)

7. My Ground Crew's still got my back. (Mom called, Dad called, Lorraine called, and Michael called! Pretty much they all warned me about Zach—but MICHAEL said he's proud of my grades.)

8. LOUIS called to "interview" me for Journalism, 'cause Michael filled him in on the Chinese girls. He wants to do a "follow-up" when I get home…

Oh, jeez, too much to list. And I haven't even mentioned Rialta. But hey, I'm ready for my Pre-Calc test, so I can stay up a while and write about stuff.

Rialta's speaking to me again. Guess how long that took? But turns out Dawntae was even sicker of Rialta's drama than I was.

Last night—November 24, over two weeks since that thing with Chaz in the dining hall—I was doing my math. "Hey, Rialta, I get point-oh-seven for Number Three, is that what you get?" I called over from my desk.

Right on cue, Rialta said, "Tae, tell Jossie she obviously doesn't need *my* help," and closed her door.

It being Day Sixteen of this crap, I shrugged at Dawntae, like, *whatever*. But Tae didn't shrug back. She bounced off her bunk—*bam*, her book hit the floor—stomped across the room and whipped Rialta's door back open.

"This is whack, Rialta! 'The flower that blooms in adversity is the most rare and beautiful of all!'"

Silence from Rialta—she must've been as stunned as I was. Finally I heard, "What the hell's *that* supposed to mean?"

"The emperor says it in *Mulan*, okay?" Dawntae snapped. *Of course, Disney.* "And I guess it doesn't really fit, but it's true, Rialta. You and Joss are exactly alike. When stuff gets difficult, you get…

ugly." Hands on hips, Dawntae darkened Rialta's doorway like she'd grown two sizes.

"Ugly?!" Rialta pouted, at the same time I objected, "Whadd'ya mean we're alike?"

"Well, maybe that word doesn't fit either, but you get all *hard*, Rialta, and so does Joss, and to me that's *ugly*, and I'm DONE with it!" And Big Bad Dawntae shrank into tears.

So we both jumped up to apologize to our ridiculously sweet roommate, and ended up apologizing to each other. Rialta admitted she didn't really believe I was trying to steal her guy. And I said, "Hey, Tae, what would a Disney Princess say about Chaz?"

"'Chaz, you suck,'" said Dawntae, and we all cracked up. So me and Rialta are good again. She even thanked me for bringing her dad to town so much. So, Number Nine on my list: I'm thankful Rialta didn't sabotage her dad's help.

And speaking of kids happy with their parents—Number Eight, Louis? His mom's girlfriend inherited some money and they've bought a house, with a phone and everything! So I get to visit him there at Thanksgiving. And oh, by the way, he doesn't know how Erin's doing 'cause they "kinda broke up." When I dived in with "when-why-how?" Louis said, "Tell you when you get here, 'kay?"

So. Number Ten: I'm thankful to get my buddy back—founding member of The Flying Burgowski Ground Crew. (Too bad The Flying Wu doesn't want a ground crew of her own.)

The Flying Wu was, however, crazy about ferryboats. She bounced like a five year-old as we stepped off the bus at the terminal. "I think we have ferries on Oahu; but I've never seen 'em. Can we go up *there*?" She pointed to the upper deck of the big white boat lumbering into the dock.

"Sure. But flying's cooler," I said in a low voice. The waiting area was crowded with people like us, students heading home to feast with their families. I nodded at a couple of Dalby grads but stuck with Vivian. "At night, from above, the boats look like big fat glowing fairies. Hah! Ferry fairies." Vivian gazed at the boat, failing to smile at my wit. "Maybe we can fly back Sunday night," I added.

She turned at that. "Not if you tell. Remember you *promised*, Joss."

Sigh. This was only the fifty-eleventh time Vivian had brought that promise up. She was so freaked out I'd told my family about her flying, I had to reassure the hell out of her before she'd agree to come to Dalby.

"I know, I know," I repeated for the fifty-twelfth time. "No telling anyone else: not Louis, not Mr. Evans. It's okay, Vivian, no one else knows…"

On the boat, she insisted on circling the upper deck the whole crossing, even as the wind made our eyes water. Felt a little like flying, except for that deep vibration under our feet. And as the foresty bluffs of the smaller islands slid by, Vivian's excitement fanned mine. *Miss the hell out of this place.*

Forget roast turkey—I'd forgotten about Lorraine's stuffing. It's like dry-bread Cinderella at the ball. Stuffing's what I did too—my face, that is—in between updates on Peach and the girls, roommate relations, and grades. Vivian ate way less— probably 'cause she's too polite to talk with her mouth full, and my family's so nosy.

I'd totally threatened them not to bring up flying, so they asked about everything else. Michael covered, "What's Hawaii Like?" then tagged off to Dad, who did, "Was the Transition to Washington Hard?" That was Mom's cue to pile on with, "Why Washington?" And Lorraine, quiet as ever, finished up with, "Small World, Eh?"

Gotta admit, my stepmom handled the topic of Zach Howe like a diplomat: "Joss told us about the coincidence of your dating the boy she met here. It's nice to see that's brought you two closer." Vivian nodded politely.

Flying stayed unmentioned—*gold star, people*. But even in my stuffing-bliss, I noticed Mom and Lorraine sharing glances when Vivian gave her brief, subdued answers. They looked like a pair of eagles spotting the same fish. *What is up with that?* Michael, on the other hand, sat up straight for once, nodding at everything Vivian said and finding parallels with fishing or band practice.

Over apple and pumpkin pie, Vivian managed to shift the focus back to me. "So, Joss, you're gonna want to catch up with your old *buddies* tomorrow, right?"

"Definitely," I mumbled. My full stomach clenched a little. "They're looking forward to meeting you," I added. *Savannah and Vivian? Hmmm…*

"Oh, that's okay," said Vivian, setting her fork down. "You need a little time with them after so *long*, don't you? I'll stay here and be a couch potato, or…"

"Or I could show you the boat," Michael offered, "or whatever."

Dad smiled like he was giving them his blessing. *If apple pie were a person, it'd be Dad.*

Day after Thanksgiving, Vivian chilled with my old *Harry Potter and the Prisoner of Azkaban* in our living room (sorry, Michael), while I checked out Louis's new house and said hi to his moms. And him. After three months.

I hadn't ridden my bike in weeks, and Louis's new house was a good twenty minutes away, up a giant hill. So I was a little sweaty when his mom Shasta hugged me breathless, her fluffy hair soft on my shoulder, and told me what a Woman I'd turned into. Forgot how much I missed Shasta's hugs; they saw me through all those years Mom lived on the mainland. Got a hug from

Janice too, firm and no-nonsense like the rest of her. And I got a tour of their new house, till Louis rescued me.

His room was twice the size of his old one—not saying much—but decorated the same way: Seattle Sounders and Mariners posters, and laundry. "Sounders did awesome this year, huh?" is what came out of my mouth as he showed me in. *Why so nervous?* Old Literal Louis would've said, "Yes, they won the championship," but New Louis just giggled. *'Cause he's nervous too, that's why.*

"How was your Thanksgiving?" I asked. We didn't hug, but that was normal—buds don't hug. I checked out his bookshelf, all the familiar titles that matched my own: the Harry Potters, the Narnias, the Tolkiens. More Star Wars and astronomy than I'm into, plus he seemed to have developed a thing for Orson Scott Card.

"Fine," Louis answered automatically. He examined his books too, like he was considering buying one. "Janice cooks better than Mom."

"Nice." My stomach felt tight, flight-engines starting to whirr. Before the Erin thing, we used to talk about his moms all the time. And fly.

It's just Louis, stupid.

I made myself look at him full-on. He was as tall as me; you'd never know one of his nicer old nicknames was Shrimp.

"So." I cleared my throat. "I know you wanna hear more about my Chinese girls. But first you gotta tell me about Erin."

"Right." Louis ran his hand through his hair, standing it up rooster-style like I've seen a thousand times. He pulled his old Mariners quilt over the mess of bedsheets before nodding at me to sit, and perched at the far end of the bed. "So, I really liked her. I mean I still like her. But you know how things…people… It was starting to change, okay?" His face was as red as his hair.

"She wanted to see other guys?" *Which is hard when your whole high school's, like, seventy-five kids.*

"No. She wanted to see…more of me," he muttered to the quilt. "You know."

"Oh!" My jets revved; suddenly I couldn't look at him either. "So, that wasn't okay with you? I mean…I thought you really liked her. Why wouldn't you wanna…" *Oh, spit it out, Flygirl!* "…get closer?"

Louis bounced off the bed. "Talked to Mom about it," he mumbled, rotating his head like a pre-game warmup. "She said you should really love the person before you get…physical." His voice dropped so I could barely hear. "And I said I didn't think I loved Erin enough."

"Uh-huh." I watched the back of Louis's head: left shoulder, center, right, back toward me. It occurred to me that he was waiting. "Whadd'ya want me to say?"

He gripped his jaw and the top of his head like a vice and muttered something.

"What?"

"Don't you want to *ask* me, Joss?" Louis flung out his arms, releasing his face to me at last. "Ask me why I can't be with Erin?" Now he looked pale, every freckle standing out. "Why I quit flying with you?"

A flood of memories washed through me: *Louis's arms twined in mine as we teach ourselves to fly doubles. Louis whisper-whooping in my ear as we sail over Whittier's Bluff. Louis in his old room, turning his back to pull on a soccer jersey, Erin perched on his bed, that cold weight in my stomach which I never let myself name.*

"Yes," I managed. *He's my buddy. My oldest friend.*

"Duh, Joss," said my oldest friend. "I can't be with Erin 'cause I'd rather be with you." His eyes were so bright blue it hurt to look.

This is really happening. Last time I had that thought was just before Zach kissed me, and wrecked me. My engines raced. I gripped the bedpost and watched my sneakers pressing onto his floor.

"So…so," I floundered, "why *did* you quit flying with me? I hated that so much!" *Wow, that feels good to say aloud.*

"C'mon, Joss," Louis said, and I looked up to see him turning red again. "Think about it."

I used to have fantasies about flying with Harry Potter; didn't even admit to myself I had them about Zach. *His breath in my ear. Chest and hips pressed onto my back.* In that post-Zach year, Louis grew a chest and hips of his own, muscles hard from soccer and baseball. No more Shrimp. And no way to control the… responses…of his body, pressed against mine.

What an idiot I am. "Oh."

"So, yeah." Louis clasped his hands and stretched them to the ceiling. I tried some head-rolls of my own; who knew warmups could process embarrassment?

"Yeah. Wow." *REALLY need to fly.* But I couldn't ditch Louis on that note. Sometimes even Flyers have to figure stuff out like a normal person.

"So whadd'ya think?" he blurted, sounding like his old self.

I stood up. My legs were quivering, but Louis knew that. *Louis knows me better than anyone I'm not related to.* "I think…"

"Could we maybe try something?" And Louis took two steps and put his arms around me.

I hugged him back. And the weirdest thing happened. My flight-energy roared stronger, but then it sort of flowed out of me. Not like that leaking feeling when Zach tried to pray me down; like my power was encasing us in a bubble.

We didn't kiss. Didn't even move our hands on each other's backs. We just stood there and held on. Louis's rough hair pressed into my cheek. It smelled like boy-sweat and felt like comfort.

At the end of our endless hug, Louis whispered, "Okay, Joss?" and I whispered back, "Yeah." We still didn't kiss.

"I better go rescue Vivian from my family," I murmured.

So we ended with a squeeze and a simultaneous, "Okay. See ya."

Neither of us remembered the interview about the Chinese girls.

A minute later, I was in the Dalby sky. Lucky that Janice and Shasta's house is deep in woods, 'cause I launched from their front porch.

Louis loves me!

The pale sun warmed my back, and oh, the smell of this place! Wet cedar and lichen with a faint note of manure.

Louis loves me.

I needed to circle for about three days.

SO amazing. And SO weird.

But I'd told Vivian I wouldn't be long. I was halfway home, tree-top level, when it hit me—I'd left my bike behind.

So I had to turn around, get the bike and ride home instead of flying. Felt the same.

"Nice time with your buddy?" Vivian and Mom asked together as I entered our living room, panting from the wind. Vivian was couch potato-ing just like I left her—*only an hour ago?*—and Mom was helping herself to Lorraine's leftovers.

I gave the world's briefest report of a life-changing event— "Fine. Louis's new house is great!"—and grabbed the last of the pumpkin pie.

Is he what I've been wanting? What if he isn't? He's my oldest friend! Who can I talk to?

Michael ambled downstairs, apparently not giving up despite losing out to Harry Potter.

"Hey," he said, "You guys gonna sit around all day? Pretty crappy tour guides. 'Cept," he added, stealing a chomp of my pie, "Dalby's not much to see, not like where you're from, Vivian."

Never thought I'd use the word "adorable" for my brother, but the way he managed to keep his eyes full of Vivian without looking at her? Mom caught my glance and we shared a smile.

"You're right, Michael. Let's take Vivian somewhere," she declared, standing and pushing back her chair.

"And you're totally *wrong*, Michael. Dalby's amazing to me," Vivian said. "Way *prettier* than Wattsville! So *green!* I want to see *everything.*" She stood up too, ditching Harry. "But don't you have to fish today? I thought—"

"Nah." Michael blushed and shook his bangs over his eyes— adorable. "Day off. Dad's messing with the boat. We could, like, show her Seal Rocks or something."

"Let's do it," Mom said. "Shoes and jackets, people."

As Michael hustled outside, Vivian whispered to me, "Your brother's adorable." She looked much brighter than her subdued Thanksgiving dinner self. *Have she and Mom been talking, Flyer to Flyer?*

"Oh, Joss, I forgot!" Mom snapped her fingers. "Savannah called. She said, quote, 'call me back or you're dead to me.'"

"Your friend with the Harry-Potter *baby*, right? Ginevra?" Vivian stopped with one shoe on, clasping her hands like she does when she's nervous.

Just what I need, another complicated old friend to deal with—too rude to say aloud. "It's okay," I reassured Vivian in a whisper, "Remember, Savannah doesn't know about Flyers. She's just—"

Savannah's just who she is. Suddenly our front door flew open; from the hallway wafted the squeak of stroller wheels, and "Helloooo! Happy Thanksgiving! Ginny says let's go ask Auntie Joss why she hasn't called us back!"

Crammed into the bed of Dad's truck, feet-to-feet with Vivian, Michael looked like Christmas came early. Up front, with Ginny's car seat, there was only room for Savannah next to Dad, whom we dragged away from scrubbing the *Flyer*. So it was pretty cozy with four of us in the truck bed, scrunched under an old sleeping bag with our backs pressed against the sides and our feet mingling in the center.

"Good thing Lorraine's gotta work, I'm not sure the truck could take another pie-filled body," Mom said, leaning toward me across the sleeping bag. "But Joss, you never said anything about Louis. How's he doing? Miss that kid."

I turned my face to the wind. "He's super busy, he has Mr. Evans this year plus Journalism, plus he's working for a landscaper." I listed all the details Shasta and Janice had given me, *since Louis was too busy turning our friendship upside-down.*

"But he says hi," I added, 'cause, well, he should've. *I'll see Louis again before I go back Sunday, right? Why wouldn't I? Maybe I could talk to Mom. Or Savannah…*

"You are so *lucky*, Joss." Under the sleeping bag, Vivian patted my knee. Dad picked up speed, and she raised her voice into the almost-yell we use flying on windy nights. "It's a real *community* here, right? Everyone knows what's going *on*. Savannah told me her parents and friends love Ginny so much, she never has to pay for a *sitter*."

"Yeah, well, Savannah would say that," I yelled back. "Ask Michael about our *community* always bugging him about college."

"Ask Joss why she left," Michael retorted from the other side of the truck-bed. With his hair flying back from his forehead, he looked like a dark version of Dad. I imagined them out on the *Flyer* together, shouting like this above the wind.

"Or try flying in a place where everyone knows your schedule," Mom added.

Vivian frowned briefly at me, but nodded to Mom. "Yeah, I guess you might feel kinda squeezed. Like those *life* jackets you were complaining about, Michael, right? But then they *save* you." She smiled at Michael as the truck bumped into the Seal Rocks parking lot, and he lit up like a little kid.

Dad parked and we bustled out of the truck, all eight of us—

or more like seven and a half. Dad insisted on carrying Ginny in her backpack, and my heart plumped bigger, seeing Ginny's little mittens conducting our hike from Dad's wide shoulders. Savannah was being polite to Vivian, not a good sign, but since Michael had gone into Tour Guide mode, I wasn't worrying about my old friend working her drama on my new one.

She sure worked it on me, though. Twenty steps along the path, Savannah turned, threw her arms around me and squeezed.

"Whoa!" I gasped when she let go. "Is that 'miss you so much' or 'you deserve to die for ditching me this fall?'"

"Both," Savannah grinned. The others continued toward the shore, leaving us two under a big fir tree, its upper branches absorbing the wind. Her grin faded as she tossed her glossy hair. "No lie, Joss, I've been pretty pissed off. It's been really hard without you."

"You have your parents, and Nate," I said weakly.

"Nate's not my bestie. You said you were gonna be there for me, when this whole thing started."

"This whole thing" = choosing to have the baby of your ex-boyfriend, son of the ex-Stander who attacked my mom? Yeah. But she's right—I did promise.

"I know," I said. "There's just been so much to deal with at school, Savannah." *Vivian… Zach… Peach and the "gulls"…* "I can't seem to keep up with everything that's important to me." *Like Louis? No way to bring him up now.*

My bestie cocked her head. She never lost the baby weight, and in the cold her face looked literally rosy, like pink petals. "Well, do less then," she said with the frown I knew from a million homework sessions. "Come home. Your semester's almost done, right? Your fancy prep school grades are okay? I sorta get why you felt like you had to leave, but I don't see why you have to stay away. Zach Howe's gone. All the Howes are gone. So what's keeping you in Wattsville?"

"Uhhh…" *My girls, of course!* But that's not the topic Savannah feels connected to. *If I don't come clean about Zach…*

"Actually," I mumbled, "Zach's there. So I should really—"

"He *what?*" Savannah screeched. "You said he was at UW! When were you planning on sharing this?" No more roses; she was all thorns now.

"He transferred," I sighed. *Idiot—shoulda seen this coming.*

"Joss, are you f---in' kidding me? Don't *even* tell me you're trying to be with him after how he did you!"

"'Course I'm not. He's Vivian's boyfriend. Or was."

"He's with her? And you're fine with that?"

"*Was*, I said! And no, it wasn't fine. And I'm sorry I never told you, Savannah, okay?" I could hear my own defensiveness. "I still don't enjoy talking about him." I'd managed to put thoughts of my Zach plan aside for a good thirty-six hours, but now my post-Thanksgiving stomach started to sour.

Savannah tossed her hair again. "I can't *believe* you. You didn't expect him in Wattsville, okay. But now he *is*, why not come home, where he *isn't?* Unless there's something else you're not telling me. In which case—fine." Hand on her hip. "Guess we're not as close as I thought."

Ouch. Guess you're right. But two and a half years of not-telling-Savannah-about-Flyers meant I couldn't exactly tell her now.

"Okay," I tried, "you know how you said Ginny changed everything?" Savannah pursed her lips, like, *duh.* "It's kinda like that for me now. I have people to take care of. There's all these Chinese girls I'm getting housing for…plus Vivian, she kinda needs me too…" I stumbled to a halt as Savannah's eyebrows puckered.

"Your mom told me about the Chinese thing, since you didn't," she snapped. *Oh, jeez.* "Sounds awesome, Joss, but there's people who take care of stuff like that." She crossed her arms and stepped closer. "Why do you need to feel so needed? Is Dalby just too small and boring?"

I pictured Dalby from high above in the sunshine, one long, curly blob lit up green and gold in the brilliant water. You can't un-know the perspective of altitude. *Flying gave me joy, then trouble, then Wattsville. Which gave me Vivian and the girls.* But I couldn't say that to Savannah.

"I love Dalby," I began, but a wail from up the path interrupted any further lady-protesting-too-much-methinks.

"Mamaaaaa!"

"Oh, shoot," said Mama Savannah, and she sprinted up the path. "We're not done, Joss!" I heard her yell as I trotted after.

We were, though. Between showing Vivian the tide pool crabs and the purple starfish slumped into crevices, and hanging onto Ginny on the sharp black rocks, Savannah found no time for Girlfriend Guilting. Except for admiring Vivian's hair, she kept her distance, collecting silvery snail shells. I held tight to Ginny's tiny fingers and tried to let the ocean's lull and my family's chatter smooth the feelings Savannah had rumpled up.

I don't NEED to be needed. I'm taking Zach down for Vivian 'cause if I don't—that's one less Flyer in the world. I could hear Michael exaggerating his fishing adventures to enthrall Vivian, and I caught Dad grinning, then Mom. Across an ancient, sea-worn log I grinned back at them both, like part of a normal family.

Trust Mom to remind me just how far from normal we are. Ginny started getting cold, and as we turned to go, Mom put her arm through mine—a first.

"Walk with me," she ordered. *Oh, boy—three heart-to-hearts in one day.*

She dove right in. "Babe, I like your friend, but I get such a weird vibe from her."

Impatience hit like a wind-gust. "Wow, Mom, look who's talking. All through dinner yesterday I was afraid you and Lorraine were gonna bust out, like, 'Pass the potatoes, and by the way, what kind of Flyer won't talk flying with other Flyers?'"

Mom looked, whaddyacallit, chagrined, but kept walking. "That obvious, huh? Well, yes, that's exactly what we were thinking."

"Lorraine too? You guys discussed Vivian?" I barely registered a huge clump of golden mushrooms in the path. *So much for my restful family holiday.*

"Yes, we did, actually, when you guys were watching the *Harry Potter* movie. You told Vivian I fly too; she knows we're a safe group. Why's she so twitchy?"

"Oh, I don't know—maybe 'cause her boyfriend tried to pray her down last month? Or 'cause she kept her flying power bottled up almost as long as *you* did?" I snapped a fern frond in passing. "'Twitchy?' Jeez, Mom, when you quit flying, you made twitchy look normal!"

Mom halted, and I saw the red spots appearing below her cheekbones. "Touché," she said. "But that's just it, Jocelyn. Vivian is flying now. Why's she so uncomfortable owning it? Unless…"

"Unless what?"

No softness in Mom's big, dark eyes.

"Zach's pretty damn alluring. And Vivian's weak. Like you said—I know a little about trying to normalize yourself to be with the guy you love." She put her hands on her hips. "If Zach finds the right way to come on, how do you know Vivian won't fold and give up her powers?"

And just like that, Sophomore Year Joss was back. "Be*cause*, Mom!" I stomped the path. "I trust her, okay? Why's everybody trying to make me rethink every single relationship? I came back for a little peace and quiet—what a joke! Might as well fly home tonight. Yeah, '*home*,'" I repeated, seeing her wince. I pushed past her. "Don't worry," I snarked over my shoulder, "I'll take my weak Flyer friend *home* with me so you guys can quit worrying about her."

In the parking lot, I sweet-talked Ginny into letting me ride with her and Dad up front. Savannah raised her eyebrows and climbed into the back without arguing. I didn't look at Mom. *Some confidantes! No WAY am I bringing up Louis.*

"Something wrong, sweetie?" Dad asked as the old truck trundled up the hill.

"I'm fine," I muttered, leaning my face into Ginny to let her play with my earring. She smelled like tide pool and shampoo. I sounded like Old Joss, like every day last year. Happy Thanksgiving.

CHAPTER FIFTEEN

WHAT WE MAY BE

After a week of rain and guilt and confusion since coming "home" from Dalby with no apologies to Mom and zero clarity about Louis...guess what's perfect? Peach's new foster-home room is painted peach! Well, hers plus Lanying's plus Meili's plus Ah Lam's—the four youngest, in the remodeled basement. The three middle girls get the blue room upstairs, and Daiyu and Jiao, honorary eldest sisters, get the double. Of all the kid-bedrooms in the Carsons' home—Twenty-seven Fir Street—the double's the only one not snazzed up by Mr. Wainwright's credit card, but the Carsons let Daiyu and Jiao decorate it with calendar pictures of roses and autumn leaves. Red's lucky in China.

"You done good, kiddo," said Mr. Wainwright in his deep movie-star voice, raising his sandwich to me in salute. The girls' housewarming banquet featured a house-shaped sandwich stack, cute pointy roof and all. The Carsons' house isn't cute—gray siding, peeling black trim —but who cares? The girls have a *jia!* Now they were crowded into the downstairs bedroom, while Translator Guy (hired by Mr. W) explained the Carsons' rules about stuff like bathrooms and bedtime.

"No, *you* done good." I "clinked" the last bit of my sandwich with my new buddy across the dining room table, and Rialta and Dee Hightower joined in with their water glasses. "You're amazing, Mr. Wain—I mean Danny. Lanying told me she loves the new paint smell in the basement! At least I think she said that."

"And those bunks!" Rialta added. "Did you see Chuntao's face when she climbed up there?"

"Well, good," Mr. Wainwright intoned, brushing crumbs off his khakis. "Anything those girls need: paint job, bunk beds, whatever. Gotta hire them a tutor, jump-start their English. Oh, and I'd like to help the Carsons install a window in that basement room."

Dee nodded. "The more light, the better. Smart of them to have the house meeting downstairs, make that room seem special. That'll help cut down on the nightmares, I'll bet. That and the bunks," she added, smiling.

"Daddy, it's almost one-thirty," Rialta said, pulling out her little digi-corder. "Let's do the interview in the kitchen before the house meeting's over."

"Interview?" Dee asked me as Mr. Wainwright followed his daughter into the kitchen.

"For our school paper. She's really into the project now." I watched Rialta and Daddy settling into the breakfast nook where so many other kids have eaten Mr. Carson's awesome waffles and felt Mrs. Carson's gentle shoulder-rubs. "She doesn't call the girls 'illegals' anymore."

"Small victories," Dee smiled. The sun suddenly zinged through the window, highlighting the remains of our feast: one sandwich, three grapes, and cupcake crumbs. Seven weeks since I found them, two days out of the Detention Facility, the girls still ate like a locust swarm. Dee stood up, a Greek goddess in red heels, and glanced toward the basement stairs. "I gotta get back to work. You sticking around till they get done?"

"Oh, for sure," I said, getting up too. "I forgot to hug Ah Lam goodbye one time and the other girls told me she cried for an hour."

Through the kitchen doorway I saw the Wainwrights' heads bent close; their voices were a cool duet of rumble and trill. I felt happy for my roommate, having dinner later with *both* her parents. Happy for the Carsons, "filling that ol' empty nest back up again," as Mrs. Carson said. Happy for the Goddess Dee, who Made This Happen. *And the girls?* When I turned to smile back at Dee, the sun hit me square in the eyes and I had to blink hard not to tear up.

Mom's voice: "Hi, you've reached the person you were calling. I can't come to the phone right now, or you know what? Maybe I can, I just don't want to. Leave me a message."

Me: "Mom, that message is getting OLD. Sorry. Hi. It's your sweet magic daughter who you love. Please pick up...Mom?"

Mom: "Sweet, huh? Which daughter is this again?"

Me: "I know. Sorry for being such a..."

Mom: "Pill? Let's say pill. Apology accepted, babe. Only because you've accepted all mine for being a hell of a lot pill-ier over the years."

I love my mom.

Mom: "You there, Joss?"

Me: "Yes. I'm very here. I'm walking down to the waterfront to meet Vivian."

Mom: "Wait, you're flying from there? It's still light, Jocelyn. I thought you started flying way far down the beach!"

Me: "I was, but I'm done with that. No one's EVER on the waterfront—duh, if they were, someone would've found the girls before me! And guess *what*, Mom," *quick, before she tweaks my mood*, "my girls moved into their new house today! The lawyer says it's world-record speed for Immigration."

Mom: "Joss, that is wonderful..." I lost her voice in the hiss of a bus stopping for a crowd of tired-looking people. "...long will they be able to stay in the U.S.?"

Me: "Hopefully forever! Their visa hearing's not scheduled yet. But the church found these amazing foster parents, they're like out of an old movie—Mrs. Carson even wears an apron!

And Rialta's dad, Mr. Wainwright? He paid for the Carsons' basement to be remodeled, and he bought new beds! So all nine of 'em can live there. He's kinda fallen in love with the girls."

Mom: "Hmm. Poor Rialta. Wasn't she already feeling neglected by her parents?"

Me: "Yeah, but this whole thing's bringing 'em all closer. And Dawntae's gonna tutor the girls next semester, and she says Rialta might too! But it has to seem like Rialta's idea."

Mom: "Ah, one of those willful types? No wonder you understand her."

Me: "Hey, I said I was sorry. Mom, of course I don't think Horizon is 'home.' And I know I should've called, like, three days ago. It's been so crazy, studying for Coastal finals. I've been skipping the dining hall so I can do my Mandarin while the roommates are gone. Granola bars are nutritious, right?...Still there, Mom?"

Mom: "Right here." [sighing] "Look, babe, three things. One, I told you, apology accepted for your little Thanksgiving hissy-fit. Two, there are other Dalby folks who need that apology more. And three—granola bars, really? Get your butt to the dining hall."

Me: "What Dalby folks? I talked with Savannah before I left. We're cool. She gets that I need to stay in Wattsville for the girls. She knows I don't have to deal with Zach."

Mom: "Uh-huh."

Me: "What?" *Why's she have to be so smart?*

Mom: "You telling me you're not 'dealing with' Zach, babe? Savannah might believe that..."

Me: "Mom, I have to go, I can see Vivian waiting for me. We haven't had Boot Camp since we got back, the weather's been so horrible, and now the sun's finally out and we have to *fly*, okay?"

Mom: [sighing again—*does she know how annoying that is?*]

Me: "I'm not ditching you, I promise. I'll call you tonight, okay?"

Mom: "It's not me you should call, Joss. It's Louis. Whatever happened last week…that boy looks like he's been hit by a bus."

Me: "Oh. It's…I'm…yeah. Okay, Mom. See ya."

A week into December, the sunset's fragile rays on my outstretched arms felt comforting. As we flew, I pulled my gloves off and stuffed them into my pockets.

"That boy looks like he's been hit by a bus."

It's been a week. I need to call. Or write. Or something.

"Hey, Joss," Vivian called from behind me. "Did you even *see* my barrel roll? I'm getting good at those. What's *wrong*?"

"Sorry," I said automatically. I slowed until her left mitten nearly brushed my wrist. *Mom's right—stupid to fly before dark,* but the sun was turning the bay into pink glass. "Do it again, I'm watching."

"Okay, here goes." Vivian tucked her chin to her right collarbone like I taught her, then dropped her right arm, letting her body follow in a perfect sideways 360. Her hair swirled. Her "whew!" and my "woo-hoo!" sounded together as she leveled beside me.

How could you doubt this Flyer, Mom? She's one of us now.

"Tell you a *secret.*" Vivian flashed a proud smile. "I've been coming out here every evening since we got back from Dalby, *practicing.*"

"Every evening?" Teensy flicker of alarm. "Like now?"

"Yeah, pretty much around sunset. I love seeing this ugly old town light up like a *postcard.*" Vivian's face glowed to match her description.

"But that's dangerous! Same time every day? Someone could See you!"

She shot me a frown. "Down here? C'mon, Joss. You mean someone could *follow* me, right?"

"Zach, Vivian. Zach could follow you." My hands were

stiffening and I started wrestling my gloves back on. "You may have dropped him, but he hasn't dropped you. I bet he wants to ground you more than ever now." Her frown hardened. "Vivian, I know how he thinks—"

"You don't know Zach like I do." Vivian's not good at looking pissed, but she was close. "He's *true*. I don't believe what *he* believes, but I do believe *him*, and he *promised* to leave me be."

"Of course he promised! Vivian, 'the devil hath power to assume a pleasing shape.'"

Before her hair whipped across her eyes, I saw her glare. "What're you talking about? You don't go to *church*."

"It's Shakespeare," I said loftily. "And it totally applies. I don't trust Zach for a second, and neither should you. Trust makes you, like, vulnerable." *Okay, Mom, you're right about that anyhow.*

Vivian's flightline dipped while she stuffed her hair back into her hoodie. "Joss, why do you have so much trouble trusting *guys*?"

"What is *that* supposed to mean?"

The sun was down now, its warm rays vanishing into dull, chilly purple. We banked our turn around the south end of the bay in silence and headed for the lights of town.

"Don't be mad, okay?" Vivian said finally. "It's just, since Thanksgiving, you've been all weird about your friend *Louis*."

Why's everyone ganging up on me about Louis? "Weird how?"

"Like not *telling* me anything! You told me about your thing with *Savannah*, how you worked it out. But you didn't even let me *meet* Louis, and every time I bring his name up you go all *'whatever'* on me.

"I never said 'whatever,'" I muttered.

"You *know* what I mean. Joss, what *happened*? I've told you my absolute worst secrets in the whole world, and you won't even tell me that you *have* a boyfriend, let alone that he just *dumped* you."

The harbor's concrete appeared just in time; my arms were suddenly lead. "Louis didn't dump me. He's…he's my best friend." *His hands on my back, warm breath on my neck…* "Just, last week, it got…complicated." We glided toward our rusty-awning landing spot, the water behind us glimmering now with the streetlights from up the hill.

"Oh, he *wants* to be your boyfriend? Well, that's—"

"Shh!" I grabbed Vivian's arm and yanked her upward, pulling her with me above the warehouse across from the awning. "Someone's there," I hissed. I glanced over my shoulder to see a figure step out of the shadow into the gloom of the street. *No one's EVER on the waterfront.*

We hovered ten feet above the dark warehouse like a pair of wary dragonflies. Then I heard it, a fast-rising murmur.

"Dear-Lord-let-those-who-stand-their-ground-defeat-all-enemies-of-Thy-grace…"

The Stander prayer! He's saying it much faster this time, he's learned…

Vivian's weight suddenly dragged on my arm. She screamed in a whisper, "Joss, I feel it! I'm crashing!"

"No, you're not!" I clutched her wrist in a death-grip and whipped toward the bay, jets in full panic roar. I heard her feet scrape the roof, then we were back over water. Vivian whimpered—*she's too heavy.* Without thought I swung my foot down to connect with something hard—her ribs?— and heard her gasp, but it worked: she revved back alongside me.

"We're too close, we gotta make it to the pier!" *None of Lorraine's old books said anything about a praying Stander's range.*

"I can *fly*, I can *fly*, I can *fly*," Vivian muttered. Her body lurched up, dragged, lurched again. "I *love* to fly, I *love* to fly, I *love* to fly."

"We love to freakin' *fly!*" I screamed into the night. My free arm was shaking with the strain. "Screw you, Zach Howe!" *How far can his prayer reach?* "Where's that damn pier?"

"We're freakin' *Flyers!*" Vivian screamed back, surging out of my grip. I saw her drop into a long shadow on the bay's glowing ripples—the pier. She landed, and stayed upright.

A second later I stood with her—only it was me grabbing for support. Vivian put her arm around my waist and we leaned on each other, sucking in creosote-scented air. Beneath our feet, the wavelets chuckled against the pilings. "Sorry I kicked you," I grunted.

"It's okay," Vivian said, rubbing her ribs. "And yeah. You were right about Zach. He's not done with us."

Us? A delayed bolt of shock shot through me. *Was he praying us both down? Was that what weakened me?*

"No kidding," I murmured. *Foiled my enemy once more—and I feel like curling into a ball.*

But I had my Slavery paper and an English project to finish, and college finals to study for. We picked our way down the uneven planks to the pavement without talking. Of course Zach was gone—*for now.*

Leaving me with the question Mom would ask, if she knew my Plan: aren't I still as much a target as Vivian?

Crossing the pavement where the girls' nightmarish container sat, Vivian broke the silence. "But *I'm* right too," she said. "About Louis. Aren't I, Joss? You're not done with *him.*"

To: <u>LouisTheRed@gmail.com</u>

Hey, it's me. Duh. Sorry I haven't called or emailed or anything since I left. I've been talking to you all week in my head. But you wouldn't know that. ☺ And I didn't exactly encourage you to get in touch, huh?

Thing is, I can't figure out how to say what I need to say without hurting you. OMG that sounds so CHEESY. I keep starting over. Argh. OK. I'll just write stuff and see what happens.

Remember last winter when I got pissed at you about Shakespeare? Must've been the last time you flew with me. We were hovering in the trees by Seal Rocks, waiting for that family to leave, remember? I was in my *Hamlet* phase and I shared my favorite Ophelia quote and you said, "Why can't Shakespeare just say what he means?" And I said, "Dude, he IS saying it." But I know you don't remember what Ophelia said: "Lord, we know what we are, but know not what we may be."

That's where I'm at right now. Me and Ophelia. I know what we are, Louis. But it's kinda getting in the way of what we may be.

I like you a big fat overweight ton. I can't imagine my life without you. (CHEESE) And I've always had dreams about somebody's arms around me, just holding me, like you did. I've never even told this to Savannah, she's so far past that. But it's really all I want. And you made my heart feel fantastic. (DOUBLE CHEESE) But you're Louis, and I'm Joss. I've spent sixteen years NOT thinking of you that way. I'm gonna need some time, to try putting your face on those dreams

-- Are you sure you want to delete this message? --

What is wrong with me? Put it on paper, Flygirl: I love Louis. I do. Wasn't I jealous of Erin? ADMIT IT. I just have to get the hell over myself and those stupid Zach fantasies. Louis loves me. Louis is REAL. Isn't that what I want?

I don't know what I want. I suck at this.

Call him, you moron. Talk it out. You know you're not gonna get anything done till you work through this.

No. Finish my report first. Then I'll call.

I reopened my Modern Slavery paper and scrolled down to the conclusion:

"In this case study, the trafficking victims' pursuit of T-visas is being aided by..."

My phone rang and I jumped a mile. Didn't recognize the number. "Hello?"

"Jossalady! The Divine Miss Vivian is refusin' to go to a pahty with me and Ah want to make her jealous. So don't tell me you're studying too, honeypie, Ah won't take No fer an answer."

"How—did Vivian give you my number, Eli?" Weird mix of pleased exasperation. "Did she also tell you, hello, I've got high school AND college classes to study for?"

"I know that," said Eli, sounding a little hurt. "Just thought it wouldn't kill ya to get out a little, before yo' curfew thang."

"Can you talk normal for once?" I demanded. "Where's Brady?"

"Studying," Eli admitted. "Okay, fine, I should hit the books too. Just thought you'd enjoy this particular part-ay," he added, temptingly.

I bit. "Why's that?"

"Harry Potter theme. I've heard your phone, *chica.*" *He noticed my ringtone?* "And to be honest, I do mightily enjoy yo' company. But no worries. The real parrrty is the end-of-term Buccaneer Bash, *arrgh.* Noooobody misses that one. Well, except wee Vivian."

"Wait," I said. "*Arrgh*, yourself. Why wouldn't Vivian go to the Buccaneer Bash?"

"Ah. Sorry. Thought you knew, darlin.' It's in Zach's dorm. So he'll be chief among the Bashers. Last I heard, Vivian was done with him—cheers to that. But why should you and Brady and I miss all the fun? We're not afraid of Monsieur Zachary."

"'Course not. But when is the Bash thing?" *The Plan. Do I still dare?*

"Two weeks. Parrrty of the year. Tell ye what, lass. Say you'll Bash with me and Brady at end of term, and I'll leave ye to yer booooks tonight."

"Deal, Eli."

But getting back to my booooks was easier said than done.

"In this case study, the trafficking victims' pursuit of T-visas is being aided by..." sheer, dumb luck, like meeting Mr. Wainwright. Like being invited to a party with Zach, whom I am NOT afraid of. Like being loved by Louis, whom I do not deserve. *"Lord, we know what we are..."*

I feel ya, Ophelia.

I wrote the lamest report conclusion ever, knowing I'd have to rewrite it. On to Chinese. *What's Mandarin for "we know not what we may be?" Arghhh.*

To: LouisTheRed@gmail.com

Hey, it's me. Sorry I haven't called or written or anything. But neither have you. School is super crazy right now and I promise I'll write more when I have time to think. OK?

Love, *(Isn't there a different way to say it now?)* **Joss**

Hah. What kind of model is Ophelia for a Flyer? She let Hamlet bring her down.

CHAPTER SIXTEEN

THIS IS HOW IT FEELS

LouisTheRed@gmail.com

☹

That was it. Then three rounds of phone-tag. And some more emojis. I needed a space much larger than my room to write back—like a giant cave, or a forest glade. The days slid by, a blur of study, and prepping my Zach Plan. Finally, after a week:

LouisTheRed@gmail.com

Hey. Using school computers SUCKS but that's all I got. Not gonna call cuz why would I? Didn't think you were so much like your mom but you are. Sorry but it's true. Guess maybe I'll see you at Christmas.

Louis

Louis's voice: "Hey, leave a message. Duh."

Me: "Hey, got your email…I wanna talk. For real. Are you there? …OK. I'll try back later. Or I'll write. Tomorrow, after my last Coastal final. Promise…'Bye."

But my college finals ended, and the blur only picked up speed. *Plan Day. How can I call Louis now? My head is full of Zach.*

I was dressing after a shower when Dawntae walked into our room saying, "Hey, Joss, I saw your friend Vivian just now in town—it was super weird."

"Yeah?" I asked, but Rialta interrupted, calling from her room, "Where were *you*, Tae? They had apple crisp tonight, Chaz was gonna give you his."

I looked up from my socks to see Dawntae blush. She was wearing a silk flower in her hairband and her favorite gray boots. "I," she said airily, "had a date, remember? With Ray, the guy from the bookstore?"

"Oh, right, with the killer eyelashes!" Socks, hoodie…*almost ready. Slow down, heart.* I forced myself to focus on Dawntae. "How'd it go?"

"Somebody brought that boy up right," Tae beamed. "Held the door, wouldn't let me pay…Telling you, my grandma'd want me to marry him!"

"Just like in *Mulan*, huh?" I said, and she lit up even brighter. *Sneakers… hairbrush already in my daypack…?* "So, Tae, what did you see that was weird?"

Plink. Plink-plink. Dawntae darted to the window. "Hey, a guy's throwing pebbles," she announced. "Like a movie! You get a date too and not tell us? Wait, there's two of 'em." She turned from the window. "Rialta, they yours? I like the one in the hat!"

My escorts! My heart gave a happy skip—nice change from all the pounding, as the Buccaneer Bash shifted from theory to fact. "Sorry, Tae, those guys belong to each other."

As Dawntae let this sink in, I wrestled with the window and yelled, "Be right down, guys!"

"Hey, you're going to the Bash after all?" Rialta appeared in her doorway, wearing her *Not fair!* face. "Hold up, Joss, I am totally coming with you."

Uh-oh.

But Dawntae chimed in, "You trying to make Chaz jealous? I heard that is one wild party."

"Chaz had his chance," Rialta said, undoing her braids. "If he's all 'whatever, gotta finish my photography project,' he doesn't have to know about the Bash." Back-together-with-Chaz Rialta is still Rialta. "Wait, Joss—you said it was semi-formal. You're wearing *that*?"

"No, no, no, I'm not Bashing," I lied. *A Flyer's gotta do what a Flyer's gotta do.* No WAY was I bringing Rialta. "Brady and Eli are just done with finals and prob'ly wanna go out for, I dunno, sweet-and-sour soup." That part could've been true. "See you guys at curfew."

"Aw, have fun," said Tae. "Gay guys are so relaxing. Rialta, it's not even nine yet—wanna go see a movie?" But Rialta wasn't done with me.

"Fine, then," she pouted, starting to re-braid. "But why's your pack so fat?"

"Christmas presents," I told her, pulling on Coastal hoodie. *Liar, liar—but it's all for the Plan.* "See ya!"

Not till the bottom of the stairwell did I realize I never found out what weird Vivian-thing Dawntae saw.

Eli passed me something that turned out not to be a joint. "No tha—wait, what the hell's this?" I demanded. "Eli, did you bite off someone's finger?"

"Bubblegum cigar. Well, half," he mumbled, chewing hard. "All yers, lass."

Brady caught my eye in the lamplight as we headed up the hill toward Zach's dorm. "Our Eli only partakes of the evil weed when he's stressing. Otherwise—candy. If life treats him right, he's gonna have no teeth by age thirty."

"Here'th to no thtreth!" Eli lisped, ridiculously cute in his fedora and Brady's high school letterman's jacket. "Finals— check. Christmas shopping—check. Nothin' to do but Bash Bucaneeringly and go home for a three-week nap."

"Speak for yourself," I mumbled around the wad of gum. "Some of us have high school finals in January." The moon was almost as big as the Halloween night Vivian flew out her window, and the air was a lot colder.

"Oh, we're so bad, corrupting youth," Brady sighed. "Well, for jail bait, Joss, you look harmless. And hot, of course," he added, seeing my eyebrows rise. "Eli should've warned you, girls dress up for this thing, but hey, at least you're not all skanky with the cleavage and the makeup."

"Eli, tell him to stop before he digs himself any deeper." Laughing is a good cure for nerves. "Don't worry, Brady, I'm totally irresistible even in jeans." *Hah—not!* "Vivian told me what to expect. She said stick to the dance floor and stay away from the punch."

"I'm bummed Vivvie wouldn't go with us," Brady said. "But her flight home is real early tomorrow, right? Plus I get that she needs to stay away. Those hot guys, man—they mess you up." He stopped in the middle of the sidewalk and cupped Eli's chin for a smooch. Clumps of party-going Coasties separated and streamed past without a homophobic glance.

Maybe Zach's homophobia's not a Stander thing; maybe it's just him. Lorraine and I never found anything about gays in those ancient texts. I nodded and smiled at people going by, thinking about kissing. And lips. And spit.

Flo Rida's "Low" was thumping so loud that my escorts and I resorted to sign language as soon as we hit the common room. Eli pointed toward the courtyard and I followed, pulling my hood way down to scan the crowd. Half the guys were wearing pirate eye-patches, bandannas or fake beards, but except for one Sexy Pirate Wench, the girls were ignoring the party theme. Brady was right: spaghetti-strap gowns, sparkly minis, Dee Hightower nails and heels. I shrank into my hoodie despite the beery heat of Coastie bodies getting their freak on. *"Next thing you know/ Shawty got low, low, low, low, low, low, low, low."* Outside was worse: pot fumes mixed with alcohol. Not the dorm you'd expect for a guy like Zach, unless he felt like a missionary about it.

Well, this girl's on a mission of her own.

Two blond girls in blue gowns—one satin, one glittery—tossed me pitying smiles. I felt WAY too conspicuous. I yanked on Eli's arm and signaled toward where bathrooms should be. He nodded and yelled something back, then he and Brady joined the herd at the kegs.

The bathroom was crowded with glitzy girls fixing their glitz. *Here goes.* I nabbed the handicapped stall as my personal dressing room, unzipped my pack, and turned myself into one of them.

Disguise is freedom. *Even Mom wouldn't know me!* Ditching my pack in a dark corner, my phone and keys in a beaded evening bag, I slithered right past Eli and Brady, now shaking their stuff to Mariah Carey's beat. I bumped Eli's arm—nothing. As far as they knew, Jocelyn was across the room, dancing harmless-but-hot. *So where's Zach in all this mess?*

"No thanks," I murmured to the third guy who tried to pull me onto the dance floor. *Mission.* I continued to circle the dancers. Black hair, red, brown—nothing golden. Not dancing, not outside drinking. *Where?*

Then I remembered: Eli said Zach would be "chief among the Bashers." DJ? I followed the throb of the music to its source in the corner, a laptop on a card table, lit by a desk lamp and barricaded by speakers. *Voilá.* Zach wasn't DJ, but he seemed to be working the lights in sync with the laptop guy. They'd both pushed their pirate eye-patches to the tops of their heads, ignoring the three girls groovin' in front of them and darting obvious glances at Zach. I saw his head nod to the beat as he scanned the dance floor, checking his lighting effects. His eyes didn't linger on any one dancer. *Yet.*

I placed myself on the edge of the crowd and pretended I was Savannah. *"I know you got that fever for me, hundred and two, and boy I know I feel the same…"* I'm not much of a party girl, but dancing's always felt good, a little like flying. *Go, body, go.* And since my body was now sheathed in black-and-silver sparkles (thanks, Wattsville Thrift Shop), padded with three inches of bra-stuffing, and capped with a wig of blond braids and a sequined beret, there was no "self" to feel self-conscious. *Jocelyn would never do this, but I can.* I hadn't left that bathroom till I'd buried Jocelyn's face under an inch of makeup.

I waited till Zach's face swiveled to my corner, and busted a quick move into the blue light. Then back to the shadows. *Ah, he's still looking this way!* I did it again, showing my gown's deep cutaway, a long oval of naked back, my golden braids waving invitation. *Hellooo.* Another flash of skin in the light. Zach wouldn't be able to smell the Flyer through all her perfume. I tried a Savannah move, butt-wriggles down to the floor and back. *"...boy I know I feel the same, my temperature's through the roof..."*

Maybe the stupidest plan in Flyer history. But Stander or not, Zach's a red-blooded guy. Currently single. And I was dressed to intrigue.

"Touch My Body" finally stopped. Guys dripped with sweat, and even us wig-and-beret-wearing females fanned ourselves in our skimpy outfits. But the next song was slow—too weird to dance solo. I looked around for a wall to lean on when someone touched my shoulder.

"Dance?" Not Zach, of course. Some guy I'd never seen before, tall, black, nice cheekbones, stripped down to a Buccaneers tank top showing stringy muscles. Slinging the satin strap of my evening bag over my neck, I slid into the guy's arms with my best Savannah smile.

"I'm Greg," he said into my ear.

"Cassandra," I murmured into his. *Always liked that name.* Cassandra swayed and shuffled, edging poor Greg closer to the music-table. On the third rotation I raised my face from Greg's shoulder and cast a glance like a fishing line toward Zach.

And he caught it across the table and held it till I rotated back around.

The song trailed away, Greg and I thanked each other politely, and I excused myself as if to use the bathroom. *Is the hook set?* I circled back around the dance floor to spot Eli and Brady, still happily sweating with the crowd and forgetting about little Joss. Then, slinky as hell, back to my corner, where Zach...*damn it, where'd he go?* The DJ sat alone.

"Hey, you as hot as I am?" My heart drumrolled. Zach stood behind me. "Whoops, that didn't come out right. Could you use a drink?"

I turned to face the Stander, enemy of flight and freedom, smiling his heart-cracking smile. I held my breath as he searched my face, but he only added, "I'm Zach, by the way," and took my arm.

"Phewww, right? Absolutely." My Cassandra-voice was basically Savannah's: higher than Jocelyn's, and chirpy, which is hard when you have to shout. "I'm Cassandra. NOT Cassie," I added for authenticity.

Zach nodded, still smiling, and jerked his head toward the other side of the room. I let his fingers on my elbow guide me toward a closed door in the semi-darkness. He opened it: a staircase. "Okay if we go somewhere a little quieter to talk, Not-Cassie?"

Cassandra smiled back, heart slowing to normal. "Okay." *I'm not some helpless drunk girl being led away by a guy—I'm a clear-headed Flyer working her Plan.*

The party thumped on through the floor, but Zach's room felt library-quiet after that zoo. He pulled off his pirate-eyepatch and dropped it on his bed. "Gotta tell ya, this is not what it looks like," he said in that warm voice. "I said something to drink and a chance to talk, and that's what I meant."

"Good, 'cause otherwise, y'know, what's a girl to think?" I

giggled. *Too cheesy.* "At least your bed's made. And no laundry pile like my brother." *Yes—authenticity.* "How come you don't have a roommate? I have two."

"Transfer student luck," Zach said, offering me his desk chair. His room was not what I expected—no athlete posters, no musicians, no "guy stuff" like Michael or Louis. Sierra Club calendar, some photos of people and a sheepdog, a poster of the Grand Canyon. Guitar case in the corner, and over the bed, a simple wooden cross. "You must be a freshman? Feel like I'd have met you otherwise."

"Yeah, we live in Benson." I'd done my homework; it's the quietest dorm and freshmen do live there. "I don't party much, but Greg invited me." *Well, kinda.*

Zach was kneeling at his mini-fridge. "Juice or soda?" he asked. "Sorry, no beer. Figure you could use the hydration, though. You're an awesome dancer."

A jolt of satisfaction sizzled through me, followed by the weirdest flash of envy: *it's Cassandra who's awesome, not me.* "Soda, please. You don't drink? That's pretty awesome too. I don't know any guys like that. Is it a religious thing?"

Zach handed me a plastic cup of Coke and poured one for himself. "Maybe," he said. "I just believe in keeping my body, y'know, the way it was meant to be." He sat on his bed, that bright face just a few feet from mine. "You think that's religious, Cassandra?"

"I dunno, but I believe it too." I was concentrating on keeping my voice high, but I wasn't lying. "Most guys just wanna get you drunk. I wish there were more like you." *Like Louis*—but I slammed the thought shut. *The Plan.*

"And yet," Zach smiled, "you followed me up to my bedroom. What's a guy to think?" But he didn't lean in, just observed me over his cup.

Guess it's up to Cassandra—she knows what Savannah would do.

"Well..." I set my cup on his night table and leaned toward him. "I kinda noticed you, when I was dancing with Greg."

"I did some noticing myself," Zach said. "Noticed you were dancing alone before, so Greg's not much of a date. I don't know any girls who dance alone." Still he sat back on his bed.

"And you don't have a girlfriend?" *Is that Joss or Cassandra asking?*

Zach dropped his eyes. "She dumped me last month. It sucked. Still sucks."

He looked so forlorn, I wanted to hug him—not in a sexy, Cassandra way. "I'm sorry," I said honestly—*but for what? That what he is hurts him? Oh, please—he wants to ground me!*

And on that wave of resolution, Cassandra took over. "How 'bout I kiss it and make it better?" she purred and stood up—I mean I stood up—movie-scene smooth, to slide onto the Stander's lap and kiss him like Jocelyn had only imagined.

Lips met lips. Flyer spit mingled with Stander.

Nothing happened.

Well, that's a lie. Zach's body startled, then responded like you'd expect if a hot girl in a clingy gown sat on a guy's lap. *That* happened.

But my Plan? Disempowerment? The Stander in shock—like Zach's uncle—and the Flyer triumphant?

Even Lorraine thought "the kissing idea has merit!"

Ha. There's a reason kissing's not in any of her ol' books: doesn't work.

But the kiss went on. Zach's lips opened to invite me in, warm and Coke-flavored. He leaned for a moment to set his drink on the night table, then his hands gripped my bare back. My shock at my fizzled Plan was melting by the second. Cassandra disappeared and it was just me, kissing Zach Howe like in a dream, his hands moving down my spine, his mouth on my throat now, my neck, back on my mouth where it somehow didn't matter anymore if my spit cancelled out his, *what a stupid idea, KISS me, this is how it feels...*

"Whoa." His voice was throaty as we separated for air. I felt dizzy, but one breath was enough, I wanted his mouth again, his hard wrestler's arms.

"You're amazing," Zach gasped at the next break. One hand went to my hair and I felt the whole top of my head move—*my wig!* I clasped his hand and moved it back to my neck, but that scare woke me out of the haze where I was somehow glued to this gorgeous boy I was supposed to be disempowering.

What're you doing, Flygirl? Take a break. I disengaged myself enough to reach toward my cup on the table. I felt two. His and mine.

His *"cuppe."*

I'd been so focused on the Kissing Plan—*stupid idiot moron*— I forgot all about the one disempowerment method I'd seen work.

Get his cup. Now.

In my lap I could feel Zach's arousal. *Can't tell which cup is which. Can't let him see.* Zach sighed, eyes closed; his hands slipped beneath the scalloped edge of my nearly-backless gown.

"I want him so bad!" Vivian said—I get it now.

I used the distraction of his desire to lift our two paper cups together, pinched in one hand. I sloshed sweet liquid into my mouth, from both, and some on my arm and Zach's pillow. Then I leaned back in. *Mmm, I've had a drink. Don't you want one?*

But it was my body Zach wanted. His fingers searched my bra hooks.

No. Bad. The Plan never got to this part. I pulled at his arms and unsealed our lips to murmur, "Wait."

He didn't. My mouth was recaptured—harder, deeper. But fantastic.

I could let him. Bra stuffing's not that embarrassing. I could find out what Savannah knows...what Vivian wants...

Vivian.

"WAIT," I gasped, and pulled away roughly to stand. My legs felt so shaky I collapsed back into my chair.

Zach put his head in his hands. "Sorry, sorry." He cleared his throat. "Told myself that was NOT gonna happen. Why's it have to be so hard?" Then a chuckle: "Ha—that came out wrong." His face reemerged, flushed like he was wearing as much rouge as I was. "Here I am doing exactly like all those other guys...sorry. Gotta cool off. Where's my..."

Zach reached for his drink. I watched him pick up a cup—mine or his, no matter now—and swallow. And sit back. Nothing.

Then his eyes flared and he clutched his chest like a man having a heart attack. His flush faded. *Just like his uncle!*

"Oh," the suddenly ex-Stander said.

I scrambled for the door. But my enemy sat there, hands on heart, shaking his head. "Wow, Joss, congratulations. You sure know how to get a guy's defenses down."

I stared at him in shock.

"Thought for sure I was gonna launch you like last time, but you were ready for me." He laughed ruefully. "Hey, when a Stander cares, he's gotta try. So, fine—you wouldn't let me save you... can you at least take off that lame wig now?"

He knew me all the time. I felt my hands go to my own chest, mirroring his. *But I won! I saw his power drain away.*

Yet somehow I was reaching up and detaching the wig clips. *I won, but he still wants me. This is how Savannah felt.* Braids and beret thumped to the floor.

"That makeup come off too?" Zach stood, smiling, and moved to me.

Leave now, you idiot. Savannah got pregnant, remember?

"Never mind, I know it's you in there." He would not unlock our eyes. "Jocelyn. What are you afraid of? You got me—now you can be with me."

"Why… aren't you mad?" I managed. My hand on the doorknob.

Zach shrugged. "I've always struggled with the Stander thing. Soul lifeguard. Wasn't lying to you, back on Dalby when I asked you to free me. Didn't choose it, didn't want it—you know how that feels, right?"

Yes. No. I love what I am.

"Well, it's out of my hands now." Zach leaned in while I continued not to flee. I could smell his sweat. "I get to be a regular guy. Get to quit worrying about your soul and just…"

And…back to the kiss. He didn't pin me to the door; I pinned myself. *Who knew Flyers and Standers could be hijacked by the same force, irresistible as flying and praying?* He wanted *me*, Jocelyn—not Cassandra in her stupid beret. Innocent, flat-chested Flyer *me*— not my powers.

"I stuffed my bra," I confessed breathlessly.

Zach laughed and nuzzled my bare shoulder, mumbling, "I know, who cares?" and I floated off the floor.

Not literally. My flight-engines were silent. I was nothing but arms and lips. "I still don't get…" I panted as we scooped each other toward his bed, "why you aren't hating me." *Arms and lips, arms and lips, there goes the bra stuffing.* "I hated you when you tried to take me down…"

"Mm, yeah, about that?" Zach murmured, his mouth on my neck. "Prob'ly not the best time, but you'll find out anyway…" now on my collarbone, "…I did my Stander job, before you dinged me. The one I came here to do." Beneath his warm breath I felt my ribs turn icy, and he added, "Think your roommate saw us while it was happening, actually."

"What do you mean?" I faltered, sitting up.

Zach gripped my shoulders and looked me right in the eye. "It's okay, Joss," he said. "Vivian wanted me to."

CHAPTER SEVENTEEN

SANCTUARY

et off me! You're lying! You're the worst person I ever met! The words I had no breath to say followed me on my dash through the party crowd, down the path to Vivian's. Still the feel of Zach's hands on my bare shoulders lingered. And the image of his amber eyes, so steady, so sure. *He's lying. Vivian's fine. Why would he say that? He's lying.*

MacDougall's windows were mostly dark. No one answered my door-pounding. Everyone was at the Bash—except the person I had to find. Whose phone was off. I stuffed my own phone back into its glittery bag. *Zach's lying...*

The party heat wore off fast in the night, leaving me freezing in my gown. My normal clothes, plus that stupid wig and beret, were back at the party. Where my enemy had played me. Through that whole lame seduction scene, that fantasy Plan—he'd *known.*

The first time I kissed Zach Howe, he'd launched me floundering into the air. This time, he hadn't counted on my resistance, or that 'cuppe.' My Plan hadn't worked...but it had. I saw the Stander's power die! But the Stander didn't care, because...

My bare feet pressed cold pavement. *I can't lose my only Flyer friend just when I've saved her. She must be fine.*

"Need some help, Miss?" It was the super-tall campus cop I'd seen some evenings in my beat-the-curfew rush.

Curfew! I snatched my phone back out to check: 10:52. "No, I'm fine," I said. He frowned at me as I hurried away, calling "Thanks!"

I wanted to fly home and cry on Mom's shoulder. But I had to find Vivian. And my flight-engines felt as numb as my feet stumbling along the sidewalk. Like it was me who got disempowered.

I made it back with two minutes to spare, fumbling my key with freezing fingers. Dawntae leapt up from her bunk as I staggered into our room.

"Joss, omigod!" she gasped, pulling on her Cinderella robe. "What happened? Did those guys mess with you?" She meant Eli and Brady—still back at the Bash, oblivious.

Rialta emerged to see me melting down inside Tae's fleecy hug. She joined us on the couch, and here's how nice Rialta's become: she waited till I stopped crying before asking, "Where'd you get that dress?"

"Never mind that," Dawntae said sharply. "What's wrong, Joss? Tell Mama."

"I've lost my friend." I clenched my teeth. "Vivian. I'm so worried, she's turned off her phone…"

"What do you mean—?" Rialta started, but Dawntae interrupted.

"Oh, yeah! Vivian! Your gorgeous Asian friend? That was it, Joss—the weird thing I was gonna tell you 'fore you split outta here! I saw her!"

My heart leapt before I realized, duh, Dawntae didn't mean "Saw" as in flying. And she saw Vivian *before* the party. "Saw her where?" I asked dully.

"Downtown. Near her café. It was just getting dark, I was hurrying to meet Ray, and there's your girl Vivian with her crazy-hot boyfriend, the blond dude."

I focused on Tae's pink-and-white shoulder.

"Looked like they were, maybe, practicing for a talent show or something? Don't know how to explain it," Tae went on. "Like, there's this lamppost? And your friend is kinda swinging on it, halfway up—she some kinda acrobat? And Mr. Hottie, he's all down on his knees at the base of the lamppost, kinda looking up, but his eyes are closed! Seriously weird, Joss. That's why I wanted to tell you."

I closed my own eyes. *"I did my Stander job...the one I came here to do."*

Rialta got up, then something soft covered my feet. "Your little toe's bleeding," she said, but no more questions about my outfit.

Dawntae stroked my hair. "Joss, should we call the cops? Did something *happen?*"

Yes! But not what Tae means. "No, not to me," I told her. "I'm fine, really. You guys're awesome." I opened my eyes to see them gazing at me in a stereo of concern. "But Vivian—she is a kind of acrobat, and yeah, she was practicing. And now she's in trouble." I heaved myself up from their comfort. "I gotta go."

My roommates looked at each other. Rialta opened her mouth and closed it again.

"Word," said Dawntae. "Rialta, you go distract the RA while Joss sneaks out. Joss, when you've found your friend, call me, and I'll do the distracting so you can sneak back in, okay?"

Rialta nodded. "Fine, I'll go whine to the RA about my obnoxious roommate Dawntae. Then you can go whine about me." *Rialta the team player,* my numb brain marveled. "But get some real clothes on her, Tae. Joss, pull my scarf over your face so the cameras can't see you."

Five minutes later, in socks and shoes and warm clothes, I darted past the RA's door, scrabbling for my phone.

It rang as I touched it. "Where the hell ARE you, Joss?" Brady yelled over party-noise as I slipped back out of Nutschel. "We've lost you in this pirate hell-hole. Are you mad at us? Please say you didn't drink the punch."

"I'm okay, you guys. I left the party." I glanced around and made a dash for the Horizon gates. "Something's…" I panted, "…you gotta help me find Vivian."

"Wait a sec," Brady hollered. The Bash beat filled my ear. "What d'you mean, *find* her?" he said a moment later, breathy as me. "We're outside, too loud in there. Vivvo's not in her room? Why'd you go looking? What's wrong?"

This time I didn't lose it. Ducking into the rhododendrons that hide all us bad Horizon kids scaling the gates, I finally felt that flare in my chest. *Still a Flyer. Time to expand my Ground Crew.*

"I'll explain. But not on the phone. Meet me behind MacDougall, where it's dark." Then I wrapped Rialta's scarf around my face.

If Horizon security got me on camera, Dean Williams will just have to wonder why a winterized mummy suddenly bust through the rhodies like a rocket and streaked away, beyond the reach of the streetlamps.

I'd never demonstrated my powers to anyone without prepping them. Eli and Brady took it pretty well when I dropped out of the dark sky to MacDougall's deserted back steps. And I learned new foreign swear words.

"I *knew* there was something about you! I *told* you, Eels," Brady said when the language finally turned G-rated. "I told him, 'there's something about our Joss, she's not a normal teenager.' It's why we hang out with you, right?"

"You just said she was extra mature," Eli muttered.

"We both have the most awesome flying dreams," Brady sighed. "All the time. You have NO IDEA, Joss, what it's like to see your deepest, oldest dream turn real like that!"

"I have some idea," I mumbled, but Brady kept gushing.

"Omigod, if you can do this…what's NOT possible? Right?" Before I could answer, Eli asked me that heartbreaking question I got from Louis and Michael when I first showed them: "Can you teach me how to do that?"

No time to let him down gently, to explain that Flyers are born, not taught—and born women. Later I'll listen to his descriptions of flying dreams, like I did with Lorraine and Mr. Evans and even Dad: *"...right over the lip of this giant canyon, and then I'd dive, but I always woke up before..."* Later I'll offer the little comfort I can give to the non-Flyers in my life: *Yes. It IS heavenly. It's even better than your dreams.* I know from my Ground Crew—despite Michael's desperate envy—that inaccessible magic is still better than no magic at all.

But right now: "No," I told Eli. "I'm sorry. But here's the thing, you guys. Vivian—she's like me. Vivian flies too." I braced myself for another burst of profanity, but the guys just stared at me. Eli had lost his hat; his hair hung across his face like a half mask. "Or she did. Zach may have...put a stop to that. He's been trying. He's part of a...a tribe, kinda, like anti-Flyers. Where I feel like I *have to* fly, they feel like they *have to* stop people from being... deviant. Like me. Zach almost stopped me, summer before last," I sped up, racing the stupefaction on their faces, "but he didn't, and tonight I took away his power for good. But—"

"What the hell's this got to do with Viv?" Eli demanded.

"Before I disempowered him, I think he got to Vivian." Felt like punching my own gut to say it aloud. "And if he succeeded, if Vivian can't fly anymore, she might be...in a bad way."

Eli and Brady shared a look that said history, understanding, trust. My eyes burned. I'd dreamed of arms around me, breath in my ear—but that look I recognized from somewhere deeper than dreams. *I want that.*

"Let's find her, then," Eli said.

After half an hour of phone calls and checking Vivian's favorite hangouts, our fear had tightened around us like a giant net. Bean There? Closed. Library? Closed. I'd taken Eli and Brady to my original takeoff spot at the waterfront. They peppered me with questions about Flyers and Standers, but no one requested a takeoff demo. Brady asked, "From here? You just, like, lift into the air?"

Eli said, "Damn."

Defeated, we huddled on the front steps of Hull Dorm. The jeans and fleece my roomies had dressed me in were losing out to the chilly night, and the guys in their light jackets looked colder. But nobody suggested going up to Eli's room.

Brady cut off Vivian's voicemail message with his finger; we'd all memorized it. "Okay, kids. I think it might be time to check Memorial."

"The hospital?" I asked stupidly. The fear-net squeezed tighter.

"You said it'd be a disaster, right? If she lost her powers just when she'd reclaimed 'em?" Brady hugged himself. "Well, where do people end up in disasters? Hospitals and..." Suddenly his eyes lit up, then he and Eli were sharing that look again. "... churches," they said together.

"Church!" Eli repeated. "We are f---in' idiots. C'mon."

Wattsville Community Church was a modest brick building I'd passed a hundred times. We heard Vivian as soon as we pulled open the door to the main part—what Eli called the sanctuary. You don't have to cry very loud to be heard in an empty church. We trooped down the dark aisle in the faint glow of the Exit signs, following the sound of despair.

My friend was on her knees in front of the table thing. Altar. I hadn't been in a church since Ginny was baptized. Standers like Zach and his uncle hadn't exactly helped me fall in love with religion. But Vivian was here, safe. So church was okay with me. I dropped onto the carpet beside her.

"Oh, you guys," Vivian whispered as Eli and Brady crouched on her other side. She straightened up, face puffy with misery. "You came."

My mouth was dry. Brady patted her shoulder. "We were worried about you, sweetie."

Vivian smiled sadly. "I'm all cried out," she sighed. "Think I've lost my voice."

"Why'd you come here, *chica?*" Eli asked. "No matter," he added.

"I miss this place since I quit attending. It's quiet." Vivian hung her head. "Joss," she murmured into her knees, "I messed up so bad."

"It's okay," I said loudly. It was so NOT okay, but I couldn't stand any more whispering. "I told Brady and Eli all about us, Vivian. They know about Flyers now. And Standers." Deep breath. "So, your power— did you feel it go?" *Why even ask?* "Why'd you let him near?"

Vivian's voice was tiny. "I was trying to get through to him." *How can a Flyer sound so weak?*

"You kidding me? Vivian, I disempowered Zach tonight! I de-Standered him! Just to find I'm too late. You knew he'd try to pray you down again!"

"It's all right," put in Brady, as Vivian's face came back up, more miserable than ever.

"No, it's not." Her voice grated. "Joss is right, I *knew*. But…" She pushed herself off the floor and sank onto the front pew, rubbing her legs. "Oh, I'm so *stupid!* I thought I could convince him that Flying can be just as—as *holy* as not-flying, that it's the *person* that matters. Reverend Gates said something like that once and I thought, Well, Zach loves the Reverend, he must be hearing the same message I'm hearing. But he isn't."

Still kneeling on the carpet, I shook my head. "Zach hears his own messages. Convert or stamp out—that's all Standers know." *They'd lock Brady and Eli in a shipping container if they thought that would "save" them.*

"So you talked to him?" I pressed. "After work? And he launched you?" Brady and Eli stared. "Why not fly away, like we did that night? Why hang onto the lamppost?"

"How do you know about…?" Vivian croaked. "Oh, who cares? I hung on because I wanted to fight *back*, Joss. For once. I'm sick of being a *wuss*."

"So you stayed up there," I continued relentlessly, "and he's below, praying the Stander prayer. You let him pray you down, after all our work." *Mom was right about you.* I closed my eyes against the throb of fury and guilt in my chest. *Stop it stop it stop it.*

Vivian snuffled behind me, then Eli's hand pressed on my head. "That's enough, Jossaroon," he said. "I don't get the s--t you're talking about, but it ain't helping. C'mon, Brade. Let's get these sad beautiful creatures back to my room and feed 'em some soup."

"Soup's good," Brady agreed, helping Vivian to her feet. I sat on the floor as they moved up the aisle.

You're good. Eli's good. I'm a selfish flying jerk. I understood why they call this a sanctuary. For the first time in my life, I wanted to stay in church and think stuff through.

But Eli reached for my hand and pulled me up. "Life sucks, lassie," he said, back to his wry smirk. "But you can f---in' *fly*. So it doesn't suck that bad for you, eh? How 'bout that."

How 'bout that. I shuffled past the peaceful pews. *I can fly. Vivian's alive. Zach is done. Louis loves me.*

A blast of phone notes yanked me back. "Prob'ly Dawntae warning me about the RA," I muttered. But it was Lorraine. Telling me…

How 'bout that. I can't delete this like an email. It's happening.

Lorraine said the coast guard got two Mayday calls from the *Flyer*. Then nothing more.

"Oh, Joss," she choked. "Your dad is missing."

CHAPTER EIGHTEEN

LOST FLYER

Forty-three minutes: that's how long it took to fly home against the wind.

Checking the time kept the fear from dragging me into the waves. 12:49. Wind blasted from the west—*where the* Flyer *went.* Outside Wattsville Bay, the first gust spun me. I dropped my head, fighting forward. A wild ocean of air, trying to swamp me. *Like Dad.* 12:52.

Dragging in the front door at 1:24 a.m., I stumbled on a Christmas tree sprawled across the floor. Lorraine the Librarian had been replaced by a Lorraine I hardly recognized, puffy-faced like Vivian, frantic. When the coast guard called an hour earlier to report no news, Mom told me, Lorraine screamed and shoved the tree over. Then my stepmother marched room to room, jittery, hands clutching, and turned out every light.

"Glad you're here safe, babe," Mom added.

She was heating soup by the light of the stove. *"Soup's good,"* Brady's voice echoed in my head—but the previous evening was gone, swallowed up. Nothing existed outside this shadowy kitchen, this dull glow of hanging saucepans. Lorraine shook her head at soup and paced the house like a clumsy ghost.

Michael was gone. Not with Dad—but he thought he should have been, Mom told me. "He needed time off for his band, so Aaron went with Ron instead," she said. "Poor Michael. He turned white and busted out of here when we got the news. Don't know where he went." She stirred the soup. "But Michael's a big boy."

Dad's a big boy too. And his buddy Aaron, filling in to haul crab pots yesterday. No, the day before. Time had become a blur, a picture so stretched you can't see the people or scenery or whatever it's trying to show you. I didn't want to see the picture anyway.

I'll go look for Michael, I wanted to say...but couldn't. I felt empty. Outside, the wind howled and all I could do was cower into Dad's red armchair, hoping for sleep. Ha. After endless tossing, listening to the wind and Lorraine's soft crying upstairs, I found Dad's pile of junk-mail scrap paper and a ballpoint pen.

5:12 a.m. Waiting for another coast guard update. Mom made cocoa.

Lorraine's on the couch, finally crashed. From her ragged breathing, she's having nightmares. Michael's still out in the wind somewhere. When I flip this piece of paper over, I read "Dear Mr. Burgowski." When I write "Dad's okay," he's okay. Vivian was okay and Dad will be too.

Mom calls softly from her kitchen sanctuary—ha, my new word. "More cocoa, babe?" But I don't want cocoa. Or soup. Every minute that passes without news is a bad minute. I'm filling all the minutes up with these words.

8:05 a.m. Words and minutes and hours later, Michael crashes back in. Lorraine sits up, rubs her eyes in the pale sunlight and starts to cry again. I numbly observe that it's turning into a nice day.

"Nothing?" Michael calls roughly, and Mom, already at Lorraine's side, shakes her head. Michael stumbles to my chair like a zombie and sags to the floor, covering his face. I pat his damp denim shoulder.

"Where've you been?"

"Walking." His voice is hoarse. "Out to the Spit, looking for lights."

"He'll be okay," I tell my brother. "Dad and Aaron have tons of experience. I'm sure they'd put on their survival suits when they made that call."

Michael uncovers his face, grayish in the daylight. "Coast guard lost 'em, Joss. All they have are the coordinates from the Mayday. The *Flyer* doesn't have an emergency beacon."

"Why'd they go out so far if they're just crabbing?" the fisherman's daughter in me can't help but ask.

"Aaron heard about these offshore banks. Swarming, he said." Michael clenches his eyes. "I didn't wanna go, knew they'd be out way past my rehearsal time. So f---in' stupid, going offshore in that wind—"

"Dad knows what he's doing," I interrupt him. "And survival suits last a long time!"

Michael doesn't answer.

"Yes, they do," Mom says briskly, rubbing Lorraine's shoulders. The sun is bringing color back and Lorraine's bright green blouse looks ridiculously cheerful. The phone rings in the kitchen and Mom hops up to check the number; the rest of us stiffen.

"It's Aaron's wife Elly," Mom sighs. "I'll talk to her. Joss, make coffee, please. Michael, get your stepmom some Kleenex and go take a shower."

9:16 a.m. Coast guard calls again to say they'd call back if they had news. The phone keeps ringing and not being them. Elly must've called everyone and now they're calling us.

Mom's putting the Christmas tree back up and says we should clean the house. My hand hurts from writing, and I'm running out of scrap paper, so fine—I'll do the stove burners. Michael's gone to bed, but Lorraine takes the broom and dustpan from Mom and starts sweeping up the broken ornaments without a word.

11:43 a.m. No news. Stove's shiny. Lorraine's scrubbed all the downstairs floors on her hands and knees. Now she's moved on to the nice clean walls, rubbing quietly, like prayer. Maybe it is. I'll help.

12:39 p.m. Louis calls. "Joss, we just heard. Are you okay? Sorry, 'course not," he adds when I don't answer. Too busy trying not to cry, hearing his voice. "You want...should I come over?"
Yes! Please!
"Hey," I manage. "I wish you would..." I glance over at my stepmother, who has taken down the hallway photo of Dad on his boat-launch day. She's rubbing the glass with her dirty cloth. "...but maybe...not right now." I clear my throat. *Too many deleted emails, too much to explain.* "Lorraine's not doing real well."
"Of course, sure, yeah," Louis says hurriedly. "Maybe call me later if you, like, hear anything—I mean if you need to talk or whatever... 'kay?" And he hangs up before I can say, *Don't go, I miss your voice so bad.* Like I'd say that.

3:10 p.m. No news. Vivian calls, or tries to. Mom says, "Caller ID says Hawaii—do we know anyone in Hawaii?" I shake my head and she lets it ring. *Vivian. Sanctuary. Disempowerment.* I just realized I haven't slept since...can't remember. *Dad's okay. Dad's a big boy.*

5:38 p.m. Pressure on my shoulder. I break the surface of sleep to find Mom shaking me gently but insistently. Raindrops are splatting against the windows; I'm on the sofa.
"News?" I croak.
"No, babe," Mom murmurs above me. "Elly's organized a vigil for Aaron. She wants everyone to gather at the post office at six." *A vigil.* I close my eyes again as she talks. "Lorraine's not up to it, she's out walking."

"It's raining," I say stupidly.

"Yeah," Mom sighs. "Anyway, Lorraine might join the vigil later. I got Michael to come; it'll be good for him. D'you think you can…?"

I can't. Eyes closed, I shake my head mechanically until Mom kisses my forehead and whispers, "Okay, Joss. You stay and rest. I love you."

When I woke up the living room was completely dark, and for a second I was back in my bunk at Horizon. Then I heard the rain pattering the roof, and reality punched me in the stomach.

"News?" I groaned into the quiet. No answer—*of course, the vigil.* My throat was dry and tight. I shuffled into the dark kitchen to drink from the faucet.

The wind had died. *Like that matters now.*

All the fears I'd held at bay suddenly ambushed. I leaned on the counter, stomach curdling. "Mom," I whimpered.

This can't be happening. Dad's okay.

I tried to visualize the vigil, all my friends and family with candles…*outside in the rain? Like Dad?*

"Dad!" It came out as a wail, like Vivian in that church.

I sprinted for the stairs, stumbled up to the dark hallway. Past my room and Michael's, rain whispering like useless comfort, to Dad and Lorraine's room. Where they last slept a thousand years ago, when the world was still whole.

He's okay.

I didn't believe it anymore. The scent of Dad's briny laundry and Lorraine's dried lavender exploded the nausea into panic. My engines sparked and lifted me off the carpet, over Dad's unmade bed. The top of my head cracked the ceiling—wonderful pain.

"Dad!" I yelled. "Where are you? DAD!" Hovering and screeching like a mid-air two-year-old.

No one ran to comfort me. *They must've heard. They're with the Sheriff now, facing the details—submerged hull, mangled rigging; bodies tangled, bluish-pale, drowned...*

"I'M COMING TO FIND YOU, DAD!" I screamed. Through the doorway, down the hall and the stairwell, flying like a poltergeist. "DADDY!" Fumbling at the front door. Then out into the rainy night.

Too late, too late, too late, my brain chanted as I jetted toward the water, raindrops stinging my eyes. *Why didn't I head out to search last night?* Below me in the village center I saw a flickering glow: the vigil. Candles for hope—*what a joke. So much wasted time, scrubbing the stupid stove when I could've been out saving him...*

I veered over the Spit, aiming for the Strait, the big water that leads to the bigger water, the offshore banks crawling with crab.

The rain blinded me. My soaked sweatshirt dragged on my shoulders. So much for those Flyer Boot Camp rules I taught Vivian: "*One layer for wind, one for warmth. Fingers and toes and ears freeze first.*" Mine froze. And I'd barely left the Dalby shore behind.

"DADDY!" I was an idiot girl who thought she could save her father without a searchlight. Or any clue where to look.

Go back. The cold burn of my fear was gelling into plain old cold. *Fly home, hear the news. Be with family.*

I dropped my shoulder, banking slowly. Rain ran through my scalp and dripped from my clenched jaw. *My power's useless. It didn't save Vivian and it can't save Dad.*

Dalby was a few blurry lights in the darkness. Dalby meant news. Reality. *As long as I stay up here...*

And with that burst of dread I rocketed upward. High, high, higher. Eyes closed against the rain.

"Dad," I whimpered, and suddenly, *I know where he is. Dad's found sanctuary, like Vivian in church. Not down in the horrible ocean— it had him long enough, but he's free now.*

"I'm coming, Dad." *He's up above.* Higher.

Lungs raw. Higher. *Sanctuary.* No feeling in my arms. Higher still. No feeling anywhere but lungs and longing.

Behind my closed eyes the darkness spread. I heard myself gasping. *This is how it feels...to lose...* The last light in the world contracted into a pinhead. *Drowning...like Dad...in the sky.*

I let the world go.

Roaring black wind. My lungs opened first, sucking oxygen out of air that finally had some. Then my eyes, stinging and worthless. My brain opened last. It saw better than my eyes. *I'm gonna die.*

By reflex my arms flung forward, my legs kicked back, flailing like my first time in the sky. Engines dead, my Flyer limbs still strained for anywhere but down.

A light! Tiny, rushing closer. Arms and legs aimed themselves, trembling. Brain sat back. *Too far. Broken. Drowning. Alone.*

A dock, long and skinny. At the tip, one rain-blurry light showed piled crab pots, kayaks. The hiss of rain on ocean rose to meet me. *Never make it.*

At the last moment, my motors unfroze to jet me across the final stretch of blackness to the dock. *Too late.* A wave swelled under me to snatch one lagging foot, and I smacked face-down in the icy water.

Nothing like drowning to jump-start your will to live. *Kick off shoes. Swim to light. Pray for a ladder.*

I scrabbled at a piling, sharp with barnacles, the dock a foot above me. No ladder. Another wave heaved me beneath the planks, smashing the top of my head. I resurfaced in panic, choking, scalp searing. In the freezing jumbled blackness, my brain smirked. *What a stupid way to die.*

In the end, the ocean itself saved me. I struggled back out for another nonexistent handhold just as the next wave hurled itself over the top of the dock—and me with it. Yay for high tide.

Gasping, I sprawled face down in a crevice between two upside-down kayaks. The rain felt almost warm after the freezing grip of the sea. Tasted sweet. My scalp stung. *Rain, rain, rinse away…*

I almost flew myself to death. Out of control—*like Mom, like Vivian.* That irresistible, propelling force…locking me into darkness. Like the girls.

Was that *me*?

"How's anyone know what they don't know?" "They don't," Dad said. *"It's everyone's weak spot."*

Dad. The horrible day came rushing back. *They left me asleep on the couch! Dad's dead and they didn't even tell me.*

The kayaks were shaking. Then I realized it was me, trembling out of control. *I can't stay here.*

I didn't want to go home.

Go.

Needles of pain shot up my arms as I heaved to my deadened feet. Sopping and frozen, I struggled out from the kayaks and crab pots and limped in my socks down what must have been the longest dock on Dalby. No more lights. No one home. No help.

On the steep, endless gravel driveway, my feet woke up, searing. *I could just lie down here in the woods…*

Finally, a road—*but which freakin' direction to my house?* My feet chose one, stumbling at the edge of the pavement. I crouched to rub them. *How can something burning feel so icy?*

Don't remember how long I walked, fighting the urge to curl up on the lumpy grass. But suddenly I was blinded by headlights, assaulted by screeching brakes, and scooped into the arms of Louis's moms.

Motherly voices: "Jocelyn, oh, my goodness, you're frozen, poor sweetie! And your head is bleeding!"

"Get in, get in."

"What happened?" Shasta began, but then, "Never mind.

Coats off, everyone—pile 'em on her." I glimpsed Louis's pale face at the driver's window as Shasta and Janice bustled me into the back seat of the VW bug, but he didn't say a word.

"It's all right, sweetie, we've got you," Shasta said, hugging me through the pile of coats as the car chugged back onto the road. "We just left the vigil—Beth said you didn't want to come, but oh, sweetie, where've you been? Here, put this on your head." She pressed something soft into my hand and lifted it to my scalp. "Thank goodness we bumped into you. Your poor family must be going nuts, coming home and you're not there! Louis, honey, you can turn around up ahead."

I heard him clear his throat. "I'm gonna drop you guys off, Mom," Louis said. "Then I'll take Joss home."

Shasta was wrong; my family wasn't going nuts, because they weren't home yet from the vigil. Louis walked my soggy self into our dark living room and I started to giggle.

"What's the matter with you?" Louis frowned, tightening his grip around my ribs as my body slumped.

"They don't...even...know!" Suddenly this was hilarious. "They're off praying for...Dad, and I...I almost just died too, and...they would've had...to pray...for both of us!"

"You're a nutcase, you know that?" Louis panted, dumping me on the couch. "Stop it, Joss." *I can't. Too funny.* "Want me to slap you like in the movies?"

"No. No," I gasped. The trembling returned, gearing higher. *Dad's dead.* "I'll...I want..."

"Shhh," Louis said, leaning over to inspect my scalp. "Bleeding's stopped. You owe my mom a new scarf."

I closed my eyes like drawing down a blind. "I want to go to bed," I told him. So Louis put me there.

"Shhh," he said again when I whimpered on the stairs. Then, in my room, "Lift up your arms." I couldn't. *Poor arms, you've done enough for one night.* "Okay, I'll do it." I felt Louis fumble at my waist, tugging upward, sweatshirt a resistant mass. "Now lie down so I can do your legs," he ordered when my top half came free.

I lay back, shaking helplessly on my bed, eyes closed, as he slid my socks and jeans off. My hands and feet burned with life, but my brain kept the blinds down. I felt Louis's hand on my bra strap. "Your underwear's soaked too," he said. His voice tightened. "And you smell all oceany. What the hell were you doing, Joss?"

Couldn't stop the shaking. "Oh…" Louis said. "You were trying to find him?" I felt his warm cheek on my cold one and his weight across my chest as he hugged me. "You're so icy," he whispered. "I gotta get those wet things off you. You mind?"

At least my bra's not stuffed this time! Giggles threatened again. My body shook harder as Louis slid his hands under my back, unclasping. The wet bra peeled away; my breasts met air. Louis made a sound like a choked sigh. *Another boy, another bedroom, another bra—how 'bout that.* I lost it.

"You're crazy, Joss. C'mere." He pulled me to sit up and yanked a dry sweatshirt over my head. "Take off your own damn panties if you think this is so funny."

"I'm sorry," I gasped. "I am crazy. Life is crazy."

"Life sucks, chica," Eli said, a million years ago. I opened my eyes and pulled Louis down next to me, clutching his warmth close. "Stay here. I'll take off my own damn panties."

Louis held me till I stopped shaking. Then he got up, fumbled in my bureau, found my old sweatpants while I added my underwear to the soggy pile on the floor. He helped me wrestle the sweats on, slid into bed next to me, pulled blankets over us both.

We kissed carefully, eyes closed. We didn't talk. He held me close from chest to hips and I felt him through his jeans and soccer jersey, but that was enough. He kept his hands on my cheek and my wet, salty hair. Slowly, slowly his heartbeat eased itself down to my own.

A while later came a gentle knock at my door. It opened when I didn't answer. I heard Mom's intake of breath, then a soft, "Ohhh." The door closed. I drifted away, a cold log of grief in a warm river.

Things I Have to Get Used To
1. Dad is gone.
2. I can't get used to that.

Okay, let's try that again. It's…let's see…nine o'clock on Saturday morning. December Twentieth. Thirty-six hours since the *Flyer* disappeared. I feel achy and dizzy, and my throat hurts. Louis comes back upstairs carrying a mug.

He kisses me on the forehead. "Lorraine and Michael are still asleep, but your mom made me eat some eggs. I told her you went out walking last night and got soaked. Oh, and you tripped and cut your head. She says I should make you drink this." The honey-lemon tea feels so good, and Louis's expression is so serious, I want to cry. But I'm too tired.

Now Louis is reading *The Hobbit* at my feet while I write in bed. Mom's keeping her distance, keeping her own shade pulled down on the world. It's a stupidly beautiful morning.

Things I Have to Get Used To
1. Dad is gone.
2. I am Louis's girlfriend.
3. Louis is my boyfriend. (Can't decide which sounds less weird.)
4. Vivian can't fly any more.
5. Zach can't hurt us any more than he already has.
6. Mom and Michael and Lorraine need me.
7. I'm done with Wattsville.

Number Seven is the only one I announced to my family, around noon. "I've decided I'm coming home for good, you guys—after my Horizon finals." *Because of Numbers One through*

Six, I didn't add. "Thanks for the soup, Mom."

"Don't rush into anything, babe," Mom told me, draping an afghan over Louis's and my intertwined feet on the couch. "Everything's crazy now. When things go back to normal, you'll feel differently. You're so close to graduating. And those little Chinese girls of yours…"

But I'd stopped listening at "back to normal." *Hah.* Dad is gone. I can write it; still can't believe it.

Under the afghan I felt Louis rub my calf with his foot. No one blinked an eye when he shuffled me down the stairs this morning and installed us on opposite ends of the couch; no pointed smiles, no questions. The day was calm—too calm, like Lorraine, drinking tea in the kitchen. Through the doorway I saw her shake her head, looking out the window like she was sharing a Parenting Moment with someone out there.

"That's so lame, Joss," Michael snorted from Dad's armchair. It was such a relief to hear his old snotty tone, my head clogged back up with tears. "Dad was so proud of you taking college classes on the mainland and now you're just gonna ditch? Like you gotta stay home and take care of everyone? Whaddya think *my* job is?"

Same as mine. But my throat hurt too much to argue. *Louis is on my side at least.* Louis knows home is where you go when things fall apart. *And we can be together, girlfriend and boyfriend.*

"Michael's right," my boyfriend muttered as my brother stomped into the kitchen. "You got too much going on in Wattsville. Your dad wouldn't want you to—"

Couldn't reach to put my hand over his mouth, so I settled for a kick. *Dad would too want me to come home.* Dad said my weak spot was not knowing what I don't know. Well, I know now: how much I have on Dalby. How messed up the outside world is. And how stupid I am for thinking I could change that.

The phone rang; everyone jumped. Mom picked up.

"Hello? Just a minute." She covered the mouthpiece and held the phone out to Lorraine next to her at the counter. "It's the coast guard. Do you…"

Lorraine jerked away like the phone was a cobra. She shook her head and didn't stop.

I saw Mom square her shoulders as she put the phone back to her ear. "His wife's unavailable. I'm the mother of Ron Burgowski's children. Go ahead."

Silence swallowed us. Michael stood frozen in the kitchen, one hand on the fridge door. From across the room I searched Mom's eyes desperately with mine.

"Yes. Ohhh…" she whispered, staring at nothing. "I see."

Lorraine clenched her hands around her face.

"I see," Mom whispered again. She held the receiver with both hands, like something fragile.

"Mom!" My voice erupted like the scream of a crow. "Say it!"

She laid the phone down on the counter without hanging up. Her lips barely moved as she reached to touch Lorraine's arm. "The Canadian coast guard found him," she murmured.

Lorraine stilled her head-shaking. A tiny whimper escaped her hands.

Mom gripped Lorraine's shoulder under her silvery hair. From the living room I saw Lorraine shiver, like something huge was rattling her from inside. "They're airlifting him to Seattle. Ron's still alive."

CHAPTER NINETEEN

FAMILY FIRST

Merry Christmas. We're one big mess. Since getting the news five days ago, all we pretty much do is cry and laugh like crazy people.

I was right: Dad and Aaron put on survival suits when they made that distress call. Mom said Dad doesn't know how long they were in the water, or how long he lay on the rocks on a teensy Canadian island, but that suit saved him.

Aaron's still missing. Mom joins the vigil every night. I didn't know Aaron real well, but it's sickening to think he went crabbing with Dad as a favor to Michael. Aaron's supposed to be enjoying a cozy, retired Christmas with Elly and their grandkids and that awesome golden retriever. That poor family. Our suffering felt endless, but it only lasted thirty-six hours. Theirs drags on.

Aaron's disappearance is gonna mess Dad up, worse than he is already. And he's bad. Fractured skull, broken arm, broken leg. Somehow he didn't drown or die of hypothermia. But no one's expecting a second miracle for Aaron.

I'm sick now. Louis distracts me, playing Bananagrams and feeding me caramel pudding—people keep bringing food!—and reading me *Harry Potter and the Chamber of Secrets* till his throat probably hurts like mine. Cuddling together's starting to feel normal—if "normal" means "whoa…this is real." I need to fly SO BAD, but Mom won't let me out of the house till I quit feeling dizzy.

"No way could you make it to Seattle, babe, and I know you'd try," she told me—after bragging about her own flight to check on Dad last night. She's staying here to take care of me.

Lorraine's been at the hospital since some nice Dalby pilot flew her there. Michael's spent the last five days doing who-knows-what down at the marina. He drags home for meals in a guilty heap—"Shoulda never let 'em go without me." He hasn't asked to borrow a car to visit Dad.

Christmas evening, the phone showed another call from Hawaii. This time I let Mom hand it to me.

Vivian: "Joss! You're *there!* Omigod, I've been going *nuts!* Of *course* you didn't wanna answer. Are you *okay?* Of *course* you aren't, you must be going *nuts.*"

Me: "No, no, I'm not! I mean I am, but it's good nuts. They found him, Vivian. He almost died, we all thought he died, but he didn't. He got washed on this island in the middle of nowhere and some Canadian lady found him unconscious on the beach and called the police and they called the coast guard and... [pausing for air]...they boated him to Victoria and helicoptered him to Seattle."

Vivian: "Oh, *wow.* Omigod. So he's *okay?*"

Me: "He's not at all okay, he's all smashed up, but he's alive! He wanted to come home for Christmas but they wouldn't let him."

Vivian: "Oh, merry *Christmas!* I guess I can say that now. Omigod, what a *miracle*—your ocean's so cold and *scary.* And you sound terrible. Are you *sick?*"

Me: "Yeah."

Vivian: "Poor *you!* I've been so *worried* since you took off— wow, a whole *week* ago. I stopped by your room before I left for Hawaii. Dawntae gave me your home number —she tried to call too. So did Eli. I can't *wait* to tell him the news."

Me: "Sorry for not answering. It was...pretty bad."

Vivian: [quietly] "Don't feel sorry. Your dad is wonderful. You're the luckiest girl on the planet."

Me: [eyes and throat clenched] *I know. I know.*

Vivian: "You still there, Joss?"

Me: "Uh-huh. Sorry. So, you in Hawaii now?"

Vivian: "Yeah. I flew home the day after I...after I saw you in the church. I was pretty much a *wreck.*"

Me: "I should've called you back. You were feeling horrible, and I just, like, abandoned you. I'm sorry."

Vivian: "It's okay. I was kinda used to not flying, right? So I'll live."

Me: "Yeah, but..."

Vivian: "Let's not talk about it, okay? I just...well, I want to wish you a super merry *Christmas.*"

Me: "You too. What's it like there?"

Vivian: "It's...*interesting*, like always. I'm helping Mom make red-cooked pork. My stepdad's watching football. But Joss, I'm so *happy* for you. Can't wait to see you in *January.*"

Me: *Yeah, about that...* "Me too, Vivian. Thanks for calling. Merry Christmas, okay?"

Hearing the defeat in her voice tightened my stomach. *Couldn't save my fellow Flyer. Now I'm ditching her and my girls both.*

Mom called from the door, "I'm off to the vigil, babe. Keep drinking that honey-lemon." I closed my eyes against a sudden sob—for Aaron's family, maybe.

They're sending Dad home tomorrow! Our day-after-day-after-Christmas present. Lorraine called from the hospital—even put Dad on long enough to mumble, "Hey, honey." Made me cry again. Who knew I had so much salt water in me?

Ugh. Salt water. I am SO going flying as soon as they let me out of the house, but I am SO sticking to the woods. I'm done with circles over Wattsville Bay. Done with Wattsville, period.

But two days after hearing Vivian's quiet surrender, my stomach still felt heavy.

A tap at my door. "Come in," I croaked. My headache had eased, but my throat stayed raw.

The door stayed closed. "Hey, it's me, but I'm hanging out here, 'kay?" said Savannah's voice from the hall. "Don't wanna bring your germs home to Ginny. No offense. I left your Christmas present under the tree—you guys haven't gotten to celebrate yet, huh?"

"Not yet—waiting for Dad." Felt good to smile an ordinary smile. "Merry late Christmas, Savannah."

"Merry freakin' Christmas to *you*, girlfriend. This is all so insane. They still haven't found Aaron, huh?"

"Not yet." I cleared my throat painfully and tried to picture Savannah in the hallway, leaning her curvy hip on my door. "What'd Ginny get for Christmas?"

"Way too much stuff. We might actually keep the outfits the Howes sent; they're pretty sweet. Ty's mom must've bought 'em."

I sipped some tea. "Savannah, are you still refusing help from the Howes? If they want to be grandparents, what's wrong with that?"

"Oh, don't get me started," Savannah sighed. "But yeah— they're helping. Kids are expensive." Her musical laugh sounded a little flat. "Know what I figured out, Joss? My parents are saints. I could never, ever be raising Gin-Gin without 'em."

I lifted my mug to the door. "Here's to saintly parents."

"Speaking of which…I saw Michael at work. He says your dad comes home tomorrow?" Savannah asked. "That's awesome. How long d'you get to be with him, before you go back?" I noticed she skipped the "fancy prep school" snark.

"Monday after New Year's. Horizon was gonna give me time off when they thought—you know—but since Dad's back, I'm just gonna bust through my finals and come home."

"Wait—home?" Up went the volume. "*Home* home? You're taking my advice after all?"

Whatever, Savannah. "Yeah. I kinda need to be here now." *And I kinda need not to be there.*

"Damn, girl, that is awesome! Giving you an air-hug! But," her volume dropped back to normal, "what about those Chinese girls of yours? Thought you were, like, in charge of 'em."

My headache crept back. "Yeah, well. You were right. They have official people to take care of 'em now. They don't need me."

"Huh," my bestie said behind the door. "I seriously doubt that. Kids always need. That's what being a mom's all about, or a mentor or whatever you are to them. But family comes first. You are absolutely doing the right thing, girl."

Suddenly I really, really needed to stop talking. I managed some more thanks to Savannah and she departed to give Ginny my virtual kiss. I closed my eyes, but my headache had taken over.

My phone rang again, jolting me out of a doze. The screen said Daniel Wainwright. *Who in the...? Oh, jeez—Rialta's dad.* I stuffed the phone under the mattress until the ringing stopped.

Then the downstairs phone started. I heard Mom pick up. Then low murmurs.

Somehow, I knew. I closed my eyes, picturing the Christmas photo of Aaron's family.

A few minutes later, another door-tap. I opened my eyes to see Mom looking in. Her face confirmed it. "Babe, that was Elly. They found Aaron."

I opened my arms and she crossed the room and leaned into them. We cried together for what might have been, and what was.

Finally! A week after his rescue, Miracle Dad was on his way home. His kids were celebrating by arguing about his hospital bed.

"He's gotta keep his head raised, Michael, he'll need bolsters!" Dang, it felt good, having my voice back. "That's why they call 'em bolsters, they bolster you."

"You learn that in college? Wow, I better enroll," Michael sneered. "This bed cranks higher, dumbass. You don't need SAT-word pillows."

"Fine." I loftily ignored his rudeness and cranked the fancy bed. "How come you didn't go with Mom to pick Dad up? Or go to the hospital at all? I would've if they'd let me."

"Had to work." Michael frowned, tucking the starchy sheet.

I frowned back. "B.s. You coulda gone anytime."

"I'm done with hospitals," Michael said, and my heart twinged with memory: *Mom, after her suicide attempt. Michael himself, when he hurled himself off Whittier's Bluff trying to be another Flying Burgowski.*

I said, "Yeah, I get that." We shared a history-heavy look across the gleaming bed.

"But Michael," I added, "it's not your fault, what happened. You couldn't have saved them, any more than I could. If you'd been there, we might've lost you...like Aaron."

He dropped his gaze. "I know," he mumbled. "Just can't stand feeling so—I dunno. Powerless, I guess. You wouldn't understand."

Powerless to help? I opened my mouth to tell him about Vivian's grounding, then shrugged. *Not bringing myself back down now.*

"Well, I think Dad's gonna love all the work you put in while he was gone. Better ask him for a raise when he gets a new boat. And promotion to, like, Lord High First Mate or whatever."

I ducked as he threw a bolster at me. *Michael's cool. Louis loves me. Dad's alive.*

I checked my watch. "Hey, ferry's here in twenty minutes. Dad still needs to eat soft stuff. Wanna make ramen?"

"I wanna go to the ferry dock, is what I wanna do," Michael

muttered. The key to Dad's truck was at the bottom of the ocean with the *Flyer*. And Mom took Lorraine's car to Seattle 'cause hers picked this week to die.

"We could bike," I suggested. "No, wait—you took your bike apart. Let's just stay here, Michael, and get lunch ready...what?" My brother was staring at me.

"Or we could fly," he said.

Flyer Boot Camp and Wattsville's hills had me in great shape, but I'd been sick for a week. And Michael was solid muscle from months of deck-handing. Attempting a doubles takeoff from our front yard nearly flattened me.

"You're too heavy," I gasped, plopping onto our front step. "Let's just wait here."

Michael paced the overgrown lawn. "No, no, there's gotta be a way." His face was lit up for the first time since I came home. "You can take off alone, right?"

"'Course." I pushed myself off the stoop into the air to hover at chest-height. It took a ridiculous effort, but Michael didn't need to know that.

"Okay. I got this. Wait there!" and Michael dashed back into the house. Half a minute later, an upstairs window opened and Michael stuck his head out. "Come get me!"

"No way!" But my Flyer body was already rising. Michael has his own powers, like innovation. And whaddyacallit—perseverance.

"This'll never work," I muttered, maneuvering into the window like a docking spacecraft as Michael slithered over the sill.

But it did work. In the air, my body accepted his weight like no big deal. So we sped over the treetops, giggling like little kids as Michael gripped my extended elbows. The clouds were high, magnifying the jagged line of freshly-snowed mountains on the mainland. Far to the north I could see the smokestacks of Wattsville's ugly side. *Two more weeks there and I'm home for good with my Ground Crew.* We made the dock parking lot in minutes, and dipped into a scratchy gap in the trees for a private landing—which flattened me again. Totally worth it.

Michael and I waved like crazy when Lorraine's little Subaru appeared on the ferry ramp, and she pulled into the parking lot, smiling like she'd expected us all along. And there was my big, strong Dad sitting sideways in the backseat, his white-casted arm carefully propped, and his face...*whoa.*

I bit down hard—*no more crying.* Michael looked like he was doing the same thing. Dad's usually ruddy face was hollowed and grayish, with stitches running from eye to jaw on the right side. The left side was dark with bruising, and his beautiful chin cleft was hidden by thick stubble.

"Aw, kiddos," Dad murmured as Lorraine lowered his window. "Looks worse than it is." His lips barely moved, but his brown eyes smiled.

Mom stuffed me and Michael into the way-back and slammed the hatchback door, then hopped into the front seat again. Dad's hospital smell filled the car.

"I'm coming home, Dad," I blurted as we wound up the hill. "Soon as I finish my finals. I want to be on Dalby now."

Dad's eyes seemed to brighten. He mumbled something—*about nut shells?*

From up front, I heard Lorraine's whispery laugh. She'd had nearly a week of Dad-translation practice. "Ron's being smart, Joss," she called. "Remember when you were going through your *Hamlet* phase, throwing all those quotes around?"

"Fun times," Michael put in.

"Well, I think your Dad just threw one back at you, right, Ron?" She caught his eye in the mirror. "He just said, 'Not feeling "bounded in a nutshell" anymore?'"

My face heated up—a weird mix of shame for selfish Old Joss, and joy that I got to start over. "Dad, you are so cool." I held myself back from hugging his battered head. "No more 'bounded in a nutshell.' Sorry I ever said that. I love it here. And yeah," I finished the quote, "I 'count myself king of infinite space.' So there."

Dad's tight lips moved. "Queen."

CHAPTER TWENTY

WHEN YA GOTTA GO

D ee Hightower was disappointed in me. She didn't say so when I told her about leaving Wattsville, but I could translate, "Well, you have to do what's best."

Yes, I do. I closed my phone to get back to Pre-Calc. *Why doesn't what's best feel best?*

I'd been back at Horizon three days; felt like ten. I'd ridden the ferry from Dalby so happy—*Dad's okay, Louis loves me; see you guys in three weeks!*

And then, from the bus, I saw the "Wattsville" sign and— BOOM. *Leaving the girls. Leaving flightless Vivian.* I labored up to my room under a load of guilt, to face the roomies I was also leaving.

Three days of defending my decision hadn't lightened the load. Now I know something else I didn't know: Rialta and Dawntae love me. I told them about Dad, and they shook their heads. I can't handle their hurt faces. I can barely handle my Horizon exam reviews. How'd I ever manage *two* sets of friends and classes?

Rialta breezed in, bundled in her new purple ski jacket and earflap hat. January had suddenly remembered itself. "It's cold as poop!" she announced. Then: "What are you doing here? My dad's down at the Fir Street house having lunch with the girls and Mrs. Carson. He said you were coming."

"I said I *might*," I answered, fighting the heaviness. "But that quiz this morning—yikes. I gotta study. The girls'll be happy to eat my share of anything."

"Uh-huh." Rialta tossed her hat and coat through her doorway but stayed in our common room, frowning. "But Joss. Coastal's still on break, right? So you could be with the girls even more now. How come you're already blowing them off?"

"I'm not blowing them off! I got 'em all Christmas presents before break! Hey," I tried for a change of subject, "can you help me with problem six?"

"Seriously, Joss?" Rialta stepped over to my desk, head cocked. "You're their Big Sister. You were practically ready to adopt Peachy—"

"Peach. Her name's Chuntao, Spring Peach, so I call her—"

"Who cares what you call her if you desert her?" my roommate demanded. "Joss, I do NOT get you. Quitting Horizon to be with your dad—great, wonderful. But since you got back, you're acting like Horizon's this tunnel you have to drive through, no stopping for anybody."

I felt pinned to my chair. "I'm leaving anyway, so what if it's sooner or later?" I mumbled.

"Ask Peach so what! Like she doesn't already have abandonment issues." Rialta shook her head in disgust. "But no—what matters is, Jocelyn doesn't like feeling guilty. So go on home and take care of your family. But quit pretending there's no side effects." She marched into her room and shut the door.

"I'm not pretending," I muttered. *I just know now what I didn't know.* But Rialta wouldn't get that. And I was still stuck on problem six.

It took Eli to unstick me. Not from Pre-Calc, but from my room. My tunnel. When my phone interrupted the fascinating wall-staring that followed Rialta's little pep-talk, I snatched it.

"Jossaroony-tunes. What is *up* with you, *chica*?"

"Nothing, why?" I said, not defensive at all. "Are you back already?"

"Nope, journeying to the Ville of Watts tomorrow. I'm at my mom's in Seattle, freezing my ass off and battling the demons of childhood. But anyhoo." I pictured him tossing his hair out of his eyes. "Ah dinna call for a pity-party, lass. I have exactly thrrrrrrree messages for ye."

Eli makes me smile. *And that look he shares with Brady—Louis gives me that look now. So, why so tense?* "Ohh-kay," I said.

He cleared his throat with a prim "ha-hem." "Item the first. Our dear Lady Vivian calls me all the way from Oahu to ask if I know why you're mad at her."

"I'm not—"

"Item the second," Eli continued calmly, "our dear friend Dee of the High Tower calls me from the Street of Fir to ask if I know why you passed up lunch with the girls today. She seems to think," he added, "that Dear Eli's got more cred with you than she does. Don't know why, since you haven't returned Dear Eli's calls either. That's Number Three, in case you couldn't tell."

My mouth was dry; I sipped some cold tea. "Eli, I'm sorry," I told him. *Drive through your tunnel, Flygirl.* "I'm not mad at anybody. I'm just trying to study for Horizon finals and get through the next two weeks." I sounded so lame. "And since I'm going home then anyway, I figure, why make things harder…"

Eli spluttered, and I closed my eyes. *Way to tell him, moron.* Add Eli to the Disappointed in Joss List. The rest of the conversation turned me into a blob of mush.

But even blobs have limits. When Eli started insisting that I organize a goodbye picnic as "guilt pay for abandoning the wee Asiatic lasses," I pushed back.

"A picnic, really? It's freakin' January. I'll take them out to Vivian's café, then we can go to the park—happy?"

"Yes. Take them to Bean There, Done That," Eli decreed, "where the Fair Vivian can dispense hot chocolate with extra whip. And you have to buy each girl her own gargantuan cookie. And take me flying."

"I can't, Eli," I told him, voice low in case Rialta was listening. "I don't want Vivian to feel bad. But I'll go see the girls now. Okay? "

But stepping out of Nutschel into the bright, freezing afternoon, I was the one feeling bad. I still suck at Pre-Calc, and now Eli thinks I'm a weasel. *Yeah—and wait till Vivian and the wee Asiatic lasses join the list of the Disappointed.*

Sweet-faced Mrs. Carson, the foster mom, soured up at the door and scolded me for not calling ahead, and for "interrupting Miss Sheldon." Lunch was history, Mr. Wainwright was gone, and the tutor he'd hired—aha, Miss Linda Sheldon— was teaching a lesson on "Parts of the Body." But when Peach caught a glimpse of me from the living room, all the girls' body parts moved toward me, and "Zhoss!!" disappeared into a giggling dogpile. Miss Sheldon, blond, with thick mascara, was not thrilled either.

But after I untangled myself, and went through nine "How ah you?"/"I am fine!"'s, and promised them "chonglet-chip" cookies if they focused on their lesson, and joined in singing, "Head and Shoulders, Knees and Toes," Miss Sheldon relaxed.

"Call me Linda," she said, with a hint of Southern accent, and Mrs. Carson, watching from her laundry-folding, shot us her crinkly smile.

After the body parts, we shared the Chips Ahoy I brought and the girls Showed-and-Told their Christmas presents: fuzzy gloves from Mr. Wainwright; hair accessories from Dee; pretty cotton nightgowns from the Carsons; daypacks full of school stuff from the church. But their favorite gifts—yay!—were the posters I'd given them three weeks ago.

Mrs. Carson approved Eli's Bean There "picnic" idea, with

herself as chaperone. I somehow didn't manage to tell her it was really a goodbye picnic. She and Linda both told me, "Come back *any* time," and when I left, I got eleven hugs.

For the first time since Dalby, all my body parts wanted to fly. I barely made it to the waterfront for takeoff in the early darkness. In spirals over Campus Hill, I thought about those Christmas posters—Daiyu's horse, Peach's kittens, each claiming a small space of self—and smiled. But I felt the smile twist, like all my emotions were fighting to claim their own space.

Round and round and round, like Hamlet: *"Sir, in my heart there was a kind of fighting..."* I flew so long I missed dinner, but Rialta was so psyched with me for seeing the girls that she ordered a pizza. It tasted like guilt.

Voicemail from Lorraine, after pizza: "Your dad's doing so much better, Joss. He says to tell you, don't come home just because of him. Figure out what's best for you and do it—that's what he wants. Me too."

What's best is home—why are you making this so hard? Lorraine said a bunch of other stuff, but that's all I remember.

Voicemail from Mom, half an hour later: "How're your girls, babe? How're you? No news, just checking in. Hope you're still feeling 'un-bounded' from that nutshell—that's why you went away, remember? Anyway, call back when you feel like it. Love you."

I didn't feel like it. *Mom's not who you need to call. Put on your big-girl panties, Flygirl.* So I closed my bedroom door for privacy and called Vivian.

Me: "Hey, it's Joss. Happy Thursday. I've never called Hawaii before—what time is it?"

Vivian: "Three hours earlier. My folks are at work; it's great to have the TV off. You studying?"

Me: "Yeah. [awkward silence] Look, I am so sorry I haven't called you back…"

Vivian: "Oh, it's okay, Joss. You have finals, right? And your *dad* to worry about."

Me: "No, no, it's not okay. Vivian, I should've let you know sooner. [deep breath] I'm done with Coastal; I'm going home in two weeks."

Vivian: "Oh."

Me: "I'm sorry! I've been too chickens--t to tell you. But I gotta be with my family now. Feels wrong, staying away. Also, Louis and I…we're a thing now."

Vivian: [so low I can barely hear] "Uh-huh. That's great, Joss. Makes sense."

Me: "No it doesn't! Quit being so understanding! I'm a terrible friend."

Vivian: [still quiet] "No, you're just…well, whatever. Is your dad doing better?"

Me: "Yes! He's in a wheelchair for now. It's weird. But when I left he was already talking about what's next. He's done with fishing."

Vivian: "Wow. He adored that boat, right? How's he gonna deal with being stuck on dry *land?*"

[downright painful silence]

Me: "Vivian, I'm so SORRY, it's my fault I didn't teach you enough, I knew how hard it is to resist Zach, and I'll never forgive myself for letting him ground you!"

Vivian: "I wasn't talking about *me*, Joss. Let it go. Hang on—" [muffled conversation] "Mom's home, she needs something. I'll be back Sunday. You can tell me all about Louis when I see you, um…"

Me: "Wednesday. I got study groups and practice finals till then, but Wednesday we're having, like, a picnic. At your café. Me and the girls and Mrs. Carson, their foster mom. It's Eli's idea."

Vivian: "A *picnic*, at Bean There? Okayyy." [pause] "Joss… you mean a *goodbye* picnic, right? How are the girls taking it?"

Me: "I…haven't told 'em yet. I'll tell 'em Wednesday."

Vivian: "Really? [another pause] Joss…if *this* Island Girl can make it in Wattsville, why can't you?"

Me: "It's not about me! I spent a whole year being a jerk to my family, and then I ditched 'em, and my dad almost died. I *belong* at home, okay?"

Vivian: "Well, if that's…oh, never mind. See you Wednesday, anyway."

Me: "Yeah. See ya. Safe trip."

Back at Fir Street next day after my English study session, Mrs. Carson handed me a packet with an apologetic look. Now that the girls are official Wards of the State, I have to fill out a six-page volunteer form and get fingerprinted. "Not sure if they'll allow that café field trip thing," Mrs. Carson added. Tutor Linda let me join her lesson on "How Do I Feel Today?" so now, along with their words—"today I'm feeling happy," "excited"—my girls know "grumpy."

Rialta rolled her eyes at the volunteer forms and vented about Big Government, but when I called Dee to complain, she shrugged me off. "Welcome to my world," Dee said. "You let a little paperwork stop you, you're not in it to win it. But hold up—you're leaving, right? Those forms'll take three weeks to process. Why bother?"

"I can still come back to visit," I told Dee. From her room I heard Rialta snort. *How Do I Feel Today? Like we discussed in English this morning: Internal Conflict.*

Saturday. Louis's voice: "Hey, it's me. Leave a message."

Me: "Hey, Louis. This feels so WEIRD—you with a phone. This is me. It's so stupid that I had to come back here just long enough to feel crappy about everything, y'know? Okay, done whining. Call me."

Sunday. Vivian's back. She just called to say that. What she didn't say:

1. How she feels, grounded for good just when she'd fallen in love with her power.
2. How she feels about Zach, who did that to her.
3. How she feels about seeing her Flyer friend who's too chicken to ask her how she feels.

Monday. Good news: the Pre-Calc practice final didn't destroy me. Better news: Mrs. Carson says I'm allowed to be with the girls while my paperwork goes through. Wednesday's supposed to be sunny. Maybe we can picnic for real, and while we're having fun in the sun, I'll tell the girls I'm leaving, and they'll be fine. We can practice Body Parts and Feelings: *My heart feels happy.*

Yeah, right.

Tuesday. Louis: "Your dad said do what's best? Well, duh, Joss— how's coming back to Dalby 'best'? Let's see, you can make a bunch of sad little girls happy and graduate early, or...hmm... run back home to be with your boyfriend."

Me: "It's not about my boyfriend!"

Louis: "Wow, thanks."

Me: "Oh, stop, you know what I mean. I thought my dad was *dead*, Louis. People don't just get over that, okay? Could you?"

Louis: "You mean if I knew who my dad was?"

Me: ...

Louis: "Sorry, that didn't come out right. Just...don't do like your mom, okay?"

Me: "What's that s'posed to mean? I'm coming home, not grounding myself!"

Louis: "I didn't say that."

Me: "But you're thinking it."

Louis: "Joss, I miss you like crazy. But if you come home and wish you hadn't, you'll be...you know. Not much fun."

Wednesday afternoon, Bean There Picnic Day, Vivian came around the café counter and hugged me before I even got my jacket off. *So much for worrying about her seeing me again.* "Happy New Year," she murmured.

I hugged her back. "You too."

The girls spotted the stack of giant cookies and started to squeal. Eli and Brady were grinning, along with everyone else in the café. I still hadn't broken my news. *Maybe after the cocoa...*

"Ooooh!" Meili pointed to some bars in shiny wrappers piled on the counter like miniature gold bricks. "Can I please have?"

"Vivian, what're those?" I asked. She stepped back behind the counter with a proud smile, and I looked again. "No way! It's the slavery-free chocolate?" She smiled bigger. "You did it! You got them to sell these instead!" *Typical Joss—forgot all about Vivian's project.*

Two minutes later, her "chonglet" bar projects were being unwrapped and stuffed into the mouths of my nine T-visa "projects." Mrs. Carson, in lavender velour sweats for the occasion, gasped, "Oh, my!" at the price of the bars, but accepted her cappuccino with a graceful nod.

"Did Prof K give you an A on your project too?" Vivian asked me, reading my thoughts.

"A-minus," I admitted. "Kinda skimpy on the footnotes. But hey—a B in Mandarin! Totally thanks to you. *Sheh-sheh.*" I saluted her with the latte she'd just handed me, and joined Mrs. Carson, Eli, Brady and the girls at our table-cluster.

Brady stole his Mickey Mouse watch back from Peach's skinny arm ("wrist, ehbow, ahm"). Men usually turn the girls stiff—even Mr. Wainwright, after all he's done—but Brady and Eli were instant big brothers. After ten minutes, along with "foh-head" and "eah-ring," the girls knew "you mine, sucka," "wassap?" and "I got dis."

"It's two forty," Brady announced, licking remnants of whipped cream. "Viv's off in twenty minutes? I wanna get in that sun!"

"We should have another couple hours of it," said Mrs. Carson. She poked the bulky laundry bag Eli had stuffed under our table. "And I can't wait to see what you kids are planning."

"Hey, you minx!" Eli swatted at Lanying as she jacked his coffee.

"You won't like that, honey," Mrs. Carson warned, and we all laughed at Lanying's clenched face when she tasted it anyway. The latte-sipping folks at the nearby tables were leaning our way like we were a sunlamp. I guess we were.

Twenty minutes later, hopped up on cacao, all fourteen of us were trooping toward Wattsville Memorial Park. Daiyu staggered in front, helping Eli lug his lumpy bag, and the rest of us Americans each held the hands of two girls. Wattsville drivers waved and smiled.

Waiting for the Walk light, Ah Lam skipped in place, pigtails bobbing. "How do you feel, Ah Lam?" I asked.

She squeezed my hand. "I feel happy. Sank you. How do you feel, Zhoss?"

I squeezed back. "I feel…" *all rumpled up* "… happy too, thank you." Sure enough, as Ah Lam and Meili turned "happy-too-sank-you" into a little song over the next three blocks, my flight-engines started to hum with stress.

Two blankets, four bags of chips, some baby carrots, juice boxes and a soccer ball: that's what Eli's bag produced. "Picnic time!" Eli proclaimed, tossing me a blanket to spread.

"Oh, good, something healthy," Mrs. Carson approved, opening the carrots. Vivian took one, but the girls attacked the chips.

"Already Americans," Brady sighed, and Mrs. Carson nodded again. *She gets it. I should be thrilled to leave my girls with her…* I dug my fingers into the grass, anchoring myself.

"Heads up, Joss!" Eli called as the soccer ball sailed my way.

If I play, I'm going airborne. "Brady, go get it!" I tossed the ball at him, Peach intercepted, and down the green they raced, hands full of chips. Mrs. Carson trotted after, a mobile purple cheer squad. "Hit me, I'm open!" Jiao shouted in perfect TV English, and my engines revved harder.

"C'*mon*, Joss," Vivian urged, jogging in place. "Grown-ups against kids—we can *take* 'em!"

Grown-ups? I jerked my head at Vivian, beckoning her closer. "Can't," I muttered. "Gotta stay sitting or I'm gonna launch right here."

Her flushed face stiffened for a second. "Oh..." She looked around nervously. "But...but it's okay, Joss, right? I mean you still can!" she whispered. "You said we don't have to worry about Zach any more..."

"Well, yeah, but I can't fly here," I whispered back. My heart expanded with gratitude—*Vivian's not bitter!*—which only revved me more. The soccer group was fifty yards away now. "You go on—tell 'em I have a tummy ache or something." I crossed one leg over the other, pressing down. *Joy? Guilt?* Given up guessing what sets the magic off.

"Oh," Vivian said in a funny voice. "Let me feel it. I want to feel it one more time." Before I could think of what to say, she leaned down from behind me and placed her hands on my shoulders. An inch from her fingertips, my power was pulsating with desire for the sky.

I closed my eyes to the weird picture we must make, Guilty Flyer Futilely Sharing Magic With Yearning Ex-Flyer. "

Vivian, I'm sorry." *Shut down,* I willed myself. *She doesn't need this.*

Vivian stayed quiet. Her fingers began to vibrate on my collarbone.

"This is too weird," I said. Down the field, Mrs. Carson hollered, "Goooooal!"

"Shhh," Vivian murmured above me. "I'm feeling it."

"Seriously, let go. You're gonna freak out the girls." The girls were a hundred yards away, *but stop torturing yourself, Vivian… you can't fly.* I opened my eyes and moved to stand up, but Vivian clamped her fingers tighter. "What are you *doing?*"

"Joss, I feel it!" she gasped. "It's coming back to life. Oh!" and she dropped her hands and sprinted across the green.

Good, she's joining in the soccer, I thought for a confused second, but Vivian was dashing for the woods. Not a deep, dark forest like on Dalby, but enough thick-limbed maples to give cover to an ex-Flyer who still believes… *Oh, this is sad.* I closed my eyes again.

I heard the girls' shouts, bright bursts of sound. "You mine, sucka!"

"I got dis, I got dis!"

"Woo-hoo!"

Except the "woo-hoo" was coming from the woods. And it didn't stop.

I'd never taken off from my butt before, but suddenly I was in the air and streaking like a bullet for the trees. *Hope Mrs. Carson and the girls are watching the ball!* Next second I almost crashed us both, sharing a mid-air hug with my Flyer friend in the treetops of Wattsville Memorial Park.

"How're you doing this?" I gasped, clutching Vivian's arms. *Stupid—she needs those right now.* I let go, and we flailed, tangling with the leafless maple. Then, like synchronized swimmers, we pushed off the same branch to hover in the lowering sunlight. Together.

Vivian was incandescent. "I don't know! I don't care! I'm not grounded!" She always sucked at hovering, but now she was a hummingbird, vibrating with confidence.

"What-the-hell?-What-the-hell?-What-the-hell?" I wanted to zip and whoop and barrel roll. But we had nine kids and a nice lady down there who couldn't handle our secret. And must have been wondering where we'd disappeared to. "Vivian, we gotta go down."

"I know," she said breathlessly, and turned a perfect somersault. "Oh, I forgot how that *feels*."

"Come on." I grabbed her hand and guided her down behind the biggest tree. "Ooh, you're scratched up."

"So're *you*!" Her eyes were shining like being scratched by a tree was the best thing *ever*.

"What just happened?" My brain raced: *Did I somehow reverse the effects of Zach's Stander prayer when I took him down? If Vivian's restored now, is he too?* But we couldn't stay there yapping. We scrambled through ferns to the path.

Vivian murmured with each step, "I don't know, I don't know, I don't know." But her smile was enormous.

"Viv-yan, Zhoss!" I heard Hua yell as we trotted out of the woods. No one missed us, so intent on their game—*thank you, Eli!* We joined in, passing, blocking, sprinting around the green in a wild free-for-all with no set teams or goals. Or maybe all one team with one goal.

"Zhoss, Viv-yan, you feeling huht?" Peach asked a short while later, looking at our scratched faces. We were sprawled in a heap, sucking down the juice boxes. The sun had dropped below the treetops—*our treetops!*—but we were all toasty with exercise, especially Mrs. Carson, wiping her forehead with a lavender sleeve.

"Oh, my," she said, and the girls joined in with chirpy sympathy. "You two find a briar patch?"

No blurting this time. We were "grown-ups" under twelve pairs of curious eyes.

"Yeah," I said cautiously. "Vivian suddenly had to *go*." I smiled at the girls; they'd learned this shorthand for "bassroom." Then I looked hard at Eli and added, "You know—*go*. She didn't think she *could*, but suddenly she *had* to…"

"And I *did!*" Vivian crowed. The girls giggled, like who wouldn't if a grown-up made such a big deal of going pee-pee in the woods?

Eli frowned. "If you're saying what I think you are…" We nodded.

"Oh, dear," said Mrs. Carson. "At your age, hon?"

"But how?" Eli interrupted. "You've been a wreck since the night of the Bash, Vivvo. You were…"

"Yes, Vivian used to feel sad," I put in, nodding cheerfully to the girls and their foster mom. "But now she feels happy. Tell us, Vivian, when Zach made you feel…uh…sad that night—how did you start feeling happy again?"

"Happy to go to bassroom?!" Peach shrieked.

"Yes, *very* happy!" Vivian laughed a mini-whoop. "Zach was saying those *words* to me, you know, and I—I had to *go* then too. But the more he talked, the less I *felt* like it…" Her voice faded, "And I haven't felt like going since."

"Goodness gracious!" Mrs. Carson looked like the definition of "baffled."

"Poh Viv-yan!" the girls chorused, and patted Vivian's arms. I was far away, visualizing what Dawntae had witnessed that December afternoon: Vivian hanging onto the lamppost, Zach kneeling. Grounding her with the ancient words.

Words. "Vivian, do you remember what Zach said?"

She looked at me like I was crazy. "What, the whole *prayer?* Of *course* not—"

"Prayer?" echoed Mrs. Carson.

Sorry, my Ground Crew's taking no new members. "Uh, I have to go to the bathroom for real—come with me, Vivian," I ordered.

"Me, too," Eli said quickly. "Brady, you mind getting the cleanup started? Be right back." He took my arm and Vivian's like a wedding usher, guiding us from our bewildered group toward the squat brick building across the green. Halfway there, he jerked his head to me. "Go on, Joss."

"Okay, yes—Vivian. The end of Zach's prayer. The last word. 'Amen.'" I squeezed Eli's wrist, like he could pass it on to Vivian; she looked dazed. "'Amen,' Vivian! Did you hear Zach say 'amen'?"

Vivian stopped, freeing herself from Eli. "What difference does that make?"

But Eli's eyebrows rose. "Ohhh," he said. "You think Zach didn't finish what he started? Tie it up with a bow?" He looked at Vivian, who was still frowning at me. "So she wasn't officially, one hundred percent grounded—she just *thought* she was?"

Back at the picnic, happy shrieks: the girls were pouncing on Brady like a pack of baby hyenas. Mrs. Carson, laughing, threw a crumpled chips bag at them.

"That's exactly what I think." I looked Vivian in the eye. "I think Zach started to pray you down. I think you were so freaked out that you thought he did. So, I think…"

"…I grounded myself?" Vivian whispered, looking wildly from me to Eli. "No, I couldn't. I loved it too much. I *felt* the power go…"

Eli and I looked at each other. Behind us, Brady started wolf-howling and the girls joined in. No one seemed to notice the three of us, gabbing on the grass.

"I got that punctured feeling, like when Zach tried to zap us at the waterfront. Leaking away." Vivian closed her eyes, narrating. "And I remember feeling like I was eight again, like when…when the Piece of Work came after me. Like I might disappear." She opened her eyes again, wide and distant. "I let go of the lamppost and walked away. So I wouldn't disappear." She swallowed. "Zach could've been saying anything. I walked away."

"Of course you walked away, darlin'," Eli said softly. He didn't ask about the Piece of Work; maybe Vivian had told him. "You let Zach think he won. 'Cause of that, Joss finds him at the Bash all cocky, and he lets his guard down. Boom. You couldn't have played it better."

What a perfect way to put it! "So yeah," I said, "I think you grounded yourself, Vivian, but Eli's right: it was like losing the battle to win the war. Now there's one less Stander, thanks to you."

"But, but…" In the dark gold sinking sun, Vivian's face flickered with emotion. "I feel like such an *idiot*! I've had such a *rotten* month, and now you're saying I could've been *celebrating..*? That makes my *head* explode."

"Ha!" Eli threw out his arms. "Try listening to you two from a normal person's point of view—abracadabra, magic powers? What-everrr. *Vamanos, chicas,"* he added, grabbing our arms again to steer us back to the picnic. "Let's get these kiddos home, then you can buy me and the Brade some hot-and-sour-soup and blow his mind like you've just blown mine."

"That was quick," Brady commented at our return, but no one asked why we never made it to the "bassroom," or why Vivian and I chose to "go" in the woods earlier. Happiness is a great mind-musher.

We started the "Clean-up Song" to finish collecting all our garbage and gear. If Lanying had asked how I felt, Vivian would have needed to translate, *My brain is Jell-O.*

When I whispered to Vivian, "So can I *please* tell Louis about you now?" she grinned and kept nodding, like she'd been saving up nods.

Still no good time to tell the girls. *Maybe back at Fir Street?*

Pulling his depleted laundry bag closed, Eli suddenly grabbed my arm again. "Hey, you magic mutant," he muttered. "Before you jet on back to your island, you're taking me flying. You or Viv, I don't care. You can fight over me."

CHAPTER TWENTY-ONE

QUEENS OF INFINITE SPACE

A week after the Amazing Flying Wu Recovery, Louis and I were boring each other to death on the phone. I couldn't stop telling him about Vivian—in code, in case Dawntae was listening through her music. And Louis couldn't stop telling me to stay in Wattsville.

Louis: "Hey, my ear hurts. And I got Mr. E's final tomorrow. Maybe we should..."

Me: "Oh, shoot! You gotta rest your brain. Last night I went to bed an hour early—that's how I survived Pre-Calc. For Mr. E, use tons of metaphors, he loves—"

Louis: "Joss. I got this. Didn't wanna talk about school—least, not *my* school. I just wanted you to know..."

Me: "I know. I *know*. It just feels wrong, being away now."

Louis: "From your Dad? Or from me?"

Me: "Both, dummy! And I don't have issues like Mom. I don't need to stay away from relationships just to prove I can."

Louis: "What about your girls? And your flying friend?"

Me: "Ahh, don't start again. Call me after Mr. E's final. But quit with the Wattsville stuff, okay? You're s'posed to be glad I'm coming home."

Louis: "I'm glad as hell you want to. But I'll be gladder if you don't. 'Night, Joss."

Next day I took my last two Horizon finals, a whole day of English and history essays. I kicked their butts. Collecting my phone from the exam monitor, I found three more messages from Eli:

"Hello, is this The Flying Burgowski? I wanna reserve a flight. Call me."

"Hey. Me. How 'bout now? Call, *chica*."

"Jossaleeeeeeen. Don't make me beg. All right, fine, I'll beg: Taaaake meeee flyyyying. *Please*."

Who knew you could totally love someone this exasperating? *My sympathies, Brady.* Heading out with the roomies into an afternoon already less dark than yesterday, I called him back.

"YES, Eli, but not now," I said before he could start. "Rialta and Dawntae are taking me out for Thai food. Where we are *not* gonna rehash essay topics," I added loudly. Rialta smiled; she's proud of her Hermione Granger habit.

"Tonight then, Jossalady? Just me, but Brady wants to watch. Ooh, that sounds dirty."

"No, not tonight either. My wonderful roomies are throwing me a goodbye party." Walking beside me, Tae gave a thumbs-up and I patted her cute panda hat. "Know how wonderful they are? They're filling out volunteer forms so they can visit the girls when I leave!"

"Oh, yeah, me too," Eli said as the roomies and I passed through the stone gates of our fancy prep school.

Gonna miss this pl— "Wait, what?"

"Yeah, me and Brady. We talked about it. Those girls are so damn cool. We wanna keep on hangin' with 'em."

"*You* are so damn cool!" I yelled, stopping sidewalk traffic. "Love you guys. And yeah—tomorrow I'm telling the girls I'm leaving. Gonna stop by at breakfast when Mom comes to take me home."

"Quick and painless, eh?" Eli's voice sounded neutral.

"Right. So you and me—we can go tomorrow morning. But it has to be early."

"How early?" Eli asked warily.

"Six. Meet in front of Hull."

He groaned. "Cruel wench! So be it. Where shall we…do the deed?"

"You'll see." Thanks to my brother, I've quit stressing about flying people heavier than me.

"Where you going at six in the morning with that foxy Eli?" Dawntae asked, opening the door of Golden Thailand.

I told the truth, sort of. "For a goodbye climb on the Coastal ropes course."

"Aaaaaaughaaaaughaaaaaaaaugh!" Eli shrieked when I stepped off our high Halloween platform next morning with him on my back. For a split second we dropped—then we were jetting alongside Vivian through the treetops into the black, predawn sky. Eli switched to cussing and kept it up our entire three-minute flight. Vivian laughed so hard she almost flew into a tree.

"Why'd you want to do this, you idiot?" I yelled over his stream of creative profanity, prying his hand off my neck for the third time.

"Always…gotta do…the s--t I'm afraid of," Eli rasped in my ear. "Accounts for my…aaaugh!…tremendous manliness."

"Eli, *relax*!" Vivian called, following our erratic flightline. "Joss has your *back*! Well, really, you have hers." She shot past, radiant in the cold, dark air. "We *rule* fear! We're King of the *World!* I mean *queen*. Queens of the *sky!*"

Queens of infinite space, I thought, but Eli was choking me again. "We can…go down now," he panted. "I'm good."

"Yeah, you are," I murmured.

How can I give these people up? But I'm not. I'm not.

We glided down to where Brady stood, still open-mouthed. Eli ruined my perfect landing by slithering into a heap on the path, but then he leapt to his feet and hugged me. "Dude, you're welcome," I said. But Eli hung onto my arms.

"Thank you," he told me, shiny hair swept back from his sharp elf face. "Thanks for being queen."

Ninety minutes later I was finding room in my trunk for the cashmere sweater Rialta gave me, when someone knocked.

"Wow, miracle, Mom's super early," I said as Dawntae got the door.

"Surprise," said Louis from the doorway.

Pretty sure I screamed. I definitely hugged him and held on, swaying like a moored sailboat as my engines sparked and whirred. Behind us, Tae and Rialta went, "Awwww…"

"Gotta move my car," Louis added when I finally let go. His face was red, but more of a proud glow than that Old Louis embarrassment. "Parked illegally."

"You didn't say you were coming!" said Obvious Joss. My own face felt warm. "I didn't think Beetle could even drive this far."

"Well, Beetle wasn't sure either," Louis admitted. He nodded to my roomies, blush fading. "Hey, I'm Louis."

"I'm Dawntae, that's Rialta, nice to meetcha." Tae's smile was huge. "Joss, you were right—he's bangin'," which I *know* I never said. Louis grinned like he won something.

"Hey, boyfriend, make yourself useful." I nodded toward my trunk. My blood felt fizzy. "We got a ferry to catch. And I gotta stop by Fir Street to say goodbye to the girls."

"Yeah, about that," said the boyfriend. "I'm not here to take you home, Joss."

I frowned at him. "What're you talking about?"

"You kept blowing me off on the phone," Louis said. "Thought maybe I'd try this in person." He stepped closer and dropped his voice. "I don't need you with me to know we're solid. And your dad—he told me to give you this."

From his pocket he pulled out a scrap of orange material and handed it to me. Rough nylon. I unfolded it, and my engines went wild.

"FLYER," said the scrap, in black Sharpie capitals two inches high. I clutched it to me. My other hand grabbed Louis's shoulder to keep my feet on the floor.

"From his survival suit," Louis murmured. "They saved it for him, like a souvenir."

I clenched my eyes. *Dad.* A year ago he could barely say the word "fly." And now... I saw our sunny table at Bean There, the shadow of his hands. *"If you handle Horizon Academy and Coastal U as well as you handle ... flying...you're gonna have 'em for breakfast."*

"He said you'd know what it means," Louis added. Still holding on, I opened my eyes to his bright blue ones. The freckles on his cheeks stood out, tiny constellations.

"You guys need a minute?" Rialta suggested.

"No, we're good. Just tell me where to park," Louis said, not taking his eyes off mine.

"We're solid." "He said you'd know what it means."

"Oh, let Joss move the car, we gotta get to know the boyfriend," Tae announced. "You need a cup of cocoa, Louis."

"Definitely," Rialta agreed. "Go stick this on his dashboard, Joss." She snatched a laminated card from her desk and thrust it at me. "We use it when my dad visits. Looks official."

Louis shrugged, fake-helpless, and handed over his keys. His face was glowing again. I let go his shoulder, still speechless, and headed carefully for the door, feeling my energy hum back to a safe purr. Down the stairwell, the FLYER scrap tight in my hand.

It was another bright, cold day, and the shabby little gray VW looked out of place behind stately ol' Nutschel. I opened the door, and Beetle's gym-bag smell reawoke the tingle in my blood, like stars unveiled from a cloud. *Stars that have been there all along.* Leaning in to deposit Rialta's bogus parking pass, I heard someone call my name.

"Viv said you were goin' home," said Zach Howe.

My head clunked Beetle's doorframe. "Yeah." I straightened up, rubbing my temple, letting my heart slow down. But my flight-power? It gave a big, fat shrug and went still.

I took a good look at the guy I'd loved and hated and obsessed over for a year and a half.

I saw a blond dude in gray sweats and hoodie, one hip leaned against my boyfriend's car. He shoved his sleeves up, showing those muscular forearms I last felt on my bare back. *Nothing— that's what I'm feeling.* That adrenalin was only surprise; my heart was already back to normal.

"I met Viv, comin' back from my run," Zach added. "She was heading to work, and she actually spoke to me. Said I might just catch you. Man, though—your dorms all look alike."

I watched his lips, remembering how they turned from soft to hard...*Still nothing.* I can objectively report that Zach Howe is nice as ever to look at. But my engines didn't care.

So I really did zap his Stander power. Not vulnerable anymore. FLYER.

"Yeah, Horizon's got this thing about red brick," I said, lame as hell. *But so what?*

"You're a strong girl. You're so, so strong," Vivian told Chuntao.

I held Zach's gaze. "But you know what?" I added, "I've changed my mind. I'm staying here. Just...haven't told Vivian yet." *Or Louis. Or anyone.* "I'm gonna reenroll at Coastal and graduate in June." The sun zinged off Beetle's chrome, cheering my decision.

"No kidding!" Zach's smile looked genuine. "Viv'll be thrilled. She was a little down, after—you know. Didn't speak to me for, like, weeks. She does seem happier now. Still needs a good friend, though. I'm keepin' my distance till she forgives me."

I could have cut through the chitchat and told him straight: *You failed. Vivian's back in the sky.*

But what for? Zach's just this guy I used to like. He does care, I'll give him that. But our precious power is none of his business—never was.

"I'm actually the one who's leaving," Zach added, breaking the awkward silence. "Just came back to get my stuff. Prayed about it with my family over the holidays and we decided I'd be happier back at UW where I started. Except for church, I never really felt at home here."

"Whoa," I said, pushing some loose hair back toward my messy ponytail. "I mean, good for you. But I never understood how you and Eli could like the same church."

Zach shrugged. "How I could like a church that helps people? Whadd'ya think?" He removed his hip from Beetle's hood. "That reminds me: I saw Mrs. Hightower last Sunday. She says you're awesome, and I should get you to bring those Chinese girls of yours to Sunday school, even though I won't be there to teach it anymore."

"Oh," I said. "Well, Dee's awesome too. I'm glad…" Couldn't figure out how to end the sentence. *Maybe I just did.*

Zach rested his hand on the car door a few inches from mine. "Hey, Joss. I get that you don't want to deal with me anymore. Really. But no hard feelings. You'll always be special to me, and I pray extra to save the special people in my life."

I stepped away from the car and slammed the door, making Zach jump back. "Yeah, you told me—cruel to be kind. Still sounds messed up to me, Zach. But keep praying. Maybe you'll figure out *why* I'm special—me and Vivian and Eli, and my mom, and your brother Rory. And why we don't need anyone to save us."

Zach's face flashed through an arc of emotions like a fast card-shuffle, came up smiling. "Maybe. Who knows? But hey." He leaned back in. The beautiful Zachs of the world will never be out-confidenced. "Viv said your dad was in a serious accident but he's doing better. Dang—must've been scary. Give him my best, okay? And that crazy brother of yours."

I nodded, marveling. *No more Post-Zach Stress Disorder.*

"Well, I'll let you go," said Zach with a little salute, and I thought, *I'm already gone.*

I pulled the dorm door open to find Louis pushing from the other side. The stars in my blood came twinkling back out.

"Everything okay? Thought maybe they were ticketing Beetle and you were fighting off security dudes." Rialta's viny little houseplant was tied on top of Louis's head with a pair of tights, tendrils twined around his face. "Dawntae thought I needed to be 'Louis of the Jungle,'" he explained.

"Gimme that." I held the plant while Louis disentangled his head. Then I set it on the pavement and took his face in my hands. "Okay, I'm staying in Wattsville. But only 'cause we're solid." And I closed my eyes and kissed him, solidly.

The stars blazed—a flood of 'em, a blanket, wrapping us in possibility. *Swooping over Whittier's Bluff, Louis's arms twined in mine...circling over the Dalby firs...*Who knew someone you've known since kindergarten could set your whole body shimmering? We held tight, flying in place. I felt my heels lift from the pavement, fueled by pure joy.

After a year and a half, messed up and stupid from Zach's betrayal, guess what? These were the arms and lips I was looking for. Not to tame me or save me. Just to love me.

"Hhhhemm."

Louis and I stepped apart with zero embarrassment.

"This your car?" It was the security guard with the fat mustache. "That note on the dash doesn't mean nothin'. You kids need the visitors' lot."

"Yes, sir," I told him, trying to get control of my breathing. "Here, Louis—I'll show you where to park." Inside Beetle, it was weird as hell seeing Louis drive, and I said so.

"Hey, at least we got one mode of transportation where *I* get to steer," Louis grinned, his face squinching up so adorably I wanted to attack him again right there in traffic.

"Driving lessons for flight time, when I come home for a weekend, okay?" I touched his hand where it rested on the shifter. "If you think you can handle flying with me now. Deal?"

"Oh, I can handle it." Louis tossed me a brand-new wicked glance. "If you can."

I might have been blushing as I pointed to the visitors' lot and Louis turned in. I felt a huge relief he'd missed Zach. Not because of guilt, like I used to feel when my fantasies outshone my real friendship. But because we got to start fresh. Solid.

Louis parked Beetle and we got back to the kissing. Paler stars this time, but—how to explain it? A broader universe. Time stopped for a while. But then...

"Hold up," said Brilliant Jocelyn, coming up for air, "What about your English final?"

"Wow, such romance." Louis ran his fingers through my scruffy ponytail, which suddenly felt beautiful. "Mr. E gave me an extension and a planned absence slip. I told him about you dropping the whole Running Start thing, and he said, 'You go tell her that being paralyzed by family might work for Hamlet, but I expect more of Jocelyn Burgowski.' Oh, and then he said, 'Tell her, "To thine own self be true."' So, yeah—what he said."

I leaned in for another kiss, true to mine own self, but my phone rang.

"Did we scare you guys off?" Dawntae wanted to know. "Rialta and I have our Psych final, but we wanna say goodbye to you first."

"Too bad, girl, you're stuck with me," I told her. "I've decided to stay after all." I held the phone away from my ear while Tae shrieked.

"Gotta go but we'll see you soon, Joss—love you to pieces!" she ended breathlessly.

"Well, you sure made her day," Louis observed, as we got out of his car. "Hey, I don't have to catch my boat home for another hour. You hungry?"

"I'm too happy to be hungry." *And dizzy. Stunned by a Harry Potter with Ron Weasley hair.* I shook my head hard. "Let's go see the girls! I was gonna stop by anyway—now I can skip the saying-goodbye part! Oh, no, wait. I'm not s'posed to barge in anymore."

"How 'bout I meet Vivian?" Louis asked. He was giving me that Eli-Brady look: *I know you. Trust you. Love you.* "You could tell her, make her day too."

I looked at my watch: almost nine. "She must have class now. Damn, wish I knew her schedule." *Didn't ask, 'cause I didn't want to think about ditching her.* But what did Zach say about Vivian? *"She was heading to work, and she actually spoke to me."* "Wait—I know where she is! Let's go get coffee."

I could see Vivian, in her brown shirt and tan apron, removing flyers from Bean There, Done That's window as Louis and I approached across the lumpy bricks where I first met her. She flung the door wide.

"Well, *hey*! You must be Louis. Joss, you didn't *tell* me he was coming!" Louis got the first hug. "Are you taking her *home*, then? Aww. I'm so *happy* for you guys."

The thing about Vivian—she *was* happy. Even though she'd wanted so bad for me to stay and fly with her in Wattsville.

I hugged her. "Guess what?" My smile and Louis's ignited her face even before I told her the news: "Louis hates me so much, he doesn't want me on Dalby. I'm staying here."

Half an hour and two hazelnut lattes later, we'd hashed out all the details. Louis would head back to Dalby to get on with his sophomore year. I'd fly over and join him for a long weekend, but first I had to meet with Dean Williams and make sure I could keep my room and my scholarship. (Almost losing your dad is a good excuse for flakiness.) And Vivian promised to help me navigate re-enrollment at Coastal. "Joss, you could take my new law class—it'll *totally* help us help the *girls*."

The café was filling up with retirees and young moms. Blue-Haired Barista Guy had joined Vivian to make drinks; turns out he's not as pissy as he was that Labor Day I first saw him. But he did put a crimp in Flying talk.

Louis checked his watch and stood up. "Well, Mission Accomplished," he grinned at Vivian. "But I still wanna see you guys, you know...doing your thing together. Next visit, 'kay? Bet you have an amazing time up there."

"Oh, *my*." Vivian clutched the edge of our table. "That totally makes me need to—wow, *thanks*, Louis. Now I'm gonna have to *anchor* myself for the next five hours."

"Ha, that's the worst," I murmured. But then: "Hey—can't Blue Hair cover for you for ten minutes?"

Vivian's dark eyes sparkled. Blue Hair rubbed his goatee and frowned when she asked. But he agreed.

One minute later the three of us stood in the empty alley behind the café.

"See you this weekend, Joss." Louis kissed my forehead. "Vivian, see you...soon. You guys be safe. Stay away from...well, you know who."

"Oh!" Vivian looked at me.

I looked at a nice, puffy cloud. She didn't know I hadn't told Louis a thing about Zach. *That's a whole big future conversation... but we have all the time in the world.*

"Right," Vivian added, nodding faithfully. "We sure will."

"Tick-tock," said The Flying Burgowski, not at all trying to avoid an awkward topic. "You got a boat to catch. And we gotta keep Vivian from launching at work and crashing onto another table."

"Okay, magic girls, gimme a preview and I'm outta here." Louis touched my cheek with his fingertips. As we pushed off, he saluted us and rounded the corner, hair glowing in the sun.

"*Act*ually," Vivian laughed as we hovered above the rooftop, waving, "that crash turned out pretty *well* for me, if you think about it."

College towns were not made for flying around on dazzling winter mornings, so my friend and I zipped two blocks to the empty waterfront and buzzed back and forth like a pair of urban dragonflies over the alley where I found the girls. Waves of asphalt-scented warmth rose from the rooftops.

"Five minutes," I warned her. "I've seen how Blue Hair gets when you're late."

Vivian's hand grazed my shoulder. Kinda-losing-then-regaining her power never changed her weird Y-arms flight style.

"His name's *Jason*," she said. "And he's totally *sweet*. He asked me out a couple of times when I was still with...Zach. I might say yes if he asks again." She glanced over at me. "Or I might ask *him*."

"Cool." *Another boyfriend to negotiate "oh-by-the-way-I-can-fly" with?* If the challenge is overcoming plain old envy instead of fanaticism—why not?

"And then next year," Vivian continued, sweeping her ponytail out of her face, "when we're rooming together, we—"

The wind gusted. "Wait, what?"

Flying alongside, Vivian turned her head to smile at me. "'*Course*, dummy. What else? I'm starting my junior year with a roommate who *gets* me for once. And *you're* gonna be the smartest Early Start freshman on the *planet*, with me telling you what classes to take."

I'm an idiot. I never thought that far ahead. But a little jet of extra happiness sent me shooting across the alley and I had to rein myself back. "Whoa. *Hell,* yeah. And we can do stuff with the girls together, and hang out with Brady and Eli. They'll love Louis…"

"Yes, and then *Louis* can come to Coastal for his senior year…" Her face disappeared behind her hair again.

My chest hurt with joy, but I forced myself to check my watch. "Two more minutes. Hey, Viv. About the girls." *Not the time, Flying B—we have tons of safe, dark flights ahead of us, gazillion hours of tea-drinking.* But my Flyer heart was on a roll. "About Peach, actually." I raised my voice above the wind. "I think she might be—it's stupid, but I have this feeling. Like she might be…or might become, when she's older… one of us." I looked at my hands, stretched ahead of me like Superman, *Fēi* Burgowski.

"Sounds ridiculous, I know," I added. "But Lorraine said something about our power kinda…calling to itself. Maybe why you ended up here, all the way from Hawaii."

My Flyer friend used half a precious minute before answering. "And maybe why *you* found the girls, Joss. Your power *felt* Peach maybe. I never thought of that." She grinned and clapped her hands before Y-ing them again, without a waver—wow, she's gotten strong! "I *love* thinking we're all connected—makes me feel so *safe!* But Joss," she added, "what makes you think Peach …?"

Time to go down; we both knew it. "Just a crazy idea," I said, slowing to drop into the alley. The sun glinted off the bay. "I'll tell you later, when we go to reenroll me, okay?"

"Abso*lutely.*" Pigeons scattered as we rounded the café's corner. Vivian grabbed me in another hug, and her silky hair draped around my shoulder. "*Nothing's* too crazy for us. We're crazy *Flyers.* Maybe Peach is, maybe not. But she's awesome no matter what, and so are *you,* and we get to fly, and hang out and, like, fight *injustice* together, right?" She headed for Bean There, calling,

"Go talk to your Dean and come back in five hours, okay?"

"Okay, see ya!" I turned toward Horizon, ready to snuggle into that groove Mr. E somehow knew was right for me. We all have one, I think, but only some of us are lucky enough to find our groove at the right time. Mom nearly died before she found hers. Michael's still looking, and Dad…he'll find a new one, I know he will. He's got Lorraine. And maybe Zach will find his groove back in Seattle. I don't care, as long as he leaves us crazy ones alone.

A nine year-old Flyer, all the way from China in a metal box? That *would* be crazy.

Which reminded me—striding back toward Horizon, sun warming my shoulders—*gotta get myself fingerprinted to be an Official Volunteer.* Who knows all the picnics and field trips and adventures we'll get into, putting the girls' American lives together? You can't pray us down, or keep us in a box. We are queens of infinite space.

THE END

ABOUT THE AUTHOR

Like Jocelyn Burgowski, Gretchen Wing occasionally needs to go for a good fly to put life's difficulties into perspective. Unlike Jocelyn, she can't actually fly. But biking, walking, and going for runs in the beautiful San Juan Islands helps. (As does scribbling longhand; singing; curling up with a good book, or baking kick-ass pie.)

If you are interested in learning more about what Jocelyn and Vivian are learning, here are some websites to consult. For slavery in the chocolate industry:

http://www.slavefreechocolate.org
http://www.foodispower.org

For issues of human trafficking:

http://www.entrust.org.au
http://crs.org
http://polarisproject.org